HER
Hopeful
Heart

VALERIE COMER

Greenwords Media

Her Hopeful Heart

CHRISTMAS AT MARANATHA INN
BOOK TWO

VALERIE COMER

GreenWords Media

I pray that God, the source of hope,
will fill you completely with joy and peace
because you trust in him.
Then you will overflow with confident hope
through the power of the Holy Spirit.
Romans 15:13 NLT

Free story?

Excited to read an entire romance series with characters in their 50s? I'm excited to write it! I'd love to offer you a free ebook novella to introduce the Christmas at Maranatha Inn series. The story is called *Her Waiting Heart*. Find out more and grab your copy at:

https://valeriecomer.com/waiting

CHAPTER
One

THESE WOMEN WEREN'T HERE to judge her.

Even after a year of teaching craft workshops nearly every Saturday morning, Wendy Clarke struggled to believe that, but the regulars wouldn't have kept coming back if they didn't like her craft offerings.

Maybe some of them even liked *her*.

She shook off the familiar feelings of inadequacy as she scanned the two dozen women smiling expectantly back at her. "Today's craft is paper-quilled apples. You'll find an assortment of paper strips in the baskets on your tables. Lots of shades of red, in case you'd like to follow tradition. Lots of other colors, in case you prefer to explore your playful side."

"Ooh!" At the nearest table, 20-something Alexia scooped up a pile of pink, purple, and green papers. "I like playful."

Laughter rippled across Maranatha Inn's dining room as the other ladies peered into the baskets.

"Let me show you how to use the quilling tools to turn those strips of papers into tight coils. Then you'll use the outline on your foam board to shape your assorted spirals into an apple. Ready?"

"I was born ready!" Alexia called.

A few minutes later, the women leaned over their projects, quilling and chatting, and Wendy wandered between them dispensing advice and encouragement. She'd put off this particular offering here in Montana. It had been the last craft she'd led in Oregon, just before her perfect life crumbled in front of her eyes. The memories were hard.

When Dave's infidelity had come to light, Wendy's peer group of homeschooling mamas vanished in a heartbeat, her name anathema. As if she were contagious, no one wanted to catch whatever virus had infected her marriage. They didn't need to worry. It was all because of Wendy's excessive weight, not something transmittable. Dave made sure she understood the reasons, but he wasn't wrong.

She'd thought those women were true friends, but they hadn't been.

How could she trust the women in her workshops? She couldn't.

Even her earliest friend group was suspect. Wendy glanced across the dining area to the inn's reception desk, where Julia and Audrey stood chatting. Wendy might have moved to Montana last year at Julia's request — along with their other chums from their shared past at Gilead Bible College — but trust them? Not so much.

"How's this, Wendy?" Alexia tilted her foam board toward Wendy, her face pulled into a pensive expression. "The result isn't quite what I imagined."

"That's the beauty of crafting. It can turn out so much better than we hoped." Unlike life.

The girl sighed. "I suppose. I always hate not doing a perfect job first try."

"You know what they say. Practice makes perfect." That was a fallacy if Wendy ever heard one. She'd practiced being a wife and mother for nearly a quarter of a century before discovering she'd failed at both. Ugh.

"Do you sell the quilling tools?"

"Not directly, but our online affiliate shop is linked on the workshop tab of the inn's website."

"I'll look that up. Obviously, I need to practice more."

Wendy touched the girl's shoulder. "Not obviously. I do think your apple is beautiful. Handcrafted items have that slightly rustic edge that only makes them more attractive than anything mass-produced."

"Hmm." Alexia tilted her head, frowning at her design. "If you say so. I did achieve colorful and playful, I guess."

"You did, for sure." Wendy patted her shoulder and turned to another crafter. "That's charming, Sheryl! I adore the Granny Smith vibe."

"Did I roll all the paper strips tightly enough?" The woman touched a spiral of neon green paper amid the design. "I decided on this color scheme to match my vintage kitchen."

"It's beautiful. You're going to display it?"

"Of course. I didn't go to all this work to hide it in a box some-where." Sheryl shook out her fingers and chuckled. "I can't believe how fiddly this was to do."

"It does take time and focus. I think the results are worth it, though."

"Agreed. And I can't tell you how much I admire you, Wendy."

"Me?" Wendy couldn't have kept the shock out of her voice if she'd tried.

"Yes, you! You have the greatest ideas. It's so fun to see what unique projects you come up with. This is the highlight of my week."

"Wow, thanks. I appreciate that." Wendy blinked back a tear or two. How was it so hard to accept praise? It seemed so long since anyone appreciated her. Even her old college friends here at Maranatha Inn were only being kind in including her again, right?

Not that Audrey was kind. They might have been childhood friends who went off to Bible school together, but these days,

Audrey did little but criticize Wendy's size and shape. None of the others tried to stop her. Had they even noticed? Audrey kept her snide comments on the down low, and Wendy wasn't into tattling. They were all grown women, after all.

Wendy took a deep breath as she looked around the tables. Everyone seemed to be done. She clapped her hands twice for attention. "Thank you all so much for coming today. I hope you've had a great time and will take home a project you can be proud to display. Next week—"

Across the lobby, Audrey squealed and dashed from the registration desk out the sliding doors.

Focus, Wendy.

"Next week's workshop is all about book carving. You can sign up at the front desk on your way out if you haven't already, or pop into the workshop tab on our website. Please come back and bring a friend! Each participant will need to bring an old hardcover book that you don't mind making into a work of art."

"Books are for reading, not chopping into pieces!" one of the women called out. A few others laughed.

"I get it." Wendy forced her attention to stay with the crafters and not with whomever had just entered Maranatha Inn. Lots of people came and went. They weren't usually a distraction. But Audrey's brother was arriving today, and Wendy hadn't seen him since he was a teenager. What would he look like now? What kind of person had he become? And why couldn't she focus on wrapping up her class?

She reached into the crate on the table behind her and lifted out her sample, a hardcover with a 3D snowman carved out of the pages.

A chorus of appreciative murmurs and excitement rose from the group.

"Okay, you convinced me," the skeptic agreed.

"I have a humungous college textbook that I can finally put to good use." Alexia waggled her eyebrows to a chorus of laughter.

The women began to gather their projects and purses while chatting with each other.

Wendy shot a glance toward the small group over by the registration desk. That man beside Audrey — the tall guy shaking the inn owner's hand — how could that be Audrey's little brother? He had hints of gray — gray! — in his dark hair. Roman Scala couldn't possibly be old enough for gray.

Hard to imagine it now, but she and Audrey had been best friends through their teen years. Audrey had resented babysitting tagalong Roman while their parents worked, but Wendy hadn't minded their little shadow. He'd been a cute kid.

After Bible college, Wendy and Audrey had drifted apart, with Audrey returning to SoCal while Wendy married Dave and moved to Oregon. Wendy hadn't seen her friend's brother since Audrey's wedding to Steve. That had been, what, over 20 years ago now? Roman had been a shy, awkward teenager.

The self-assured man with the trim beard by the registration desk held little in common with that pimple-faced youth. He chatted with Audrey and Julia then tilted his head back and laughed. He looked good in jeans and a casual, untucked button-up.

Wendy blinked and turned back to what she was doing. What had that been again? Right. Gathering up quilling tools then sweeping up the scraps of paper. In an hour, this space would revert to being the dining room of the finest restaurant in Jewel Lake.

And Wendy would be back to being invisible.

Roman Scala slung his arm across his sister's shoulder. "Audrey. It's been too long."

She turned to hug him. "It has. I'm glad you're here, but Mom and Dad must be livid that you left SoCal."

He shrugged. "They're furious with me anyway for selling my share of the company to Leo. I may have worked there since high school, but it was never my dream job. Not like Dad's and Uncle Emil's."

"It wasn't a dream with them. It was an all-holds-barred fixation." Audrey shuddered.

"Anyway, I'm ready for a new chapter, and I thought I'd check out this part of the world and hang out with you for a while. This inn is impressive."

"I'm sure it's nothing to you after all the exotic places you've been."

He eyed her quizzically. "Why would you downplay it? You have to admit it's quite the architecture. Your friend has done an amazing job here. I'm grateful to rent a room for a few months while I see if my business ideas will fly."

"You're right. It's cool. Wait until you see the fitness room on the third floor! Julia took all my ideas and created a classy space, albeit a bit smaller than I'd hoped for."

"Nice! I can't wait. I definitely need a regular workout to keep in shape. Too much desk time makes for a flabby Roman, but I'm hoping my new gig will get me out and about more."

"Tell me again what you're planning?"

He grinned. "As if Gen X could understand a Millennial's job creation."

"Please! I'm not that old."

"I've made a career of figuring out what people want, sourcing it, and getting it to them—"

"It's called market research, bro. It has a name."

Roman smirked. "So, now my job will be to figure out what people want to see, experience, and eat in the northwest... and show them where and how to do that."

"Tourism marketing. Who's paying you?"

"The public. The platforms."

She raised her eyebrows at him. "Uh huh. I wasn't born yesterday."

"Gen X…"

"Shut up." She swatted his arm. "Have respect for your elders."

"I'm starting a YouTube channel, an Instagram account, and a blog."

Audrey's nose wrinkled. "You're serious about this."

"Yep. It's not like I need a huge income, though it would be nice for it not to bleed. Cousin Leo paid decent money for my half of the import company."

"Must be nice."

He searched his sister's face. "Are you hurting financially? I thought you were taken care of."

"I'm okay. Don't worry about me. Things with Steve were complicated, as you know, but he didn't have anyone else to leave his savings to besides his ex-wife, so he never changed his will. Plus, I built a nest egg of my own."

Roman would make sure his big sis never needed for anything. Their parents had been furious when Audrey and Steve split… they'd welcomed their son-in-law into the bosom of the company then hadn't been able to deal with the divorce. Steve had stayed on the inside, and Audrey had stepped away to become a fitness coach and instructor. Her career choice hadn't made their parents any happier.

Water under the bridge, especially with Steve's death a few years ago. His funeral had been the last time Roman had returned to SoCal until this summer when he'd met with Leo and a pack of accountants and lawyers to hammer out the deal. Only when the ink was dry had he dropped by his parents' home with his bombshell.

Montana had to be more welcoming than SoCal. His big sis had always been there for him. Now he looked around the inn's stunning lobby and adjoining dining room, where a group of women appeared to be wrapping up a workshop of some sort. A curvaceous woman with curly blond hair moved among the attendees. The facilitator, no doubt.

The woman smiled at one of the participants, and Roman blinked. He knew that smile. He nudged his sister. "Who's that?"

Audrey looked over and sighed. "Wendy."

That was Wendy Bilson? No, wait, she'd been married, but he didn't recall her married name. "I'd recognize her smile anywhere."

"You always tagged behind her like a puppy hopeful for a scratch behind the ears."

Roman laughed. "Puppies know who's on their side. Hey, maybe once I'm settled, I can get a dog."

"Not while you're living at Maranatha, you won't. We're not a pet-friendly establishment."

"Too bad, but I won't be staying here forever, just until I figure out if I can make a go of it. Either way, I'll be moving out eventually."

"If you need a dog fix, Chris — you remember her? She lives in the old farmhouse about a quarter of a mile past the inn. She's in charge of the Christmas tree farm and has a couple of dogs."

Chris. Chris. He wracked his brain. Thin woman with short hair who seemed super awkward around people, if he had the right person in mind. "Thanks for the tip."

"Do you want me to show you to your room? You know the drill, right? There's a breakfast buffet every morning between six and nine-thirty. We don't serve lunch, and dinners are by reservation Wednesdays through Sundays only. You can fix basic meals in your room if you like, and there are several restaurants in town."

"Good to know."

Chattering, the workshop attendees streamed toward the front doors, and he and Audrey shifted further out of their path. No one paid him any attention, but he overheard gushing over how talented Wendy was and how great a teacher. The women each carried a piece of stiff paper with a raised apple design on it. He couldn't quite discern how that was a craft.

Roman glanced across the dining room and almost caught Wendy's eye, but she looked down, brushing her hand across a table. Looked like she was gathering scraps together.

"Excuse me." He stepped around Audrey and strode toward Wendy.

CHAPTER
Two

BE STILL HER HEART, that tall hunk of manhood was coming straight toward her. Maybe if she ducked into the kitchen…

But why? He was Audrey's little brother. She'd spent many, many hours with Audrey and her tagalong when they were kids. But that child had turned into an absolutely gorgeous man with a devastating smile focused straight on her. Who'd allowed him to grow up?

Dave. Remember Dave.

Dave the Cheater? *That* Dave? She didn't owe any allegiance to him. Not anymore. Not that she was looking to replace him the way Shyanne, the hussy with the bikini bod, had displaced Wendy.

"Wendy? Is that you?"

She dared look up at the man who stood only a couple of feet away. "Oh, hey! Roman? Long time no see."

"Wow, it really is you. Do I get a hug?" He opened his arms.

The appropriate answer should be no, but she couldn't get the word out. Neither could she stop herself from stepping into his embrace.

Self-control had never been her strong suit. She only needed to look into a mirror to be reminded. Now, however much she'd like to burrow into his embrace — what scent was his cologne? — she forced herself to accept a quick squeeze and step back. "You've changed," she blurted.

When Roman laughed, the skin around his eyes crinkled and his dimples peeked from his short facial hair. "Yeah? People do that in 20-some years, but I'd have known your smile anywhere."

Meaning he wouldn't have recognized the rest of her, which was fair. She'd been largely pregnant with Theo — or had it been Selah? — at Audrey's wedding. No doubt, she weighed more now than she had then, not that she'd stepped on a scale in years. Some things were best left unknown.

"Thank you. It's good to see you. Audrey mentioned you expect to stay at Maranatha for several months?"

"That's the plan." He rocked back on his heels. "I sold my share of the family biz to my cousin, and I'm starting a new venture here. We'll see how it goes."

"Wow, that's a big deal. Quite a change."

"Yep. It couldn't come soon enough for me. I was tired of living overseas and trying to foresee what Americans would want to buy next. When Leo and I got on a video call, and I realized he had hopes of steering the company in a tangential direction, I saw my chance to cut ties."

Tired of living overseas? Wendy hadn't visited more than half a dozen states. Maybe someday she'd get the chance. It was hard to imagine it being blasé.

But that was neither here nor there with Roman. "Congratulations on starting fresh."

"Thanks. It will be a lot of work, but fun work, if you know what I mean."

"Sure. That's the best kind." Teaching workshops was that for Wendy, but it wasn't a nine-to-five. The rest of her position at Maranatha involved a mix of social media and cleaning rooms after departing guests. Someone needed to do it.

Roman still stood there, looking totally at ease. "Tell me everything you've been up to since I saw you last."

"Not much. Homeschooled my six children but found myself at loose ends when my husband filed for divorce." She winced inwardly. What a loser. She'd never even held a job since working at the coffee shop during Bible college.

"Six! Wow. I remember two little ones at Audrey's wedding."

Which meant it had been Theo she'd been expecting. "Those two littles are parents themselves now."

He shook his head. "That's just crazy talk."

"I know, right? I don't feel old enough to be a grandmother, but I guess that's what happens when your kids are in their mid-20s." And she should slap her own face, because neither Roman nor his sister had children, meaning their parents, now likely in their 80s, had no grandchildren. Way to blurt out the wrong thing.

Roman's smile held. "That happens a lot, I hear."

"You never met the right person to settle down with?" Not that it was any of Wendy's business.

"Never did. I've had a few brief relationships, but things never worked out, long term." He shrugged. "It's okay. I came to grips with it a long time ago. There are distinct advantages to being solo."

Wendy couldn't think of a single one, but then she'd forever be linked to Dave through their children. The next event they'd both be forced to attend would be Faith's high-school graduation in May. Wendy could put off worrying about that for a while yet, though.

The inn doors slid open, and Pam bustled in.

Wendy gave herself a shake. No doubt the chef expected the dining room to be spotless by now, and here Wendy was, head in the clouds, chatting with an old friend. She could call Roman her friend, right? He wasn't only Audrey's brother. She'd had a relationship with him, too. She'd read him stories, pushed him on the swing, and cheered at his soccer games. He'd been her honorary little brother, and she really needed to keep that firmly in mind.

Starting right now.

She waved at Pam, who came toward them, arm-in-arm with Audrey.

Audrey spared Wendy a mere glance as she turned to Pam, her shoulder angling slightly to exclude Wendy. "Pam, remember my baby brother, Roman? Roman, this is Pam, the chef here. Wait until you try her cooking! I reserved you a seat at dinner tonight."

Pam and Roman exchanged greetings, and Wendy backed away. She hurried to the closet for a broom and swept up the last remnants of her quilling class, listening to the three of them chat just beyond the tables. She hadn't missed the cool look Audrey had given her as she'd cut Wendy out. Almost a warning, but for what?

Wendy wasn't some loose woman bent on destroying Audrey's brother. The three of them had a shared history. She'd been a fixture in his childhood. It was natural for Roman to want to catch up with her. It didn't mean anything.

She didn't want it to mean anything. *Couldn't* want it to.

Dave might be the moving-on kind, but Wendy most certainly was not. She'd dedicated her entire life to being the perfect wife and mother.

Uh huh, tell yourself that.

If she'd managed perfection, she'd have a toned body like Audrey's and still be Dave's doting wife. Instead, when the going got rough, she'd defaulted on her family and retreated to Montana to lick her wounds.

That's not exactly what had happened. Right?

Well, kind of. She'd stuck it out in Woodburn for another year, wrapping up Ezra's senior year and teaching a reluctant Faith tenth grade. When Faith began mumbling about her dad supporting her plan to finish up at the public high school, that had been all Wendy could bear. The other five were out of the nest. Adriel and Silas were married with babies, Theo was working in Portland, Selah away at college, Ezra working construction and living with his dad... Faith had been the final straw.

So, yeah. Maybe Wendy *had* run away, but it felt more like she'd been shoved. After all, Dave the Cheater had kept the house and moved Shyanne in. What was Wendy supposed to do? Congratulate them? Not on her life.

She looked around the now tidy space, hoisted her supply crate to her hip, and headed for the elevator without a backward glance.

"Welcome to Maranatha, Roman! We've heard so much about you."

He'd been about to take his seat at the dinner table next to Audrey. Now he paused and extended his hand to the slim woman who'd greeted him. "Christina, right?"

She angled her head and shook his hand with a firm grip. "I go by Chris."

"Got it." He waited until she seated herself before taking his own chair. "What do you do here, Chris? I'm sure Audrey told me but, to be honest, she talks so much it all blurs after a while."

His sister's sharp elbow caught his arm. "Hey!"

Laura, whom he'd met earlier, laughed. "Isn't that the truth?"

Audrey glared at her friend. "I feel picked on."

Chris glanced between them before turning back to Roman. "I have a degree in forestry with a minor in horticulture. I moved here early on with Julia and George to take over the Christmas tree farm, which had been neglected for quite a few years."

He nodded his approval. "Very nice. How big is it?"

"Twenty acres of mixed conifers. We're coming up on our second season of selling them."

"If you ever need a set of muscles, let me know. I'll be doing far too much sitting around with my laptop, and some fresh air and exercise will be a welcome change."

Chris's eyes narrowed. "I'll keep that in mind but, so far, I've managed fine on my own. Just because I'm female doesn't mean I'm weak."

Oops. Backtrack. "I didn't mean to insinuate you were. Let me rephrase that. If you ever need an extra set of hands, let me know. Also, I hear you have dogs I might need to visit."

Had the set of her narrow shoulders relaxed any? It was hard to believe she had strength in that small frame but, hey, how would he know? Maybe she could bench press a ten-foot spruce.

"Walk up the road anytime. Luna and Duke will be happy for company."

Meaning Chris would not? She didn't seem particularly welcoming for all that she'd greeted him first. Roman looked around the table. All of Audrey's cohort was here except one. "Is Wendy coming for dinner?"

"She often takes meals in her room. Staff quarters each have a small kitchenette. Maybe she stocked up on salad." Audrey smirked.

Roman frowned. Why was that funny? Considering the two had been best friends for years, they seemed cool toward each other now. Mind you, he hadn't kept up with his childhood buddies, either. He'd gone overseas fresh out of college while many of them began settling into SoCal careers and relationships. Roman's life was so different from theirs that links had dissolved.

He'd flown solo ever since, with dozens of superficial friendships at the office and in the churches he'd attended wherever he'd found himself. Anything deep? Not so much. He'd certainly never formed bonds like his sister had with this group of friends, though the bonds seemed to have frayed, at least a little. Maybe that was just life.

"She said she was stepping out this evening," Julia said. "I know she needs to recharge after leading a workshop."

Roman nodded as though he understood. He'd have to catch up with her tomorrow, not that it mattered. Except it kind of did.

He could use a friend in Montana, and she was the most likely candidate. Sisters didn't count.

The inn's front doors opened, and Julia glanced over. She dabbed her cloth napkin over her mouth then set it down as she rose. "That must be our other long-term guest. I'll be back shortly."

Julia crossed the space and shook hands with the man before stepping behind the desk. They chatted a while longer while she keyed into the reservation computer. Then she came around again and walked beside him to their table.

"I'd like everyone to meet Bruce Leland. Bruce, this gentleman is Roman Scala, another guest who's here until the New Year."

Roman stood and shook the man's hand. "Pleased to meet you."

"Likewise." The man smiled and nodded then greeted the women as Julia introduced each one.

"I'll get you a plate from the kitchen," Julia said.

"I've got it." Audrey surged to her feet and hurried off, returning a moment later with a plate heaped with roast beef, mashed potatoes, and a medley of roasted vegetables.

Roman had only taken a couple of bites of his, so he tucked in, listening to the conversation. He knew why *he* was here in Montana — to get reacquainted with his sister and start a business — but what about Bruce? Not every middle-aged man could relocate for a few months at a time. Didn't he have a wife and family?

"What brings you to Montana?" Audrey focused her smile on the newcomer.

Roman winced. Awkward. He hadn't realized his sister might be on the manhunt again. She'd been fully dedicated to capturing Steve back in the day. Then she'd been equally devoted to changing the poor dude into her ideal man. Hadn't worked so well, hence the divorce.

"I'm a writer, and I needed a change of scenery for inspiration."

Ah. Bruce might be a potential friend, after all. "I write, as well," Roman put in. "I've done travel articles for several big blogs and am starting my own. What's your angle?"

"I write novels." Bruce held up both hands. "And before anyone asks, no, you won't find any of my books under Bruce Leland. I write under a private pen name."

Great. A guy with secrets.

Julia's eyes brightened. "I wonder if we have any of your books in our library! Are you famous?"

The man shrugged. "My stories are popular in certain circles. But enough about me. Tell me about yourselves." He turned to Chris. "You're on staff here?"

Roman tuned out the discussion. He might be looking for someone to hang out with in the area, but it wasn't going to be this new guy. The whole idea of keeping one's basic identity hidden seemed wrong.

Wendy was still his best bet for an actual friend. They went way back, after all.

CHAPTER
Three

"ROOM FOR ONE MORE?"

Wendy startled at Roman's low voice at the end of the pew. "Um, sure." Not a lot of it, mostly because she took up more than her fair share. And also, she didn't want to be squished up against him. It wasn't seemly.

Ha. Dave had done far more than sit too close to a woman in church. He'd been increasingly too busy to attend services in the final couple of years. How had Wendy made excuses and turned a blind eye to the cracks in their marriage?

Now, she edged closer to Chris, who shifted over toward Laura, all while they kept singing, "Will Your Anchor Hold?"

The lyrics had been hard to sing before she'd been distracted by Roman at her side.

We have an anchor that keeps the soul steadfast and sure while the billows roll; fastened to the Rock which cannot move, grounded firm and deep in the Savior's love.

Wendy didn't feel much like she'd been anchored amid life's stormy waves. Granted, she'd been a greenhouse seedling before, with little experience of turbulence. Maybe she was mixing metaphors. Maybe she'd had no clue how to cling to her anchor *or* how to dig her roots into God's love.

God did love her. Right? She knew He did. If she tossed aside her belief system, she'd have nothing left, so she'd clutch it like a drowning person clung to a rope.

What if she discovered her dependence on God was just as unmoored as her dependence on Dave had proved to be?

Nope. Not going there. God was loyal. Trustworthy. No other tenet was acceptable.

The worship team led the congregation in a couple of other songs. Wendy sang along quietly. She'd once sung with conviction. Not anymore.

Thanks for cutting my confidence off at the knees, Dave. Thanks for dashing cold water on all my optimism.

No, her hope was in the Lord. Not in Dave. She was done with her cheating ex, but how to carry on? Even moving to Montana hadn't made enough difference. She'd had to bring herself along, after all.

Finally, they sat, and the moment of reckoning arrived. Everyone in the entire pew had to squish closer to make room for Roman, but he didn't seem bothered by it... even though it was Wendy's fault. If she were skinny like Chris or Audrey, there'd have been plenty of room.

Ugh. Why couldn't she stay out of the junk food and learn to love exercise? Audrey would gleefully help her, but that was a fate Wendy couldn't face. Maybe she should just stay fat and happy. As though the two went together.

They once had, or at least, she hadn't noticed if they didn't.

The offering plate slid into her line of vision. She passed it to Roman, who handed it to the usher. Most people gave online these days, but Creekside Fellowship still passed the plate, as well. Wendy had begun giving here once she'd decided to stay in Montana indefinitely, a decision she still grappled with.

Pastor Marshall Smith mounted the steps to the platform. The man didn't look healthy, though he wasn't as overweight as Wendy was. He mopped his brow with a white handkerchief as he took his place behind the pulpit. Rumor had it that he was considering early retirement due to health issues. As it was, the youth pastor preached almost as often as Marshall did. Both provided many interesting tidbits, but nothing life changing, at least not for Wendy.

"Will your anchor hold?" Marshall began. "There will always be storms. I'm facing one myself, as many of you know. Storms are a fact of life, and they offer us a choice. Hold on... or let go. Grow in our faith or turn our backs."

Wendy had chosen the third option by default: drift.

"There's no middle ground," Marshall went on.

Oh, yes, there is.

"If we're not actively growing, we are loosening our grip."

Ugh. Wendy hated when he made sense.

"Does God *send* those storms into our lives? Or does He simply use them to grow us spiritually? There's no indication in the Bible that God purposefully causes hardship. It isn't God's plan to break us. Rather, He desires to grow us, and trials play a part in that. Let's pray together as we dig into the Word this morning."

Wendy bowed her head along with everyone else. This was a sermon she didn't want to hear, yet a teensy bit of her heart responded differently, with interest if not eagerness. Answers would be good, but Marshall wouldn't likely say anything she hadn't heard dozens of times before. She'd stopped seeking understanding a while back.

She'd once tried to compare her suffering to Job's but abandoned that idea quickly enough. Wendy was not righteous like Job. Neither God nor the devil would ever hold her up as a godly example that needed testing. Plus, the book was as confusing as all get out. The man's erstwhile friends said a lot of things that seemed to make sense — about how he'd brought all this trouble on himself through some random-but-unknown sin he'd committed — until the ongoing narrative shot down their arguments, leaving the true reason for his suffering unrecorded in scripture.

Roman shifted on the pew beside her, slouching down a little. His shoulder bumped against hers, and she forced herself to stare straight ahead at the pastor even while she caught Roman's glance in her periphery.

Nope. Not looking at the man who'd turned her head upside down in the past 24 hours. He was still supposed to be an awkward adolescent, not a grown, gorgeous man. He was still supposed to be Wendy's little brother, not… this.

And Wendy wasn't going to be distracted by him. Not now, in church, and not in day-to-day life at the inn, either. He'd likely be busy, and she'd rarely run into him. They could wave and say hi like any two acquaintances whose lives occasionally intersected.

Right. He'd be at Maranatha for months. He was going to be extremely difficult to ignore, but this would be the first test of her self-control that she would not only pass, but ace. If she could do that, then she could confront her weight. She'd be able to tackle anything. All she had to do to prove her own strength to herself was to ignore Roman Scala.

Easy peasy.

Only… not.

It seemed Wendy must be avoiding him, but Roman couldn't figure out why. She'd turned to Chris after the service and chatted so long that it became awkward for him to wait for her attention, so he'd finally left. E-reader in hand, he'd hung out by the fireplace in the lobby most of the afternoon, but she hadn't passed through, nor had she come to the dining room for dinner.

On the plus side, he'd had an illuminating visit with Julia, and he was excited about partnering with her for his business. He'd feature Maranatha Inn in some of the earliest videos for his new channel, and she had connections to other locals he might also like to check out.

Best of all? She'd cited Wendy as adept at handling the inn's social media and suggested they work together on the segments featuring the inn.

Pretty sure he'd remained calm as he agreed, rather than revealing his inner fist pump.

Why did it matter if Wendy ignored him? That was the question he'd grappled with last evening as he sat out on his balcony watching the setting sun cast a glow over the Christmas tree farm. The bucolic view was incredibly soothing after the pandemonium surrounding his Jakarta apartment building. Now, all the turmoil lay within him.

Why did Wendy matter?

That was the question, but the answer eluded him. Was it only their shared background? Her seeming sadness? Or was there something more? If so, he couldn't name it. He felt sorry for her, the way her ex had dumped her, but it wasn't simply that, either.

Mentally, he set the question on a shelf in the back of his mind, where he could take it out and examine it later, once he had new insights. For now, he'd just be her friend, though she didn't seem to want that, either.

But she didn't seem close with any of the others, except maybe Julia. It looked like Chris had her own set of issues, and Audrey clearly looked down on Wendy. Laura? Roman couldn't say, but she hung out with Audrey, which likely meant her views were similar. He'd only met Pam briefly as she didn't live at the inn, and he'd been here fewer than 48 hours now.

Now, on Monday morning, he sat in the lobby once again.

"Good morning, Roman!"

He looked up to see Bruce Leland exiting the stairwell, a backpack slung over one shoulder. There were many guests, of course, but Bruce was the only other person booked in for a long stay. A couple from Atlanta had a suite on permanent retention. Apparently, they had family in Jewel Lake and often made the trip, but he hadn't met them yet.

Roman rose and gripped Bruce's hand. "It looks like a beautiful fall day. The sun is shining and all that."

"It does look pleasant. I heard there was a decent hike to that bluff overlooking the lake, so I'm checking it out this morning. Want to come?"

"Ah, no, not this time. I have an appointment shortly." At least, if Wendy agreed to meet with him at Julia's behest. "If it's worth it, though, I'd be happy to come another time. It sounds more fun than a treadmill."

Bruce laughed. "You'd better believe it. I can't think why anyone would rather exercise indoors than in God's great outdoors."

"Uh… rain? Snow? Bugs? Travel time before you can even start?" Hence, Roman's home gym had always been well equipped. He'd worked extensive hours, and a long run on the treadmill every night kept his head from exploding.

"I guess those are valid concerns, but not on days like today. It's too nice out."

"You have fun and let me know. Maybe I'll check it out sometime. Where's the trailhead?"

"Follow the road from Jewel Lake that goes through the Agate Bay subdivision down below. It's another five or six miles, the guy said. He also said I couldn't miss it."

"Sounds good, although some of us can miss anything. Speaking for myself."

Bruce chuckled. "There's that."

"So, you write adventure fiction? Protagonists who hike and love nature?"

"I'll never tell." The man grinned and waved as he headed toward the main doors.

Roman sank back into the leather love seat and glanced at his watch. Maybe he should suggest he and Wendy walk while they talked about social media. Maybe strolling side by side would seem less intimidating than facing each other over the coffee table in the lobby.

Intimidating? Why had that thought even cruised through his head? Ridiculous. They'd known each other nearly all their lives... or at least, *his* life. Okay, they'd known each other for a segment of about ten years. Roman had been three when Wendy's family moved in down the street. Which meant Wendy and Audrey had been twelve. Wendy's parents had moved to Seattle while the girls were in Bible college, so that had been the end of seeing her often.

Now, he looked up as she exited the staff elevator and turned his direction. He jumped to his feet. "Hey, Wendy!"

"Hi." Her smile looked strained. "Julia said she wanted us to meet?"

Why did she need to make it sound like a hardship? "Yes. She mentioned you do all the inn's social media and advertising, so I took the liberty of looking up the accounts. You've done great! And you get a fair bit of engagement."

She sat on the edge of the love seat across from him as he settled back into his spot. "Yes, people seem to like the content."

"Can I pick your brain about how you choose what to share? Julia mentioned she'd like us to work together on my segments about the inn."

"Segments about the inn?" Her pretty face pulled into a frown. "I'm not following."

"Oh! I'm sorry. I thought you were there when I told everyone my business plans. I'm starting a kind of tourism site for the region, called *Roaming with Roman*. I'll be running on YouTube and a blog — I've already begun setting up the website — with a profile on Instagram, as well. Maybe Facebook. I haven't determined yet if that's where my audience hangs out."

"Okay?"

"Julia and I worked out a deal regarding a few promotions for Maranatha Inn. We'll do a video on the inn itself, another on the dining experience with Pam being an award-winning chef, and one on the activities that bring extra life to Maranatha."

"Activities? You don't mean…?"

"I mean your workshops."

But her head was already shaking. "Oh, no. We couldn't possibly do that."

CHAPTER
Four

"FOR THE GOOD OF MARANATHA INN?"

Roman's kind words and smile nearly did Wendy in, but the fear of being prominently and permanently displayed as a fat person remained stronger. She shook her head. "There's no need to feature me. Please don't."

He tilted his head and studied her so long it made her squirm. "But you're a major draw at keeping the community engaged with Maranatha."

"No, that would be Pam. Without her cooking style, meals here would be mediocre. The restaurant is a local date-night favorite, and over the summer, tourists discovered it, as well."

"I'm already planning to feature the restaurant, because you're not wrong. Pam is a huge asset to the inn and the community, from what I've discovered thus far."

"Also, the Christmas tree farm. That's another way the inn connects with the community, right? You'll see once the season arrives! People come from miles around to pick out their trees and take in the Maranatha experience."

"How would you define the Maranatha experience?" Roman set his tablet on a stand and unfolded a small keyboard in front of it on the coffee table.

Maybe Wendy could breathe after all. "Interesting question." She pretended to think. "We straddle two worlds, really. The inn itself with all the guest rooms and suites caters mostly to tourists. We are trying to establish ourselves as a destination. We're close to the Ski Bowl. People love waterskiing on the lake and hiking and geocaching around the hills."

"Yes, Bruce mentioned he was hiking Miner's Rock today. You've been in Montana for, what, a year now? Have you been up there?"

Her eyebrows shot up, and it took force of will not to laugh and point at her flabby figure. Did she look like someone who hiked? Not so much. "No, I haven't."

"Maybe we could do it together sometime."

"No, thank you." She'd seen the bluff overlooking the lake across from town. The elevation gain on the trail would be enough to have her panting and heaving in the first three minutes. She'd never put herself through that, especially with someone watching. Judging. Not that they didn't already do that. She knew Audrey did, but Wendy also judged herself.

Roman pursed his lips and looked down at his tablet.

"Some of our guests go horseback riding at Happy Trails Stables at the bottom of our road. I'm sure you've seen the sign."

"I noticed it, but I haven't popped in there yet. Have you—?"

Wendy shook her head. "I don't ride." It looked positively terrifying, honestly.

"Julia suggested I talk to the owners there about a feature. She said it's fairly new."

"Yes, they've only been in business for about a year now. It's owned by three sisters in their 20s, daughters of one of the area's prominent ranchers."

Roman tapped into his keyboard. "Human interest story there."

She nodded, not that he was looking.

"Okay." Roman glanced up. "Back to the Maranatha experience. You mentioned the draw to tourists. What else?"

"To locals, of course. The restaurant and the Christmas tree farm couldn't function on tourism alone. We have to be a regular destination for residents." Uh oh. He was sneaky. She could see what he was doing now.

"And part of that is your Saturday workshops."

"Yes… but it's really the participants and projects you should be showcasing, not me."

"You're the common thread, the genius that pulls it all together."

Her gut clenched as buzzing encircled her head. "Genius? That's a laugh."

"That's what Julia calls you."

"Oh, that's silly. She's just being a kind, supportive friend."

Roman leaned back and studied Wendy. "I was standing over there by the reception desk when your workshop closed on Saturday. I overheard the women chatting with each other about how great you are. What a good teacher. How interesting and fun your project choices are."

Wendy's head shook rapidly without a conscious thought. "I taught homeschool forever, including some co-op classes and moms' nights out. The crafts are just little diddly things to pass the time and get people together. Please don't mistake me for anything special."

"But… you *are* special."

Tears sprang to Wendy's eyes. Hopefully, he wouldn't notice. How long had it been since anyone had told her that? Peculiar, maybe, but not special in a positive sense. "I'm not," she whispered.

"God's unique, favored daughter."

She gulped a breath and pasted on a smile. "One of many, right? But enough about me." Divert, divert, divert. "What else do you have planned for your channel?"

"I'll start with a focus local to Jewel Lake, then expand outward. I'm not sure how far."

Wendy managed to suck in air. "So, you'll be staying at

Maranatha Inn while doing local segments, then move on to a hotel or resort in another area?" She'd looked forward to seeing Roman again, but now she couldn't wait for him to move on. The reality was that he'd changed from the small child and awkward teen she'd once known, and the grownup version unsettled her in ways she did not wish to contemplate.

He shook his head. "I expect to be away for a few days at a time, but I'll mostly be working from here. This is where my sister is, so it will be my home base."

Right, Audrey. Once Wendy's best friend, now her sharpest critic, who went beyond rolled eyes and judgmental glances to snide remarks. Audrey had a naturally slim build. Sure, she honed her body, but it was easy for her.

It wasn't easy for Wendy. Food called to her in ways Audrey couldn't possibly understand. Not vegetables, either, though a little greenery here and there probably hadn't killed anyone yet.

"What businesses downtown do you recommend as unique and interesting?"

Wendy forced her attention back to Roman. "Have you been to the Golden Grill? Probably not. You've only been in town a couple of days."

"Golden Grill? Audrey mentioned it."

"You should take her for lunch there sometime. It's unique in that the owners are absolutely obsessed with the Golden Girls sitcom, and it shows."

Roman glanced at his watch. "Would you like to go with me for lunch today?"

"I meant you should ask your sister."

He angled his head and grinned at Wendy across the coffee table. "She's busy doing who knows what. But I'd love to take you."

Would he accept no for an answer?

It had taken longer than Roman could have guessed to convince Wendy to accept a lunch date. Well, not a *date*, simply a meal with a friend. Now he pointed his SUV down the hill toward Jewel Lake. "Give me directions?"

"Um, sure, but if you've driven around at all, you've probably discovered the park just off the waterfront. The Golden Grill is on the street alongside it."

"Oh, I've seen the park. Looks like a great, relaxing refuge in the middle of things."

"Yes. It's popular. It has a playground as well as a path all around the duck pond and benches to take in the view, so it appeals to people of all ages."

"Perfect." He focused on the short drive, since Wendy didn't seem inclined for casual chit chat. She was clearly uncomfortable with him, and he couldn't for the life of him figure out why. Her ex had eroded her self-confidence, but why would that extend to Roman? They'd known each other forever!

He couldn't say they'd been friends. With a nine-year age difference, he'd likely been more like a bothersome gnat, though she'd never made him feel that way. Unlike Audrey, who'd made her annoyance with babysitting him clear. Not Wendy, though. She'd been patient and kind.

Now, the age difference didn't matter, did it? He'd rarely thought about the ages of people he befriended in the past 20-ish years, once he'd begun to feel secure in his own skin.

Bingo.

Wendy didn't seem to feel that way. Who knew self-confidence had little to do with chronological age?

He turned onto Garnet Drive, where city hall presided over the end of the park that spanned several blocks toward the waterfront. "Where should I park?"

"The Golden Grill is near the middle, so wherever works for you."

"Ah. There it is." He found an angle parking spot. They'd have to cross the street on foot, but traffic was light. He imagined it was busier during summer months than on a random Monday in late September. With any luck, he'd still be in Jewel Lake to see the next tourist season for himself.

Hmm. Why did that seem like an interesting thought? He'd planned to make the region his home, but staying in Jewel Lake itself had kind of depended on how he and his sister got along after years apart. She was all the family he had... at least, family who was speaking to him, which did not currently include his parents.

But Audrey wasn't the only pull to Jewel Lake. He'd been excited to hear Wendy was here, too. How had he thought he'd relate to her after all this time? Peers? Friends?

He hopped out of his SUV, planning to open Wendy's door, but she was already struggling to exit. He turned to look at the park with its golden leaves while waiting for her. No one wanted to be stared at while performing a simple movement. Finally, he turned toward her with a smile. "Ready?"

"Sure." Her smile seemed forced.

Was his company really that unwelcome? He glanced both ways and, seeing no oncoming traffic, headed across. She walked beside him, keeping a vehicle width between them until they approached the restaurant. He held the door, sweeping a bow. "After you."

"Thank you." Her glance landed somewhere beyond his face.

A middle-aged woman stood at the podium. "Table for two?" She looked between them with interest.

"Yes, please."

"A table rather than a booth, please," Wendy put in.

Aw, Roman would have preferred a booth by the window rather than a table in the middle, but whatever.

"High-top?" the woman asked.

"No, thank you."

He trailed Wendy as she followed the host, then took a seat across from her. The woman set two menus on the table and mentioned drinks. Wendy asked for water, and Roman echoed her.

Roman studied his menu. Everything from liver and onions to lunch salads to Reuben sandwiches. "What's good here?"

"Everything, from what I hear." Wendy closed her menu. "I think I'll have the pear gorgonzola salad with grilled chicken."

"Mmm. Sounds good, but I think I'm hungrier than that."

When the server appeared, he asked for a burger, fries, and a side salad. Wendy hesitated before placing her order. While they waited, Roman looked around and stifled his low whistle. "Wow, you weren't kidding me about the sitcom vibe. It's... intense."

"Isn't it, though? Pam can't handle coming in here. She says all the huge faces on the posters creep her out."

He chuckled. "I can understand that. I might have to focus on you so I can block them out."

She looked down to where she straightened the napkin-wrapped flatware bundle. "I'm not much to look at. The sitcom stars are much prettier, although dated."

He angled his head and studied her. "Why do you do that?"

Wendy's cheeks pinked. "Do what?"

"Deflect. I get the feeling you don't see your own worth."

She chuckled but didn't meet his gaze. "Oh, I'm pretty sure I understand how much I'm worth." She tucked her hands into her lap.

All her body language screamed exactly what it was she believed. "Beloved child of God," he said quietly.

"Sure." She managed a smile.

"You don't believe me."

"Of course, I do. I know God loves me. He loves everyone."

"Which doesn't detract from how much He personally loves you, Wendy Clarke." He'd nearly said Bilson but caught himself in time. She hadn't been Wendy Bilson in decades. Decades in which he hadn't known her. Decades in which she'd been married, given birth six times, and eventually been discarded.

Roman didn't know the woman across from him. Not really. He had memories of the teenage Wendy, but that was it. At Maranatha, Laura had been far friendlier, but Roman didn't much care. She was probably nice enough, but he kept seeking Wendy out.

Why? Was it just that he couldn't bear to see anyone sad? Anyone putting themselves down?

If it were something more, he wasn't sure he was ready to acknowledge it. They'd only been back in the same setting for two days. It had to be that she was still somehow familiar from a shared past.

That was it.

For sure.

CHAPTER
Five

"YOU WHAT?" Wendy pulled back from her computer in the staff lounge downstairs and stared at Julia.

Julia frowned. "I gave Roman the passcode to the staff elevator. It's not like he's a regular guest, not with him being Audrey's brother plus working on advertising projects for the inn with you.

"But... he's a guy."

"Someday we might have a male staff member who lives downstairs. I don't see it happening, but it could. We have a vacant suite now that Pam has moved out."

"But..." Wendy pursed her lips. The staff area had been her sanctuary, although Audrey had once brought her brother down to see her quarters. Now he had access whenever he wanted, and no male should have easy access to women's spaces.

Back when Wendy counseled at Bible camp, that would never have happened. The male and female counselors had been kept firmly apart during sleeping hours, and for good reason. Were things different in their 50s? And Roman was only 46.

Only.

He made her so uncomfortable. If Julia had mentioned she might offer Roman access, Wendy would have pushed back, but it was too late. "Well, it's your call, I guess."

Co-ed spaces were a thing, but Roman saw too much. Too deep. A few days ago, he'd called her out on God's love for her. She'd changed the subject, but she'd been able to tell he'd seen through it and allowed her to deflect.

See? Ridiculous. He made her uncomfortable because he pointed her to God? But that was only part of it. A small part. Mostly, he made her uncomfortable because he actually saw her, Gwendolyn Marie Bilson Clarke. In under a week, he'd penetrated right into the insecure core of her, the part she'd managed to hide from everyone else.

But now she wondered. Did everyone else see her doubts, too? Maybe they marveled that she tried to cover up a canker sore that was obvious to everyone.

Ugh. She hated herself.

Julia settled onto the secondary desk chair. "Wendy, is everything okay?"

"Sure. Why wouldn't it be?"

"I didn't think it would be a problem with Roman. I'm sorry I didn't consult you, but it wasn't because I don't value your opinions."

Hopefully, Julia wouldn't see the tears that Wendy blinked back. "I'm being silly. It's totally fine."

"I feel like you're carrying the weight of the world on your shoulders. Is there anything I can do to help?"

Wendy glanced back at the Maranatha ad she'd been working on. "Am I letting my work slip?"

"Not at all. I didn't mean about the inn. I meant as a friend."

Julia was the kind of person whom everyone liked because she was genuinely interested in them. She'd been their mother hen in college, and she hadn't changed a whit.

But opening up would be painful and confusing for them both. Wendy couldn't do that to her friend. Julia had enough going on with managing Maranatha Inn. "I'm okay."

"If you ever need someone to talk to, please pick me."

"Thanks. I'll keep that in mind." Wendy managed a smile.

Julia gave her a searching look then squeezed her shoulder before heading to the elevators.

Wendy watched her go. Across the space, beyond the covered patio, rain drizzled grayly, unendingly, a metaphor for life.

She gave her head a shake and turned back to the advertising dashboard. The click ratio from the newest ad to the reservation app looked solid, and actual bookings reflected a reasonable uptick. She'd need to come up with another idea in the next few days but, for now, she could relax.

Next, she checked enrollment for Saturday's workshop. Whew. Near capacity. Who knew so many people had old hardcovers they were willing to desecrate? She consulted her list and began setting up another workshop offering. It seemed Jewel Lakers liked to peer a few weeks into the future.

"Hey."

Wendy started to see Roman standing close beside her chair. Inside her bubble. "Hi! I didn't hear you coming."

"I wasn't trying to sneak up on you. You look deep in thought."

She shook her head and rolled her chair a few inches away from him. "Just copy-and-paste for future workshops. The registration form is all set up and only needs each week's pertinent information."

Roman grabbed the back of the chair Julia had vacated and pulled it closer before settling into it and adjusting the height for his tall frame. "Systems are super helpful."

"Yes." Wendy saved the page and exited the program. "I can finish that up later. What can I do for you now?"

"I didn't mean to interrupt."

"It's fine. I can do that any time I have a few minutes. Julia mentioned you wanted to talk about her campaign."

"Sure." He nodded. "I'd like to film segments around the inn and briefly introduce Julia for the first one. But... I have a problem."

Wendy eyed him. "What's that?" Not that she wanted to know... or maybe she did.

"I've scanned dozens of different YouTube channels in various genres, and there are a few ways the videography can go. Some creators use a selfie-stick, but I don't personally love that option. The narrator is bigger than life in a fair segment of the screen. Another option is for the narrator to shoot what he or she sees and never appear onscreen, so there's this disembodied voice blabbing in the background. Some, of course, go back and forth between the two views."

Wendy allowed herself a chuckle.

"But the best channels seem to have a camera person who never — or rarely — speaks. Sometimes the narrator is showcased and, at other times, it's the project or view or whatever is pertinent in that genre."

She pinned her smile in place, but what was he getting at?

"From the inn's ads and social media, you've got a great eye for the camera. I consulted Julia, and she said it was okay to ask you if you'd be my camera person."

What? No! "I couldn't do that."

"Why not? I can pay you, if that's a concern."

"No, that's not it."

"Julia said she can spare you for a couple of hours a day, if you were willing."

Wendy gulped for air and closed her eyes. "She's right that anyone can do what I do here."

A warm hand settled on her knee, and her eyes flew open to take in Roman just inches away.

"You're doing it again."

"Doing what?" But she knew what he meant. She scooted her chair far enough that his hand dropped away.

"Downplaying your worth." His gaze was so intent, so kind, that she couldn't look away. "Don't do that, Wendy. You bring a unique flavor to Maranatha Inn with both your workshops and the inn's social media presence. We're not asking you to give up either of those things. Julia meant she could pinch-hit house-keeping in your stead for a few weeks while you help me."

Wendy blinked. "Julia… would clean guest rooms?"

"Why not? She doesn't seem to me to be the kind of boss who wouldn't do any of the jobs around here that need it."

"I never expected this." And still couldn't believe what he'd told her. "I don't think I'm that good at videos."

"I beg to differ. I'm not asking you because I'm desperate. I'm asking you because I have seen solid evidence that you have a good eye for what engages viewers."

She choked back the, "Really?" that wanted to erupt. He'd only call her on it again. "I don't know what to say."

"How about yes?"

Roman's gaze seemed to bore through her eyes and clear into her soul. He seemed to see something in her that no one else ever had. Not even Dave. Maybe especially not Dave.

"Okay?" Her response came out weak, breathless. This was such a bad idea.

"You won't regret it. We're going to have a lot of fun together."

Precisely what she was afraid of.

Roman grinned at Wendy. That she was having second — or perhaps third — thoughts was clearly written across her face. But she'd agreed, and he'd hold her to it. He didn't want to think too deeply about why, but it wasn't only the success of his new venture he had in mind.

Nope. No more contemplation on that score.

He slid his tablet in front of her. "Here is one of the scripts I'm working on. How would you video this?"

Wendy scanned the narrative. "A pan of the property, zooming into the front doors. Julia throws them wide and welcomes the guests — er, the camera — in. You'd be onscreen from about here —" she tapped a block of text "—and then shown talking to Julia. I could then pan the lobby and dining room while you converse with her."

Roman nodded. "I can see that." He leaned over the tablet and scrolled down further. "How about here?" Now he was close enough to Wendy to feel the heat from her body. To inhale the fragrance of her shampoo. If she were wearing perfume, he couldn't make it out.

Creeper. He leaned back. What in the world was he doing, sniffing his sister's best friend? He hadn't exactly been doing that. He also hadn't exactly *not* been doing that.

Sheesh. Get a grip, Roman.

And she was talking about camera angles, so he refocused on her melodious voice. He'd enjoyed listening to her sing softly beside him in church. She had a nice soprano, and it was probably her low self-image keeping her from belting it out like Laura had from a few seats over.

Right. Back to the project. Back to the rainy day. "Guess we can't film that first one today with all the drizzle, but we could do a practice shoot of the second one, just to see how well our ideas mesh."

Wendy hesitated. "We could. Perhaps after lunch?"

"Sure, if you need to wrap up your current project first, that will work." He was itching to breathe life into his ideas. He wanted fresh, fun, inviting content, not zombie-level. He'd listened to too many creators drone on. After some testing videos, he was fairly confident he could do better, but he wouldn't know for sure until they were filming actual content.

It took a bit of ego to think he could make it on a cutthroat platform like YouTube. That he had a great voice and a decent enough image to edge in front of other creatives. Who did he think he was?

No. He wasn't traveling that road again. He'd done all the soul-searching and research over the past months. He had a decent shot at it, if he could pull his vision together. Wendy would be a valuable asset.

"Okay." Wendy moved his tablet to the side and jiggled her computer mouse.

"We could do lunch together first. Doesn't the Copper Carafe have a deli menu?"

Wendy's head whipped toward him. "Um, they probably do, but that's okay. Thanks, anyway."

"Everyone needs to eat, so unless you have other plans…" *Way to sell it, Rome. You're gonna have to do better than that with your channel or it will sink without a ripple.*

"I… never mind. Thank you, but perhaps we should keep interactions to a business level."

Was that a brush-off from a woman who wouldn't even look him in the eye while she said it? "I thought we were friends who'd just become business buds. Friends do lunch. They hang out."

"I'm not sure how to say this, because I'm sure it will sound like I'm full of myself."

Not even if she tried.

"But I don't think it's appropriate. You're my friend's younger brother, and I don't want people to speculate. It's not seemly."

"Seemly?" Roman managed not to laugh. "Now there's a word you don't hear every day."

"It means appropriate." Wendy looked down at her hands clenched in her lap.

"I know what it means, but I have no idea what is unseemly about a man and a woman who are friends having lunch together. Or… more."

"People will think there's something going on." She hesitated, and he strained to hear her muffled words. "And we all know that could never be."

Roman studied her profile. Her face flushed, her shoulders hunched, and she seemed fixated on her hands. He took a deep breath and let it out. Here went nothing. "Why could it never be?"

He'd startled her into looking at him, if only for a few seconds, before she turned away again. "A man like you would never be interested in a woman like me. Not *that* way."

"What kind of way?" Maybe he was rude to persist, but he couldn't help it. Not when she'd started down this path.

"You know." The flush in her cheeks deepened. "A, a relationship. Dating. I'm sure you never thought people might assume that. I'm warning you what a small town is like, what Audrey and my group of friends here are like. Audrey would not, well, be impressed."

"You and Audrey are friends."

"We were, once upon a time."

He could barely hear her, so he leaned even closer. "What happened?"

"She thinks I'm an idiot for mourning the demise of my marriage. She..." Wendy scrunched her eyes shut. "She's always after me about my weight. She doesn't approve of anything about me."

"My sister has her own set of issues which have nothing to do with you."

"Well, it sounds like it has something to do with me when she looks at me and calls me fat." A tear squeezed out the corner of Wendy's eye. "I'm sorry. I shouldn't be talking like this about your sister." She pushed the chair away and stood.

"Wendy."

"What?" She gulped but didn't look at him.

"You're a beautiful woman."

"I'm fat."

"You're a beautiful woman." He couldn't deny she was perhaps heavier than many women, but that didn't mask her attractiveness.

"Thank you."

"You don't believe me."

"How could I?" She gestured to her body. "Evidence."

"There is far more to beauty than body shape. You have an

amazing personality, too." He'd imported enough beauty products for the family company to know he trod a fine line, but that didn't keep it from being true. Even if she didn't seem predisposed to believe him. "You're thoughtful, and creative, and—"

"I'll meet you at 2:00 in the lobby." Wendy hurried down the corridor to her room and shut the door behind her.

Roman stared after her. How could he convince her? Maybe it wasn't his job to do more than pray for her. Not yet.

He hadn't been lying. She had many stunning qualities, and he'd love to get to know the real Wendy better, the one beneath the self-deprecation she wrapped close like a protective cloak. Was he going to need to talk to his sister about adding to her friend's issues?

Maybe he ought to pray about that, too.

CHAPTER
Six

IT TOOK every minute of those three hours for Wendy to gather her nerve together to meet Roman in the lobby. If she had anywhere to go, she'd have seriously considered fleeing Maranatha Inn completely, but there was nowhere. Not back to Oregon. She didn't have it in her to compete with Dave for their children's love and attention.

In an abstract way, she knew they could love both parents, but in reality? In reality, they had to choose. Ezra and Faith had picked their father, while the others pretended neutrality.

Enough. She checked the batteries in her camera. She'd bet a lot of content creators used cell phones, but hers was an older, basic model. She had a good camera and knew how to use it, so it was the obvious choice.

For a long moment, she stood inside her suite, trying to control her breathing. "Lord? Please help me. I don't know what I'm doing. I don't know why Roman wants me to help him with this. I'm no good at it or anything else except maybe a few simple crafts." She had to be honest with God, after all. "Thanks for the ability to do them. I appreciate it. But I don't know how to navigate this thing with Roman."

It wasn't the videography. So long as she was behind the

camera, all would be fine on that score. It was… well, it was Roman himself.

"God? I can't be attracted to him. I know it's ridiculous to even think about it, so if You could just remove these silly emotions from me, I'd really appreciate it a lot. He's my friend's brother. My former friend." Was restoring that relationship even an option? How?

It was 2:00. Wendy cast one more fervent plea heavenward before making her way upstairs to the lobby, where Roman and Julia sat chatting by the fireplace.

Roman rose as she approached, a smile wreathing his entire face from the laugh lines around his eyes to the dimples bracketing his mouth, partially hidden in his trim beard. "Hey, Wendy!"

"Hi." She managed a smile for him then looked at Julia. "Hi, Julia."

"Hello, Wendy."

Awkward. Her fingers tangled in her camera strap. "Why don't the two of you sit there and talk about the history of the inn while I film?"

Julia chuckled. "The inn's history is quite short."

"Good. Then the segment won't be long enough to bore anyone."

"That's fair."

"Let me check the lighting and figure out angles. I'll be moving around the space. Don't mind me."

Roman resumed his seat beside Julia, angled toward her. "If we keep talking while she does that, she can get an idea of volume, as well."

Good point.

Julia nodded. "Have you met our neighbor Monte Newman yet?"

"I don't think so."

"This whole hillside used to be one large tract owned by Monte's parents. He bought the section to the north of us from his parents years ago and, after their deaths, he and his sister, Sheryl Johannesson, divided the rest of the land. They sold part of it to Happy Trails Stables and part of it to George and me to build Maranatha Inn. Monte and George were great chums in their youth, and we'd been back in touch occasionally over the years. I didn't know Monte's wife, Karen, all that well, but I did enjoy spending time with her when we all got together."

"It must be nice to have great lifelong friends," Roman replied.

Wendy zoomed in on his face for a quick moment then out again. Natural light from the window shone more on his face than on Julia's.

"Yes, it's such a blessing to have friends like Wendy and the others who came to rescue me when I needed help launching the inn."

Wendy couldn't help the snicker. Oops. She didn't dare allow herself into any of the official videos.

Julia turned toward her. "What's so funny, Wendy?"

"You rescued us — at least, me — more than we rescued you."

"I'm so glad it's been mutually beneficial. That's the best kind of friendship, isn't it?"

Roman rubbed his bearded chin. "I haven't stayed close with anyone from my youth."

Julia refocused on him. "It's beautiful and hard at the same time, like many things in life. George was there for Monte when Karen died. And now... Monte has been here for me following George's passing."

Wendy swallowed the observation that Monte clearly hoped for more with Julia, but then Karen had passed on years ago, while George's demise was relatively recent.

She lowered the camera, hit replay, then adjusted a setting. "Keep talking. I've almost got it."

Roman nodded as she resumed filming. "I've come to see how much I've missed, not having a tight group like you do. I always envied Audrey that."

And Wendy was part of that sisterhood. Julia had invited her to Montana. Pam and Chris, especially, had been very welcoming. She had the least to do with Laura, and Audrey... well, Audrey was mostly critical, though she'd complimented Wendy a couple of times about the workshops. She'd even participated in one over the summer and seemed to enjoy it.

Was the issue all in Wendy's head? The issue where she felt like the least deserving to be here, like she was on the fringe. She didn't have major life skills to offer, not like Pam in the kitchen or Audrey in the fitness room or Laura with her experience running her own bed-and-breakfast in Maine. Chris was clearly in her element operating the Christmas tree farm.

Only Wendy had nothing... but here she was, filming a video for social media. Roman said she was good at it, and he wasn't completely wrong. Her content did get a lot of likes, clicks, and comments.

Who knew photographing her kids and the other students in their homeschool group could hone a valuable skill? Or planning all those events and fundraisers? She'd been good at that, too. Granger had asked her to help plan a fundraising event at Creekside Fellowship last Thanksgiving and had hinted he'd like her to help again.

She, Wendy, had skills. Who'd have guessed?

She blinked back emotion and refocused on the conversation in front of the fireplace.

"What's the key to a long-lasting marriage like you and George had?"

Uh... why would Roman ask that? Was he considering marriage? With whom? Wendy had seen no signs he had a girlfriend. Not the way he'd been focused on drawing her out. Oh. But no. Her imagination was running wild. He couldn't possibly be considering *her*!

"We kept Jesus first. I know it sounds cliché, but that really was our key. We read the Word together. Prayed together. Encouraged each other in our individual walks with the Lord. If both parties truly desire God's best, I believe He blesses that. George took seriously his mandate to love his wife as Christ loves the church. He never pulled the 'I'm the master of this house' thing on me. We both worked on submitting to each other like Paul advises in Colossians three."

I'm the master of this house.

Wendy heard the statement in Dave's ringing voice. Wasn't that the biblical way, for the husband to be the head of the wife, and for the wife to submit? She'd have to check out the chapter Julia mentioned.

"My dad was authoritarian like that," Roman mused. "Still is, really."

"Okay, that's enough," Wendy cut in. "I've got some footage to work with. Let me play with it and see what you think when I'm done."

Because she couldn't handle any more talk of what made a good marriage. Had hers been doomed from the start?

"I can't believe you asked Wendy to be your videographer."

Roman looked up as his sister stormed into his line of sight. "Why not? She's good at it."

"You know why not."

He tapped to save his notes and set his tablet aside. "Actually, I don't. Maybe you could enlighten me." She was going to, anyway. Might as well pretend to be open.

The rain had cleared off enough that he'd taken his 'office' to an Adirondack chair in the gardens behind the inn. It seemed Audrey had seen him from the windows or deck and decided it was time they had a sibling chat. Oh, yay.

Audrey perched in the large chair kitty-corner from his. "Wendy's in a bad place, Roman. Surely you can see that."

"You mean because her self-esteem is suffering?"

"Because she can't even take care of herself."

Roman forced his eyebrows to stay in place. "She's a competent adult. As far as I've noticed, she showers and brushes her teeth."

Audrey slammed her hand against the wooden armrest. "You know what I mean. She's crazy overweight, and she won't do anything about it. It's like she doesn't even care about her health."

"Sis, you know I love you, but why is that your problem?"

"What on earth do you mean? She's my friend! Of course, I care that she's unhealthy."

"Is she your friend?"

"Well, duh! We've been chums since we were kids. You know. You were there."

"Friends hang out together like you two did back then."

"She was fun then."

This should be enlightening. "And she's not fun now?"

"Not really. She's… mousy. Such a downer."

Mousy? Not the word Roman would have used, but whatever.

"We might've once hung out together, but now she avoids me. She can't take a little helpful advice."

Roman shook his head. "You don't see it, do you?"

"I don't know what you're talking about."

"No one wants to hang around people who don't approve of them. Around people who criticize them all the time."

She huffed a breath. "It sounds like you're on Wendy's side. You always were. You followed her around like a hopeful puppy. It was disgusting."

Roman gritted his teeth. "You're doing it again."

"Doing what?"

Could she really not see how hurtful her words were? "I don't think it was awful for me to like being with Wendy when I was little. She saw me as a person. A much younger person, sure, but someone with feelings and hopes. She hasn't changed. She really sees people."

Audrey stared at him. "How does she see you now? You're

still following her around, but it's not as cute as it was when you were five and told her you wanted to marry her."

Roman chuckled. "I wonder if Wendy remembers. I'd nearly forgotten."

"Who knows. I wouldn't ask her if I were you."

He raised his eyebrows at his sister.

She huffed. "She'll think you're trying to start something up now that you're both adults. Dave divorced her for a reason, Roman."

"Steve divorced you for a reason, too."

Audrey narrowed her gaze. "Who says it was Steve who filed?"

"That's what he said, but I'm sure it was mutual. My point is that every divorce has reasons. Some are likely better than others, but in the end, it's the same thing."

"Just because you've never even been married."

"I was impressionable enough to see what our parents' marriage was like. And I had a front-row seat to you and Steve." He shuddered. "Frankly, it didn't look all that inviting."

Audrey deflated back into the wooden deck chair. "You're right. It wasn't that great. As for Steve, he just wouldn't listen to me. He worked too much. Ate too much junk food. Wouldn't get any movement in his days. The more I tried to help him, the worse his habits became."

"Sis, you know I love you."

She eyed him sideways. "Nothing good ever comes after that line."

"Has it occurred to you that you might be your own worst enemy?"

"I don't know what you mean." Her arms crossed over her chest.

"Don't you?" Roman wanted to say more. Way more. But then... wouldn't he be doing the same thing she did?

"I can't help if I'm more insightful than most people," she muttered.

Give her the benefit of the doubt. "Not everyone is ready to hear it, especially if they're somehow missing the love you feel when you're telling them." It *was* love, right? He sincerely hoped so.

"Great. Now my little brother hates me, too."

"Never. You can't push me away. You're stuck with me."

Audrey's eyebrows rose as she studied him.

Roman spread his hands wide. "You can try, I guess, though I'd much rather you didn't. We've each got enough problems without antagonizing our only sibling."

"Tell me. What's got your tighty-whities in a knot?"

That was an image he could do without. Also, he wasn't about to give his sister more ammunition. "Life. You know how it is."

"Uh huh."

Clearly, she wasn't buying his deflection, but he'd stand firm. No way was he telling her, of all people, how much trouble he was having keeping Wendy Clarke out of his head. And out of his heart.

CHAPTER
Seven

WENDY STEPPED off the elevator and glanced furtively around. She'd emailed the video link to Roman, so hopefully he was up in his room viewing it... but no.

He rose from the love seat by the fireplace. "Wendy! I hoped to catch you."

Catch her he had. Likely without meaning to.

"That video looks great! You're making me believe we can really pull this off."

"You're quite photogenic and have an easy way in front of the camera. You're the one who made the video look so good." Was she giving away too much? "You and Julia. She's the same."

"A good photographer can bring out the best in nearly anyone."

"Thanks, but it wasn't a challenge." Not that way. The challenge came in not replaying the footage a thousand times after she'd completed the edits just to watch him in action and see his smile reach his eyes. See those dimples crease his cheeks.

Remember Dave.

But why should she? Their marriage had been dead for a couple of years before they'd buried it, and *that* had been several years now.

She didn't deserve another chance. Not that Roman was asking for one. And if she did, someday when she was maybe 70, it wouldn't be with a man nine years her junior.

Dave married Shyanne, who was 20 years younger. But it was different when the man was older.

How?

She didn't know. It just was. She didn't make the rules, but they were clear enough. *Thou shalt not date a man nine years younger.*

Where in the rulebook was that?

"You okay?"

Wendy gave her head a shake. It was bad enough when her thoughts wandered this direction in the privacy of her own room. Far, far worse when Roman was present. What if he could read her mind? He'd laugh his head off.

No, he wouldn't. But that didn't mean he felt the same as she did.

Which was an attraction she absolutely should not feel. Audrey's little brother! Imagine being Audrey's sister-in-law. Wendy shuddered. Now there was a fate that should help her keep this infatuation in check.

That's all it was.

Wait. He was talking. "Pardon me?"

"I hope you're only thinking good thoughts. Maybe about more videos we can make together."

"Um, sure. We can make more."

"Great. I've got a list a mile long. Some of them are no doubt better ideas than others." Roman bit his lip and looked at her.

She did not look at his lips. Not for long, anyway. "That's how it is with my workshops, too. Some look great on paper until I drill into the logistics. Then many concepts fall by the wayside."

"I want to take you for lunch, Wendy. I want to talk about these videos and maybe…" His voice trailed away, but his gaze remained fixed on hers.

Wendy could feel the heat building on her cheeks. Gah, it was hard to keep her thoughts in check when everything showed on her face. "Maybe what?"

"Wendy, I like you. I like you a lot. I want to spend time with you."

She blinked. Pulled back.

Roman shook his head with a rueful grin. "Too much. Too soon. I'm sorry. I get it."

"You can't possibly mean it." Even though she'd been thinking it herself. It had been her little secret, a wee obsession she used for comfort, like Selah had sucked her thumb as a toddler.

His dark eyes looked straight into hers. "I absolutely mean it. You're a terrific person."

Was this when she reminded him she was overweight? That his sister almost certainly would not approve? No. He could see. He knew she was fat. And he knew Audrey better than Wendy did.

"I…" Great. Now she couldn't even form sentences.

Roman offered her puppy-dog eyes. "Please?"

Something between a gasp and a laugh leaped from her throat. Not very ladylike at all. "I'm sorry. I just remembered you making that same begging face when you were little."

"I don't want to remind you of five-year-old Roman. That was 41 years ago. I may have grown up just a little since then."

"Quite a bit, if we're being honest." She prided herself on candor, even if it meant pointing out her own flaws. Roman probably had a fault or two as well, but she couldn't think of any at the moment. Besides being related to Audrey.

He grinned. "I like honesty almost as much as I like you."

If she'd been reading his words in a romance novel, she'd be fanning her face right now, because that heart-melting statement was what every woman wanted to hear. "Thanks." Probably.

"So, lunch? Are you needed for anything here this afternoon, or can we head into Missoula? There's a farm-to-table restaurant with great reviews I'd love to check out."

Oh. He meant he wanted to do research for his channel. That

made more sense. "Okay. We can do that. Should I bring my camera?"

Roman shook his head slowly. "This is a date. We don't even need to talk about work today if you don't want to."

She gulped back panic. "A... a date?"

"Yes, please."

Dave... but Dave was not a consideration. It turned out he'd broken their marriage vows prior to Shyanne. Business trips? Ha.

Wendy was not tied to Dave anymore. Yes, they shared children and grandchildren. She missed the babies and their parents. Thankfully video chats were a thing. But still. She didn't need to feel guilt where her ex was concerned.

Dave was history.

Was Roman her future?

Wow, nothing like allowing her mind to leap off on tangents. But she couldn't turn Roman's words any other way. He'd been clear. He wanted to date her, Gwendolyn Marie Bilson Clarke. Why was anyone's guess. The man was hot. Any woman would be lucky to snag his attention. Why would he look twice at her? Because the only kind of hot she was had to do with perimenopause.

"We could leave in half an hour," Roman was saying. "No need to change, though. Casual is fine. We'll have lunch and see what catches our eye to do this afternoon. Next time, I'll have a plan in advance, but today, we'll just wing it. Is that okay?"

Next time? There'd be a next time? How could he know she wouldn't embarrass him today? He didn't know her capacity for it, but having true hope for the future might be beyond her current abilities.

Roman promised himself a four-mile run on the treadmill tonight. He was going to need a way to come off the highs of the day. A solid workout should do the trick, although that would put him on Audrey's radar. Maybe he could take a page from Bruce's book and run outdoors. How far was it to Jewel Lake town limits? Probably a couple of miles. He'd take that route instead.

But first, the actual date. Wendy had agreed! She was nervous, but then, so was he. More was at stake than last time he'd taken a woman out a few years ago. Had he somehow been waiting for Wendy all along, not even knowing she might ever cross his path again as a single woman? God worked in mysterious ways.

He whistled as he trimmed his beard. Did she like it? Did Dave have facial hair?

Stop it, Roman. Dave doesn't matter.

Except he kind of did. Not that Roman feared Wendy might return to her ex, but, well, they had six kids together. It was easy thinking of pursuing a relationship with her until he remembered her children... who were mostly in their 20s. What would they think of their mom dating anyone, let alone a man so much younger? He shuddered to think.

We'll cross that bridge when we get to it.

But a mind honed with decades of market research wasn't likely to let it go for long. He was jumping ahead. He knew that. Either of them could decide at any time that this relationship wasn't a good thing.

It wouldn't be him. He was all in.

He stared at himself in the mirror above the sink, the trimmers poised half an inch from his jaw.

He was all in? Like... the forever kind?

The man in the mirror stared back, looking about as thunderstruck as he felt.

Roman had never contemplated permanence before. Not in his place of residence, and not in a relationship. Everything had been casual, fluid. No promises spoken, hinted at, or dreamed of. Ever.

And Wendy was a flight risk. She didn't believe in her own worth.

Do you really know what you're doing, Roman Scala? Because this is not a woman to trifle with.

The clock was ticking. He forced himself to finish the trim while the weight of that truth settled on him. If he would be the one to sever things, she'd lose any ground she'd gained in her battle with herself. If she were the one to call it off, it would almost certainly be because she heeded that inner voice.

How could he ensure that didn't happen?

He couldn't. Wendy was a free woman. Only God could work that out in her life, and He wouldn't force Himself on her. Wendy had to take the steps herself.

All Roman could do was pray for her and patiently show how much he cared.

He was a man of decisive action. If he didn't jump on a potential product, another company's rep would, and the Scala import company would lose out. He wasn't in that business anymore, but the mindset lingered.

Patience was not his forté.

Or… it hadn't been. It had better be now. He patted his pockets to confirm his wallet, phone, and keys were in place, saluted at himself in the mirror, and headed to the lobby.

Wendy stood in front of the fireplace with her hands clenched together. She'd changed into a pair of black leggings and a long sweater and carried a small purse slung over her shoulder.

He grinned at her. "Sorry if you had to wait for me." That's what he got for giving himself a stern talking-to in the mirror.

"It's okay."

Probably a mother of six had learned to get herself ready in two seconds flat. She wouldn't have had much time to primp during those years. Maybe Wendy had never been the primping sort.

She started toward the doors, and he followed her as they slid open automatically.

Roman set his hand on the small of her back. "My SUV is right over there."

Wendy shifted to create a bit of distance between them. Maybe that was a good idea, in case anyone watched from the inn. What did it matter, though? They were getting in the same vehicle and wouldn't return for hours. If Roman had his way, he'd pin an announcement on the bulletin board beside the inn's front desk.

He pulled open the passenger door, and she stopped a couple of feet back, staring at him. "What, no one ever opened the door for you before?"

She shook her head slowly.

Clearly, Dave didn't know how to treat a woman. His loss was Roman's gain. He waited until Wendy had seated herself and reached for her seatbelt before closing the door and rounding the vehicle. In a few minutes, they passed the Happy Trails Stables sign.

"Do you know the owners there?" Roman asked. "Julia suggested I do a feature on their business."

"Yes, I've met them. There are three sisters in their 20s. One of them, Alexia, has taken many of my workshops. She has quite an artistic bent."

"Introduce me sometime?"

She hesitated. "Sure."

Roman angled toward the interstate and glanced over. "Why the pause?"

"It's just…" Wendy turned slightly in the seat. "You'd probably like one of them better than me."

"Girls in their 20s?" He allowed his eyebrows to spring upward. "Not a chance. I'm not looking for someone that much younger than me."

"But a woman nine years older?"

He reached over the console and covered her clenched hands with his. "I didn't set out to fall for you, Wendy Clarke, but it seems to be happening nonetheless."

"I didn't…"

"Didn't what?"

She glanced his way. Too bad he needed to focus on merging into the other lane.

"I didn't plan to find you attractive, either."

Mental fist pump time. But the grin could not be kept under wraps.

CHAPTER
Eight

CINDERELLA HAD NOTHING ON WENDY.

Oh, the bliss of being treated like a princess for a few precious hours. It would all come to a screeching halt when they pulled back in at the inn and Roman's sleek black Jeep turned into a metaphorical pumpkin. There'd be no glass slipper left behind that fit only Wendy, so she'd enjoy this day as much as she possibly could.

They'd had a fabulous lunch, and she'd done her best not to be overly self-conscious about eating in front of him. They'd each ordered a salad, which had helped. At least, she hadn't had to watch him eat a juicy burger and a plate of fries across the table from her like the other day. Left to her own devices, she would definitely have ordered something like that, but she didn't want him to judge her habits.

Any more than he likely did now, not that he'd said a word.

After all, she'd already pointed out her plump figure to him, and he'd called her beautiful. The man needed his eyes examined. That was it! Although he was too young for cataracts.

Too young for her.

Nope. Not going there. Today was for the memory banks, like the scrapbooks she'd made for her kids as they grew, only she wouldn't dare record today in any sort of hardcopy others might discover.

Roman's arm brushed hers as they exited the Missoula Art Museum and stepped into the late afternoon sunshine. "That seemed up your alley."

"All kinds of art. For sure." It was the sort of place she'd taken her children for field trips in Portland. Art fed her soul.

His fingers tangled with hers.

Accident? It didn't seem like it, since he didn't pull away.

Who knew a 55-year-old woman's hand could tingle when touched by an attractive man?

"We're not far from a park by the river. Want to go there for a bit? Then we can find a place for dinner before heading back to Jewel Lake."

"Oh, no! I have a reservation at the inn for dinner." Why hadn't she thought to cancel?

Roman smirked and pressed against her arm. "Not anymore."

Now the heat of his touch spread further. "You canceled?"

"Sure did. Mine and yours, both."

"Oh…" That meant someone had known they were going out before they ever left the inn. "Who was at the front desk?" Hopefully she'd managed to sound casual.

"Laura."

"So, everyone knows."

His grip tightened. "I don't mind, but does it bother you?"

"Uh…"

"Hey." He stopped and turned toward her, now grasping both her hands as he searched her face. "Are you embarrassed to be seen with me?"

"What? No! It's not that."

"Then what?"

She huffed and looked down. She couldn't even see her own shoes below her belly. "The reverse."

"Wendy? I'm not embarrassed to be seen with you, if that's

what you're concerned about. I like you. I think you're beautiful and kind. I thought we'd established that already."

How long could it last? "But that's today."

"Pretty sure I won't change my mind tomorrow."

"How could you not?"

"Wendy."

Before she realized why he'd dropped her hands, he cupped her face between both of his. What was he doing? And why did she want to close her eyes and lose herself in his tender touch? Would he kiss her? Did she want him to? Sort of...

"Wendy, in some ways, I'm an impulsive guy. As a scout for my family's import company, I grabbed gadgets and patents and technologies on what might have seemed a whim to someone not in the business."

All she got out of that was impulsivity. But the rest of his words began to sink in, as well.

"My brain works very quickly, but it does work. I don't make decisions without running the probabilities, and then I stick with my choice. So, my interest in you may seem sudden and fleeting, but I can assure you, it's not. I know myself. I know that I have never felt this sort of attraction to any woman before. I kind of figured I'd be single forever, and I was mostly okay with it."

"Because of your parents. Because of Audrey and Steve."

"Neither couple made marriage seem particularly attractive, that's for sure. I'd decided if the Apostle Paul could find contentment and purpose in a solo life, so could I. It wasn't like my nomad life was conducive to a wife and kids."

Wendy grasped at that last word. "You want children?"

He shook his head slightly, his gaze fixed on hers. "I once thought I might. I like kids just fine, but I don't need them to fulfill my life."

"My baby days are over." Wendy felt like clapping her hand over her mouth, only Roman's hands were still in the way. His thumbs traced gentle, electrifying circles on her cheeks.

"I figured as much." His grin reached his eyes.

One of the things she loved about him.

Oh. Not that kind of love. Just general appreciation. Roman was genuine. He felt deeply and didn't seem to feel the need to hide his responses. Maybe it was the Italian in him. Weren't they noted for romanticism?

"I don't want to scare you, Wendy, but I do have an end game in mind."

"Oh?" Her voice squeaked. Great.

The humor in his gaze fled. In its place, he searched her eyes with solemn ones of his own. "I don't think we're ready for that exposé."

What was that supposed to mean? Also, he wasn't wrong. He already overwhelmed her with his focused attention and gentle touch. Her heart felt full to bursting, like she couldn't take any more. Just knowing this sweet, kind man cared for her would take a while to absorb.

Now Roman leaned forward and pressed his lips to her forehead. Then he stepped back and took her hands once again.

She'd been branded like a calf in a corral, like she belonged to him now. It wasn't an altogether unpleasant feeling. For a split second she'd thought he would kiss her properly, but now she had something still to look forward to.

If he didn't change his mind tomorrow, despite what he'd said.

But there was nothing in what she knew of him to cause that doubt. It was all on her side, because Dave had proved she wasn't desirable.

No. All Dave had proved was that Wendy wasn't desirable *to him*. It didn't mark her worth in every regard. But could she really believe that? Deep down inside? She took a shaky breath.

"You okay?" Roman asked softly.

"Maybe? I think so."

"Let's go find the park."

It had taken all of Roman's willpower not to pull Wendy fully into his arms and kiss her. She would have had no question whatsoever about his feelings for her if he'd done that, but he'd listened to the still small voice that warned him it was too soon. Much too soon.

What he'd told her was true. He wasn't into second-guessing himself. He never had been. He'd given everything to his job overseas for 25 years, but he'd signed it all away to cousin Leo with a bare minimum of mulling. Dad had been livid. Said Roman was impulsive and foolish. Even questioned his parentage, as if there'd been any doubt that Roman was his father's son.

Today had been perfection. He'd held Wendy's hand. She'd told him about her children and grandchildren, and even that hadn't fazed him. They'd fed the ducks and found shapes in the puffy clouds and laughed at jokes that likely weren't particularly funny.

As he drove up to the inn, he still wished he could kiss her, but no. He came around the vehicle, opened the door for her, and gave her his hand to help her out of the seat.

"Thanks for today," she whispered.

"My absolute pleasure," he replied, then watched her walk toward the door before driving to the parking lot.

When he entered the lobby a few minutes later, Wendy was nowhere to be seen. He'd suspected as much, then realized that Audrey stood behind the registration desk with her arm linked through Laura's. Both stared at him from beneath raised eyebrows.

"Good evening, ladies." He headed toward the staircase but, of course, he wouldn't be that lucky.

"Roman." Audrey's voice.

"Yes?" He turned slowly.

"What, exactly, do you think you're doing?"

Last-ditch effort. "Going to my room?" He covered a fake yawn.

"With Wendy."

"I'm sure she went to her own room."

Audrey came around the end of the counter. "You know what I mean. What were you doing with her today?"

"It's called a date. We had lunch, went to the museum, fed ducks at the park by the river, had a lovely dinner, and came back to the inn."

"Your childhood infatuation with her never faded?"

He stifled a laugh. "It definitely ended."

Audrey's eyebrows shot up. "Then how do you explain—"

"First of all, I'm an adult. I don't have to explain anything at all to you, but I will, because you're my sister and the only family member still talking to me. Or, at least, until tonight. Tomorrow is up to you."

She scowled at him.

"So, here's the deal. I hadn't thought of Wendy in years. Yes, my 'childhood infatuation' with her, as you so eloquently worded it, disappeared a long time ago, replaced with fond, but infrequent, memories. I did not invite her on a date because of our history."

"Then why?"

"Why does any man ask a woman out?"

"You can't possibly be attracted to her, so maybe you feel sorry for her. You don't have anything in common with her."

"Why can't I be attracted to her?"

"Have you noticed her shape?" Audrey's hands waved a wide silhouette.

"Yes?" Roman shrugged. "But I'm not sure what that has to do with appeal. I like that she's smart and kind and creative."

Audrey's nose all but curled. "I guess some men prefer their women with love handles."

Roman glanced at Laura, who lifted both hands in a what-can-

I-say gesture. He turned back to his sister. "I really don't think this is any of your business. You and Wendy are friends. At least, you once were. She is so much more than the shape of her body, just like you are."

Audrey's hands slid down her sides as her eyes narrowed. "What are you saying?"

"I'm saying that personality counts for so much more than looks. For the record, though, because I'm being perfectly honest, I do believe Wendy is beautiful."

"Gah! I don't know why I even bother."

He tried his best to pin his mouth shut, but he just couldn't do it. "You mean your fixation on working out? If some men are attracted to heavier women, you're wondering why you bother with your obsession with weight control?"

She stalked a few steps closer. "Shut your face, little brother. You've no right to talk to me that way."

Roman held his ground. "Audrey, you're my sister, and I love you. But you don't get to trash-talk the woman I've chosen to date. I am 46 years old. You were married, divorced, and widowed long before you were my age. My life is mine to live, and I will make my own choices. I suggest you take a good hard look in the mirror at who you've become and the attitudes you've embraced, and then talk to God about it."

"Is there anything else you'd like to add?" Audrey ground out through clenched teeth.

Roman tilted his head to one side and stared at his sister until she shifted slightly. "Not just now, thank you, but I'll let you know if something comes up."

"Whatever." Audrey flounced to the elevator and stabbed the button.

Movement from the corner of his eye caught Roman's attention, and he glanced back at the registration desk.

Laura offered two thumbs up and a firm nod.

And here he thought she was just like his sister. Maybe that wasn't true, after all.

The elevator doors opened, Audrey entered, and the doors closed.

"Way to go, Roman."

He turned back to Laura. "I'm not proud of how I spoke to my sister."

"You're right, though. You needed to stand your ground, and she needed someone to call her out on her stinky attitude. I hadn't realized she resented Wendy quite that much."

"I can't figure out why. Do you have any idea?"

Laura shook her head, chewing on her bottom lip. "It's like she's jealous of her, but why?"

"Jealous?" Roman's eyebrows hiked up of their own accord. "I don't see that at all."

"Not of Wendy's weight, I guess. But there must be something. I know Audrey picked up Wendy in Oregon last year on their way here, so they must have still been talking to each other at that point. I didn't arrive until a few days later, but the ice was already present."

Roman shook his head. "I don't get it." Maybe once he'd calmed down, he could try to figure out what had happened. Not tonight.

"Also? Wendy is a lucky lady to have you in her court."

"I appreciate that. Thanks, Laura." As he took the stairs two at a time, Audrey's other comment slid back into his mind.

You don't have anything in common.

Aside from shared history, his sister had a point. He was into travel and fitness. Wendy had asked few questions about the places he'd lived. As for fitness, Audrey was right. Sauntering those few blocks this afternoon had seemed to tire Wendy.

Was he interested in her only because his sister thought it was a bad idea? What did he really see in Wendy? Smart. Kind. Creative. All those things, yes, but were they enough?

CHAPTER
Nine

WHY COULDN'T Wendy spend the day in hiding? Living at Maranatha Inn with all her old so-called friends felt like swimming in a fishbowl. Naked.

Last night, she'd rushed past the front desk to catch the elevator before the doors closed. Not that she hadn't seen Audrey and Laura. Not that she hadn't heard Audrey's strident voice demanding to know where she'd been, why, and with whom. Like it was any of her business.

But Wendy wasn't being paid to cower in her quarters. She'd need to clean several rooms this afternoon, which meant she needed to check the social media and ad accounts this morning, which meant she needed the computer in the staff lounge.

Thankfully, Roman was unlikely to appear downstairs without warning. Back in Bible school, a guy would have called out "man on the floor" as he entered the women's dorm. No such rules applied at Maranatha.

Rules weren't relevant at all. If women in their 50s couldn't be trusted to make good judgment calls, humanity was a lost cause. And Wendy had not used good judgment yesterday. First, she shouldn't have agreed to Roman's insane request for a date.

Even if she'd gone, she shouldn't have enjoyed it. Shouldn't have quivered at his gentle touch, lost herself in his brown eyes, shouldn't have wished for a kiss.

How could she face him today? Face her friends, because surely everyone knew where she'd been? Audrey and Laura certainly did.

The only saving grace now was Audrey's schedule in the fitness center upstairs. She wouldn't deviate, not even to put Wendy in her place, not when there was a yoga class or whatever she did on Thursday mornings. Wendy wouldn't know. She hadn't set foot in Audrey's domain since her initial tour of the property over a year ago.

She was as put together as she could be, considering all the tossing and turning for the past eight hours. Now she listened at her door, but the staff corridor seemed quiet except for the laundry facilities at the far end. Time to earn her keep.

Wendy straightened her shoulders, marched to the nook at the back of the staff lounge, and booted up the computer. Before it could run through its start-up sequence, the elevator chimed, and the doors opened.

She braced herself for an angry Audrey, but it was only Laura. *Only*, nothing. The two women had been chumming around together for the past year, much like they had back in college. Could she pretend she hadn't seen Laura?

"Hey, Wendy."

Nope. No pretense. No lying. She'd taught that to her kids — Dave apparently hadn't received the memo — and she wouldn't stoop so low now. "Hi, Laura." She stared at the computer, willing the screen to clear.

"I just want you to know that I think it's pretty cool."

Wendy blinked. Before she knew what she was doing, she turned to Laura. "What is?"

"You dating Roman."

"Really? But Audrey hates me."

"That's her problem. She's just envious."

"That's crazy talk. He's her brother! And besides, she's so much more put together than I am. I'm nothing to be jealous of."

Laura's smile gentled as she took a seat nearby. "You really don't see it, do you?"

"See what?"

"You're awesome."

"I'm fat."

"Fat isn't a personality trait. It's a body shape." Laura didn't need to say it, but Wendy could practically hear the rest of it. Body shapes could be changed more easily than personalities. Yeah, yeah. At least, Laura didn't deny the truth.

Wendy jiggled the mouse and logged into the ad program.

"I'd like to kick Dave where it hurts."

Laura's tone was so conversational Wendy couldn't help the little giggle. "Pam said the same thing."

"I knew I liked Pam. But seriously, he did such a number on your self-esteem, and I want little more than to give him a piece of my mind. No holds barred. He's such a jerk."

Wendy couldn't deny it, but she'd also tried very hard not to vilify him in front of the children. He was their father, after all.

"Surely you're not still in love with that scum."

A sigh escaped, and Wendy turned to Laura. "No. But we were married nearly 25 years. I'd begun planning our silver anniversary party when he told me not to bother, as we wouldn't be together by that point."

"Ouch."

Aside from Julia, Wendy had been married the longest. But Julia and George had been happy to the end. Wendy had no reason to doubt her friend's testimony to that effect. "What happened with you and Gord?"

Laura's lips tightened. "Gord wanted kids… a son, specifically, to carry on his family name. I guess he figured I was a good bet, obviously fertile, since I had a toddler when we met. What we didn't know was that complications during Michael's birth had made it difficult for me to get pregnant again. Seemingly impossible."

Wendy had popped out babies practically on a whim. How would she have coped if she hadn't been able to? "I'm sorry. That must have been incredibly difficult."

"It was." Laura huffed a humorless laugh. "Gord was obsessed with sex. He had the most insane drive to see a miniature of himself. So, when we didn't conceive, he hauled me to a fertility specialist. We did all the things, succumbed to all the tests, and aside from some minor uterine scarring that shouldn't have been a big problem, they found nothing wrong. He was fertile. I was ovulating, but conception wasn't happening."

"Hence the divorce?"

"In the end, that seemed to be the biggest contributor. And by then, I was happy to be rid of him. I felt... well, I felt like an object good for only one thing, you know?"

She meant sex. And yes, Wendy did understand. She'd been quietly relieved when Dave's interest had waned. She hadn't even guessed he'd taken it elsewhere.

"And I couldn't even do that right, since I didn't get pregnant. Gord grew to despise Michael as a symbol of something that should have been his but wasn't. That was the last straw. I kicked him out on his rear."

"You're stronger than me."

Laura maintained eye contact while shaking her head. "That's not how I see it. You're an amazing person, Wendy. Remember, I've met your girls. They know what a great mom they have."

Wendy gulped. Selah and Faith had visited Maranatha at Thanksgiving and Christmas last year and for a week in the summer. "I feel like a failure there, too."

"I haven't met your other kids since they were young, but I'm proud of you for leaving Oregon and everything you knew. I'm sure it's been hard — I hate being this far from Michael and his family, too — but you needed a clean break, and you got it."

"I feel like I abandoned them." She'd never said that out loud before, but it was true. She'd put up a token front but when Faith had chosen public high school, Wendy hadn't been able to take any more. There'd been nothing left that she hadn't failed at.

"I could be wrong, but I don't think that's what happened."

Wendy glanced at Laura and twisted her hands together. "No? You weren't there."

"I think you needed some space to regroup and figure out who you are without Dave. And… I'm guessing you weren't able to find that space there."

Wendy let out a sharp exhale. "You have a point." Dave had done little but flaunt Shyanne in front of Wendy. Any time she'd grasped a shred of self-composure, the happy couple had been in her face again.

Seeing 30-year-old Shyanne dote over Adriel's little girls like a proud grandmother had been the final straw.

Clean break, indeed. From going in circles mourning Dave to going on a date with Roman Scala? That wasn't a clean break. It was insanity.

But was it?

Roman was going stir crazy. He'd done as much prep for his channel as he could. Now he needed videos to upload, but Wendy was busy. She had the inn's media to do, her weekend workshop to prep for, and three guest rooms to clean.

He wanted nothing more than to spend all day with her, but she had responsibilities, and he was at loose ends. He'd poked his head into the fitness room, thinking he'd log a few miles on the treadmill, but his sister's glower changed his mind. He'd said, "hi," and carried on.

The fall day beckoned, but for the first time since he could remember, he didn't want to explore it solo. He should, though.

Maybe check out Bruce's recommended hike, or poke around downtown, or something. Anything. But he stayed riveted to the view beyond the lobby's semi-circular window.

"Hey, Roman."

He turned to see Bruce approaching. The man wore a fleece jacket with a backpack slung over one shoulder. "Hi. What are you up to?"

"I'm headed up the road to the Christmas tree farm."

"To write?" The backpack contained the guy's laptop, right?

Bruce shrugged. "Maybe. First, I need inspiration."

"If I knew what kind of books you wrote, maybe I could help with that." Anything to deal with someone else's concerns rather than his own.

"I'll never tell." Bruce grinned, which kind of removed the sting.

"I haven't had a look at the tree farm."

"You could join me if you like."

"You know, I just might do that. You think I need a jacket? It seems pleasant."

"It gets cool in the trees. On the other hand, you might have a different internal thermostat than I do, so it's your call."

It was a good opportunity to envision how he'd present the tree farm in its own episode. He could chat with Chris, maybe, and get a feel for her goals for that part of Maranatha. "Give me five?"

"Sure."

Roman made it back to the lobby in three, followed the other man out the sliding doors then fell into step beside him. "Where do you hail from, Bruce?"

"A little mountain town in Colorado. You?"

"SoCal originally. A dozen countries since then. Most recently Indonesia."

"You were in the import business, I understand."

Roman nodded. "Until I sold my half of the family biz to my cousin a few months ago. Time for a new direction."

The man laughed. "This is different, all right. Plus, I hear you took our resident crafter out yesterday."

"News travels quickly."

"Those women seem like a tight group."

"My sister doesn't approve."

"Siblings, huh? Who needs them?"

"Spoken like a veteran." Roman chuckled.

"My older sister is a doctor in Spokane, and my kid brother is an architect in Denver. For years, they've been after me to pursue a real career."

"Writing isn't real?"

"Not according to Bob and Sally."

"If you're making enough money to live reasonably comfortably…" Roman let his voice drift away, not quite asking a question. Would Bruce take the bait?

"Close enough."

They entered the block of trees with its rows of pines, spruces, and firs. Roman breathed in deeply. "How do manufacturers of car fresheners miss the mark by so much?"

"Right?" Bruce chuckled. "Those are nothing but chemicals, but this—" he waved at the forest "—is nature like God designed it."

"You're a man of faith then?"

"Ransomed by the blood. Saved by grace. Blessed."

That about covered it. "Amen."

Roman had seen Bruce in church last Sunday, and he could use a friend, but what kind of friendship could exist if one party kept a big part of himself private? Roman was an open book and could think of no good reason to hide any part of himself. Did the other guy write twisted, sexy stories God wouldn't approve of? But Bruce said he was a believer, so he'd know he couldn't hide that from God. Hmm.

"Duke! Luna!" Bruce dropped to his knees and two dogs leaped on him. He rubbed the head of the smaller beagle and gave the chocolate Lab a hug around the neck.

The beagle bounced over to Roman, who bent and scratched the pup's long ears. "Which one is this?"

"Duke. He's three. This lady is Luna, and she's about a year older. Aren't you, pretty girl?"

The dog licked Bruce's face, and he laughed.

Roman liked dogs well enough, but he drew the line somewhere before slobber.

Bruce roughed up Luna's face, which the dog clearly adored. Then he patted her head and rose to his feet. "Where's Chris?"

The dog bounded off, the smaller one cavorting around her heels.

Roman eyed Bruce. "You know these dogs pretty well." Did that extend to Chris? He'd been so busy with Wendy, he hadn't noticed.

"Yeah. Our old dog, Brody, passed away last spring. By the time I felt ready to get another one, I'd decided to do a bit of traveling. Spend a few months here and there. Not every lodging choice allows pets, so it seemed best to wait, but I've missed having a canine companion. Luna and Duke fill in nicely for now."

He'd said 'our,' but it didn't add up. Roman eyed his new friend. "You're married?"

A shadow crossed the man's face. "I was, for 18 years. My wife passed away of a rare form of cancer a few years ago now."

"I'm sorry, man. Cancer is a nasty thing."

"Sure is." Bruce took a deep breath and exhaled as he turned in a slow circle, his arms spread out. "Makes a man grateful for every breath, you know? God knows the number of our days. Nothing surprises Him like it does us. However hard it gets at times, there's comfort in knowing that God's got it."

"I know what you mean." Not that Roman had experienced that sort of heartbreak. He'd held people distant enough that not much drama had penetrated. How had Wendy found her way into his heart? It certainly wasn't because she'd tried.

"Hey! Hi, Bruce." Chris came down a gap between trees,

pushing a wheelbarrow, her face lit up. Then she noticed Roman, and her smile faltered for a second. "Hi, Roman! What brings the two of you out to my domain?"

Bruce said nothing, so Roman jumped in. "A need for fresh air and to see some four-footed creatures."

The dogs bounded closer again, and Roman bent to pet them. He'd probably imagined Chris's restrained greeting.

CHAPTER

Ten

"ISN'T THERE a law about when you can start playing Christmas music?" Wendy asked Julia.

Julia beamed from ear to ear. "Thankfully, no! Don't you just love it?"

"I do love it. In December... but it isn't even November yet. We'll be doing pumpkin carving at next week's workshop, and somehow 'O Holy Night' doesn't seem like the right soundtrack."

Julia giggled. "That sounds like fun. I could run with it."

Wendy shook her head slowly, holding Julia's gaze.

"Oh, if you could only see your own face right now."

"It would be telling you no way."

"It would. Truthfully, it's never too early to remember our precious Savior's birth, you know? And I won't be playing carols 24/7 for the rest of the year."

"Whew." Wendy shuddered dramatically.

"Did you actually listen to the song that was playing when you came in? It's called "Hope has a Name" by Kristian Stanfill. It's fairly new as Christmas music goes."

"I didn't notice it, no. Something about new carols sounds like an oxymoron. There's so much tradition wrapped up in Christmas, and that's how I like it."

"Let me play it again for you."

"I need to prep for today's workshop. We're doing cinnamon stick candleholders today."

"You can listen before you set up. It's only about four minutes long."

"Right. Of course." But Wendy hadn't been kidding. Traditions were not to be trifled with. There wasn't any need for change. *New* carols, indeed.

On the other hand, Dave had royally upended her life. Maybe clinging to her former rituals didn't make sense. It wasn't like she could turn back the years and gather her young family around her on Christmas Eve to listen to Luke chapter two again. Dave had always read the story in his deep voice then prayed with the children.

What had happened to his faith? It had once been real, hadn't it?

"Here, listen." Julia tapped at the sound system controls behind the reception desk and music swelled.

The artist's clear, powerful voice began to sing of Jesus's birth and how He'd come to set people free from captivity. The Jewish people didn't understand for whom they'd been waiting. Not really. But… their future hope had arrived encased in flesh. Their Messiah had a name. Jesus. Emmanuel. They hadn't seen Him coming. Not the way He arrived, lived, and died.

Wendy didn't want to get sucked into the entire song, but it happened, anyway.

"Right?" Julia's voice had a triumphant ring to it. "Isn't that amazing?"

The song's invitation to those who were broken and in need of God's healing drove straight to Wendy's heart, and she blinked away sudden tears. "Yeah. I had no idea."

"I'll send you the link, so you can watch and listen to it anytime. It's become one of my favorites."

"Sure. Thanks."

"Hey, are you okay?"

Wendy managed a smile. "Sometimes it's hard, you know?"

"Aw, sweetie. Come here." Julia held out her arms.

Wendy stepped into them and returned Julia's hug. "Thanks."

"Want to talk?"

"I'm not sure." But if Wendy were going to unload on anyone, it would be faithful Julia.

"Is it Roman?"

She sighed and glanced around to make sure they were still alone. "Partly. Partly that Audrey hates me."

"She doesn't hate you."

"Really? Because you're clearly not seeing what I'm seeing."

"She's just… concerned."

"She has two big 'concerns'." Wendy air-quoted the word. "One, I'm offensively overweight, and two, I've apparently seduced her brother."

Julia opened her mouth and closed it again, shaking her head. "She cares a lot."

"Attacking people is an interesting way to show it."

"I know her methods aren't always the greatest, but her heart is in the right place."

"Toward you, maybe, but me? She despises me."

"Despise? That's such a strong word."

"You're sweet. Of course, everyone loves you. Also, you're our boss now." Wendy held up her hand to stop the protest she could see forming on Julia's lips. "Trust me, though. I'm not making up Audrey's reactions. Surely, you know that."

Julia sighed. "True, I've seen some concerning things. Should I talk to her? I don't want divisions in our group."

Wendy shook her head. "And have her think I was tattling on her? No way."

"I'll pray about it. Maybe God will present an opportunity for a conversation."

If only God cared that much about Wendy's problems. She'd once thought He did. How naive of her.

"Would you like to come for dinner to my apartment tonight?"

Wendy forced a smile. "Not tonight. I'm sorry." It was hard to believe that Julia would choose her friendship over Audrey's. Being close to both of them? Impossible. And Audrey was the better choice. She had more to offer Maranatha Inn than Wendy did. Not just anyone could run the fitness center, but the workshops were just a fun little add-on. Also, anyone could create ads.

Okay, maybe not that easily, but social marketing was a common skillset. Wendy was far from alone in her abilities.

"I'm sorry I haven't followed up with Audrey with what I've seen. I wasn't sure it was my place, but if it's affecting how we run the inn, I guess it is. I hate being confrontational."

Wendy huffed a laugh. "Trust me, I understand. It's so much easier to turn a blind eye when you finally realized someone you care about has been doing things that don't add up."

"Now we're talking about Dave."

Didn't all roads lead back to him? But maybe they didn't have to. Not anymore. Wendy braced her shoulders. "Just saying, conflict is hard for people-pleasers. I only want everyone to like me, but they don't."

"I like you. A lot. You're a friend I value a great deal, and I'm so glad you're here at Maranatha. Your talents are wonderful and helpful, but it's *you* I treasure."

"Because anyone could do the things I do here. You don't really need me."

Julia's hands held Wendy's shoulders as she looked deeply at her. "You're right about the projects and duties, but didn't you hear me? I'm glad it is *you*."

Yes, she'd heard. It was just so hard to believe. "Thank you. I'm trying to accept statements like that at face value." Like when Roman said she was wonderful.

"Roman's been good for you."

"When I'm with him, I think so. When I'm not, I have to agree with his sister. I'm not good enough for him. He's... he's so amazing, and I'm someone's discard."

"That's the past, my friend. Not the future. Light shines in the darkness, like the song says." Julia searched Wendy's face. "Have hope in Jesus."

"Hope is a great sentiment. Truly. And I liked that song, but it doesn't change anything."

"It does, though."

Wendy was done with this conversation. How could she make her friend understand the clamoring in her head? She believed in Jesus, and she'd cling to that until her dying day, but had God really buoyed her during the last few years? Maybe a little, but not like she desperately needed.

Maybe because Wendy was too much like Lot's wife in the Bible, who'd turned to look back at her old life when the angel of God had clearly told her not to. The woman had turned into a pillar of salt, never to breathe or walk or love again.

Wendy might not be a literal statue, but she'd felt the bonds strangle her in what seemed a similar way. She'd been all but paralyzed before she left Oregon and moved to Montana. She still wasn't sure it had been a good idea. She'd abandoned her family to Dave and Shyanne, but she'd needed air. Needed distance to get clarity, like Laura had reminded her.

"I'm praying for you, Wendy, with the words of Romans 15:13."

Wendy stared at her friend. "I don't recognize the reference offhand." Did she want to?

Julia placed both hands on Wendy's shoulders and looked deeply into her eyes. "It goes like this: 'I pray that God, the source of hope, will fill you completely with joy and peace because you trust in him. Then you will overflow with confident hope through the power of the Holy Spirit.' There's no true hope, no confident hope, without Jesus. And that's why I celebrate Christmas 12 months a year."

Wendy wanted to turn that last sentence into a joke to mask her discomfort, but... she couldn't. "Thanks, Julia. I need a friend like you."

"That's why God brought us back together. We need each other. All six of us."

Roman lingered across the lobby from the dining area where Wendy stood in front of a group of women, holding up a roll of white ribbon, from what he could tell from here. Would she feel harried if he took a seat and watched? Or maybe it wasn't even allowed, since he hadn't paid for a workshop. Huh. He could do that another Saturday. Too late this time, since the class was well underway.

"The dining room will smell amazing with all that cinnamon."

He blinked and turned to the registration desk. How had he not heard Julia coming up behind him? "Cinnamon?"

"Wendy's making cinnamon stick candleholders for all the tables, and we'll put battery-operated tea lights in them. The workshoppers have the option of a rustic look with burlap and holly or white ribbons and glass beads. I've opted for the more formal look for the dining room."

"Uh, that sounds nice." Guess he'd see when the dining room switched from its fall look? "She seems to have lots of ideas."

"Yes. There are fewer participants this time. Maybe because it's a much simpler craft than some of them, but that's okay. More older ladies are here than usually come. The pastor's wife and the church secretary are sitting over on the far side."

The women in question looked to be 60-something, not that he was an expert. Women were strange creatures with their hair dyes and Botox and layers of makeup. His gaze wandered back to Wendy. Was her hair color natural? The hue seemed like what he remembered from years gone by. Maybe blond strands faded into gray less noticeably than some colors.

Not that it mattered. His own hair had started to turn at the edges. Rite of passage, maybe.

"Granger!" Julia squealed. "Wow, it's been ages since we've seen you here!"

Roman turned to see the couple who'd just entered the inn as Julia ran and embraced them both. He'd met Pam, of course. She was the inn's chef, but she didn't live on the premises since she'd apparently married a while back.

"Granger, meet Roman Scala, Audrey's brother. Roman, our very own military hero, Granger Durand! Oh, and he's also Pam's husband." Julia beamed.

Roman extended a hand. "Nice to meet you. I've heard all about your romance from my sister. She's a fan."

The tall, angular man chuckled. "That's saying a lot, coming from Audrey."

Roman liked him already. "She might not have used those exact words."

"No doubt."

"Talking about me?" Audrey breezed in from the sitting area on the other side of the lobby. "Hey, Granger. We've missed having you around. My little brother needs a real man around here to look up to."

Roman shook his head but couldn't help rolling his eyes. "Anyone else have a bossy big sister who thinks she knows what's best for you? I mean, it might have been true when I was six, but maybe not so much 40 years later."

Granger chuckled. "I have a sister like that, too. Welcome to the club."

"See? Roman needs a mentor, and here you are." She turned to Roman. "Where were you earlier? I was looking for you."

How to make him feel like that six-year-old again. "Bruce and I went for a walk up to the Christmas tree farm. We hauled some brush for Chris and played fetch with the dogs. Why? What did you need?"

"Bruce?"

"Our resident author? That Bruce." Not that he knew another. Audrey shook her head. "I didn't realize he knew Chris."

"She has meals here sometimes," he pointed out.

"Not often." Audrey tapped her chin as she frowned.

Seemed Audrey thought she was needed to run interference for all her friends as well as any male visitors to the inn. Wait. Did that mean she suspected... was Bruce interested in Chris? Stranger things had happened, Roman supposed. It wasn't any of his business. It wasn't any of Audrey's, either.

Pam turned to Julia. "I want to go over the menus for the next few weeks with you. And Granger needs to talk to Wendy about the outreach event at the church. We forgot she'd still be teaching her workshop."

Outreach event? Wendy hadn't mentioned anything to him. Maybe she hadn't had a chance. It was hard to deny that she seemed to be avoiding him the past few days, though. At least, he hadn't caught much more than a glimpse of her in passing. Maybe she'd been working on this church thing.

He turned to Granger. "What kind of event?"

"Last year, we hosted a turkey dinner in the Creekside Academy gym. That's the Christian school across the parking lot from the church. Anyway, Wendy and Pam helped me put together a meal and a program and gifts for the children—"

"Granger dressed up as Santa Claus to hand those out!" Pam interrupted.

The man's cheeks pinked a little as he shook his head. "No big deal. The goal was to bless some of the families in Jewel Lake who are struggling to get by. We had a lot of donations for the whole thing, and it seemed to be a success."

"Total bull's-eye," Pam chimed in.

"So, we're doing it again." Granger eyed Roman. "You wouldn't be interested in helping out, would you?"

The man was here to plan with Wendy? Easy decision. If she was in, so was he. It would be a chance to work together with her on something she couldn't easily avoid. Right? Totally worth it. "I don't know what you need help with, but sure. I'm game."

A smattering of applause came from the far end of the space, and Roman turned to see the crafters begin to stand and gather their things. Wendy looked up and noticed the group of them by the front doors. She lifted a hand in acknowledgment. Maybe to Granger? Roman couldn't be jealous of the guy for working with Wendy, not when he was a newlywed himself and clearly besotted with his wife.

That didn't mean Roman would step aside and let others have access that he could have himself. Not since he'd realized they needed more in common.

"Great." Granger nodded firmly. "Laura will be along in a few, as well. I look forward to hearing your input."

Julia turned to Pam. "Let's sit down by the fireplace and look at the menu you brought."

"Sure." Heads together, the two women strolled to the other side of the lobby.

Granger started toward Wendy as the group of women flocked toward the doors.

Roman took a step to follow him, but his sister grabbed his arm. "Don't think I don't know what you're doing."

He sighed and turned back. "Audrey, until you have something nice to say about Wendy, I'm done talking to you about her. I'm not going to apologize for liking her. When you like someone, you want to do things with them so, yes, I'm going to help out if I can, to spend time with her. You? You can deal with it."

CHAPTER
Eleven

"HI, GRANGER." Wendy set the remaining cinnamon sticks in her crate. "Is Laura joining us?"

"Yes, and I roped Roman in, as well."

She couldn't avoid looking at Roman. "That's great." Why couldn't he leave her more space to adjust? This whole happily-married-to-explosion-to-divorce-to-dating-again thing... she needed time to adapt.

It had been three years. Nearly four.

That homeschool-mom friend of hers had remarried 18 months after her husband died. But death was final. Geni hadn't had to wonder if her marriage could be revived.

Dave had left no room for revival, either, but wasn't God in the resurrection business? Did Wendy still even want Him to be?

Laura jogged over. "Sorry I'm late. The time got away on me." She pulled out a chair across from Wendy and seated herself like the drama queen she was. "Oh, hi, Roman. Joining us?" She smirked as her gaze toggled between Wendy and Roman.

"Granger here invited me, and I thought, why not? I don't have a whole lot to occupy me, so if I can be of use, I might as well be."

Laura winked at Wendy.

Wendy looked down as the men took places on the two remaining sides of the table. She'd been so sure Roman would be bored with her by now.

"I've been thinking." Granger opened a spiral-bound notebook and laid it on the table. "What do our struggling friends need more than anything else?"

"Jesus?" Laura suggested.

"Always Jesus," Granger agreed. "And since our outreach event is at Thanksgiving, at the onset of the advent season, we start by being grateful for what we have and for who we are in Christ."

Roman nodded.

"But I was thinking of hope."

That word again. Wendy looked down at her hands folded in her lap.

Granger went on. "Many of our friends are locked in bleak despair. Depression, even. Life has kicked them in the teeth so many times that optimism is a distant, vague memory. They have stopped believing things could ever get better. My daughter is a case in point."

Wendy had met Melissa a few times, but this also described herself.

Granger looked across the table at Roman. "My daughter is a divorcée with two kids. She has a job, but she's just barely making ends meet. She's starting to ask questions about Jesus, but the next step seems to require more effort than she can summon."

"Hope…" Roman mused. "One of my favorite verses is this. 'For I know the plans I have for you,' says the Lord. 'They are plans for good and not for disaster, to give you a future and a hope.'"

Years ago, Wendy had memorized Jeremiah 29:11 in a different version, but Dave had pointed out that it wasn't relevant to believers today. "Wasn't that a promise for the Jewish people in Babylon?"

"Specifically, yes." Roman turned to her, and she couldn't

avoid meeting his gaze. "But the principle is transferable. There are plenty of New Testament verses that speak of the hope Jesus brings us, as well."

What was the one Julia had mentioned? Romans something, but Wendy couldn't remember the exact reference.

Laura leaned on the table. "Julia shared Romans 15:13 with me earlier today."

Wendy stared as her friend thumbed into her cell phone. Had Julia made the rounds with her attempt at encouragement? Had she proclaimed the same verse over Chris and Audrey and Pam?

"It reads like this: 'I pray that God, the source of hope, will fill you completely with joy and peace because you trust in him. Then you will overflow with confident hope through the power of the Holy Spirit.'"

Granger nodded. "Now *that's* what I'm talking about. The kind of expectation that sets the theme for the first Sunday of advent. It's all about the hope ancient Israel clung to that God's promised Messiah would come. That we have today in that same Messiah's second coming. God was faithful to His promise to send Jesus in the first place, so we can trust He will do it again."

There had been many times in the past few years Wendy had wished today was the day the skies would split wide open with Jesus' triumphal return. It hadn't been driven by eagerness, though. More by despair at facing another day of being the unwanted, discarded ex-wife.

That was not the image of what Jesus desired of her.

Wendy blinked back the sudden threat of tears. Jesus wanted her to look forward to His coming with joy and anticipation, not merely to escape today's unpleasantness or embarrassment. Had Wendy truly suffered? Not in a physical sense but, yes, emotionally. She'd just wanted to crawl in a hole and die, so she wouldn't have to face the ridicule or feigned sympathy of her former friends.

She was supposed to have it all together. She'd thought she

did. Even now, her face heated with the realization of how blind she'd been. How naive.

"I like hope as a theme." Laura's voice interrupted her thoughts.

Right, Wendy was in a meeting. She needed to get a grip and listen to the conversation. Add to it, if possible. Pretend she knew anything at all about the subject.

"Very timely," Roman agreed. "How are you thinking of presenting it?"

Granger turned to Laura sitting beside him. "Would you be willing to sing 'Will Your Anchor Hold?' I know that's not a Christmas song, but then again, this isn't billed as a Christmas event."

Laura hummed a bar with a thoughtful look on her face. "Yes, I can find a soundtrack for that, I'm sure. Good choice."

"Have you heard 'Living Hope' by Phil Wickham? That one will be under copyright, but the church's licensing agreement might cover it as a solo."

Laura shook her head. "I'm not familiar, but I'll check into it. You could ask Caleb about the legalities."

Granger played drums on the worship team that Caleb led, so that seemed logical.

"Okay. Look it up meanwhile, and see what you think."

"Can do."

Granger turned to Wendy. "Any other ideas for the evening?"

Time to be on point. "Is Pam handling the food again?"

He nodded. "I convinced her that keeping the same menu as last year would simplify the drill. Besides, it worked out well, so why reinvent the wheel?"

"It was delicious, and the church women—"

"And a few men." Granger's eyes crinkled as he interrupted her.

"Right, and a few men — did a great job following Pam's excellent instructions. So, if the menu is taken care of, that's a big chunk of the planning done. And Laura will sing a couple of special songs and lead a few carols…?"

Laura nodded.

"We need a speaker. Eli did it last year. Maybe he'd like to do it again, or maybe he's feeling stretched."

"I plan to ask him." Granger made a note.

Wendy went on. "We did the decorated Christmas trees last year as door prizes. Do we want to do that again, or something else?"

"It was great, but it was really a lot. I don't think we can expect local businesses to put in all that work every year."

She was getting warmed up now. "Any other ideas?"

Everyone looked at each other and slowly shook their heads.

"I'll see what I can come up with for an activity then. I think you're right about the businesses, Granger, especially since we're already asking them to donate gifts. Are you up for playing Santa again this year?"

"I could." Granger glanced at Roman. "I'd offer you the job, but you'd need a wig to cover your dark hair."

Roman laughed. "On either you or me, padding's a requirement."

Not if Wendy played the role, but that was never a woman's job, thank goodness. She and Dave had never perpetuated the Santa myth in their home… and she didn't even know if Adriel followed the same path with her two littles.

Why was Wendy so far away from her grandchildren? She'd missed so many baby snuggles since moving to Montana. At least Adriel had video-called more often in the past few months than the first while.

Granger scribbled a few more lines in his notebook. "We'll need to do the door-to-door thing downtown for donations. Wendy, you're looking into door prizes or something similar. Laura, you've got music. Pam's got the food covered. I'll see if Eli wants to speak. Anything else?"

"What's my part?" Roman's gaze caught on Wendy's. "Maybe Wendy and I could visit businesses for donations."

Wendy started to shake her head. Didn't she have enough to do already?

But this was a good cause. Wasn't it?

"Okay."

Roman kept his fist pump inside his head as Laura and Granger left the table, heads together about music. "Hey, I didn't mean to put you on the spot."

Wendy's smile seemed forced. "It's okay. I'll make time."

"You're busy. I get it. I can do it on my own, but you've lived here for a year now, so you probably know a lot of the people, and I don't."

"I don't go downtown that much, but a few of the business owners attend Creekside." She looked down.

"Wendy?" He kept his voice quiet and gentle.

"Yes?" She peeked at him then looked away.

"Did you not have a good time the other day?"

"It was... nice."

"I was going for more than nice. Maybe romantic?"

"Roman, you know this thing between us isn't going to work."

His gut knotted. "I don't know that. I like you, and I know you like me. My sister can go fly a kite." Had he covered the bases?

"It's not just Audrey."

"Wendy." He scooted around the corner and slipped his arm around the back of her chair. "We can work through it together, whatever it is." Not that he didn't know the cause. Once again, he'd like to damage Dave's face for the pain he'd inflicted on Wendy. On the other hand, if Dave had been an attentive husband, Wendy wouldn't be here, wouldn't be free to be loved.

But she'd have been happy, and that mattered most. Hadn't Roman decided long ago that singleness was a good life?

"I don't know."

He rubbed her shoulder and felt her pull slightly away from his touch. "I'll be here. I'm not going anywhere."

"You should find someone else to care about, like maybe Granger's daughter, Melissa. She's about ten years younger than you. Maybe she's willing to have more babies than the two kids she has."

"She's probably very nice, but she's not for me. Didn't I tell you that babies aren't a dealbreaker?"

"You say that now."

"If I'd been driven by wanting children, I'm sure I could have settled down with someone by now." He paused for a second, contemplating that alternate history. "But I think I've been waiting for you all along."

"You can't talk like that."

"Why not? It's true. I feel like God has something big planned for us." Yeah, maybe he'd stuck his neck out too far, but lying wasn't his thing. "Please give me a chance. A real chance. I don't want scraps from you, Wendy."

"Scraps?" Her gaze bounced off his.

"Like an amazing day and then nothing."

She gulped. "When I'm with you, anything seems possible. When I'm not, I remember all the reasons it can't work."

"Then let's stick together, so possibility — hope — is the controlling narrative. None of us needs to live in the depths of despair. That's not God's desire for His children."

"But it's hard."

"Let me help you. Let me remind me of your worth."

She shuddered before her shoulders pulled back against his hand. "I'll try. But Audrey..."

"Audrey isn't the one who wants to date you."

"Thank heavens."

Roman chuckled. "True, that. But it isn't any of her business. This is between you and me and God."

"But she's your only sibling."

And Wendy had none as he recalled from their childhood. "I've lived on a different continent from her for decades. I can do it again if needs be."

"Oh! I don't want to move far away."

He caressed her shoulder. "I'm not asking you to. It's Audrey. I'll toss her in a rocket bound for outer space if required. I won't let her come between us. Okay?"

This time her eyes stayed focused on his a little longer. "Okay."

He wanted to kiss her in the worst way, but the first time would not be in the dining room at Maranatha Inn with Julia and Pam discussing food nearby or Granger and Laura chatting by the elevator.

"When would you like to shoot a video? Does tomorrow afternoon work for you?"

"Maybe."

"We'll go to the Christmas tree farm. It smells so amazing there this time of year, not that smell translates on video."

"I don't get up there often. I should, though. It's not that far."

"Not far at all. We could walk it every evening. If you want."

She swallowed audibly. "We could. I should get out more. Be more active."

"I'm up for that with you anytime."

There was a fine line somewhere between accepting her as she was and inspiring her to be a healthier version of herself. Audrey leaned way past encouragement into hostility. She may have damaged their former friendship too much to regain it.

Roman's inclination might be too far into the acceptance side, because his sister had a point. He might not have Audrey's same addiction to fitness, but how could he and Wendy carve a future if she didn't even care? Walking together, even if it started as a mere brief amble, was a step in the right direction.

No pun intended.

CHAPTER
Twelve

ROMAN LEANED over Wendy's shoulder and watched the replay on her camera. "That's a wrap." He inhaled the scent of her... hopefully not too conspicuously. "I like it. What do you think?"

"I should have tried a wider angle there and gotten more conifers in."

"But then Chris would have taken up less of the screen, and the focus is on her in that section. You did a pan of the tree farm earlier."

"True. I... never mind."

Roman rubbed her shoulder. "What? You can tell me."

"I'm trying to be content with the way God made me."

He did his best not to give his head the actual shake her words demanded but couldn't stop the twitch completely. Why had her brain gone there right now? He murmured, "Hmm?"

"I'm fat. I know you've noticed. It's impossible to miss." Wendy slid her hands down her sides.

"You're beautiful."

She turned, forcing his arm to drop from around her shoulders. "Thank you, but I'm also fat."

How did a man respond to that? Did she carry excess weight?

Yes, but he refused to add to her burden. It wasn't his place to pressure her on the topic, and it didn't affect how he felt about her. He wasn't quite ready to name exactly how he felt, mostly because she stayed slightly aloof even though they'd now worked together for a couple of weeks on creatives for his channel. "What made you think of that right now?" Hopefully a safe question.

Wendy looked away. "Pam told me about a horseback ride that starts at Happy Trails and goes up the hill behind the Christmas tree farm. She saw horses at the top, so it seems to me that would be a good place to shoot a video of the area."

"Hmm. I remember hearing about that spot, too." He still didn't get the connection, though.

"I'm too heavy to ride a horse, and I'm too out of shape to hike up the hill. It's several miles, according to the map."

"Ah." There really wasn't a valid response to her assumptions, since she was no doubt correct on both counts. "I see what you're getting at. I could go up there, take a video with my phone, and we can edit it into mine if it turns out."

She bit her lip. "You could take my camera."

"Nah, I'm not familiar with it. I use my phone camera for everything."

"But the quality…"

"My phone is excessively smart."

Wendy managed a weak smile. "How do you stay so fit?"

Roman blinked. Her brain was bouncing more than usual today, or maybe she was finally comfortable enough with him to loosen her thoughts. "Working out. Running. Hiking."

She grimaced and looked down. "I should have known that's what you'd say. I can't imagine lifting weights or whatever."

He opened his mouth. Closed it again. Talk about navigating a minefield. It wasn't his place to give advice, even though she'd broached the subject. *God? How do I handle this?*

"I don't know if the output from your phone will have a similar enough tone to the rest of the video we've already shot, but if you want to give it a try, go for it. Although it's probably fine the way it is. I shouldn't have brought up the topic."

"Wendy, come here." He stepped in front of her and wrapped his arms around her.

She held herself rigid against him.

"It's okay, *tesoro mio*. It's okay." He rubbed her back.

"What does that mean?" She sniffed.

What had he said? Oh... was she ready to hear it? "It's Italian for 'my treasure'."

"Your... treasure?"

"Yes. That's how I feel about you, Wendy." It went a whole lot deeper, but this was a good start. "I'm so thankful God brought us both here to Maranatha Inn. I've loved every minute I've spent with you. I never would have seen this coming when I was a kid." Man, that chuckle sounded awkward.

She relaxed enough to rest her head against his shoulder. "You were an adorable child."

"That was then, and this is now. Am I still adorable?"

A tiny chuckle shook her frame. "You might be."

He maybe shouldn't go here... but what could it hurt? "Audrey reminded me I was always besotted with you. I'd almost forgotten I'd proposed to you once upon a time."

"Oh!" She tried to push away, but he kept his hands on her hips.

"Do you remember?"

"Of course. I've only been proposed to twice. By you, and by Dave."

"I was crushed you turned me down."

"You were five years old."

Roman chuckled. "It just proves I had good taste even then."

"Is that what it proves?" She took a step back, and his hands fell to his sides.

"That's how I see it. You've played an important role almost my entire life."

"No." Wendy shook her head. "We didn't see each other for decades. That's not an important role."

"I think I held all women to the standard you set all this time."

"You can't have." Her voice dwindled to a whisper.

"I can't prove it, but I suspect 'what would Wendy do' lurked in my subconscious."

"I can't have been that important to you. I was an awkward, chubby girl… I guess some things have never changed."

"You've changed. You've gotten better."

"You mean bigger."

How he wished she'd let him hold her tight, but with every utterance, she backed up another step. "I mean better. Your heart is gold, *tesoro mio*. You were kind to a little boy whose parents shuffled responsibility to a big sister who didn't want to be bothered with him. I can't thank you enough."

"Like I said, you were adorable. What was not to love?" Her eyes widened as her face flushed.

"Am I still lovable?"

"Of course, you are! It's me who's not."

"Oh, Wendy. You are truly a treasure, not only to me, but to God. To all your friends here at Maranatha."

"Not to Audrey."

"She's not so fond of me right now, either." Had Roman been too blunt with his sister? No. She needed to keep her nose out of his business. She also needed to stop bullying Wendy.

Wendy needed to stop bullying herself.

How could he prove to her that he loved her for who she was — oh, no. Now he'd admitted it to himself. There was no going back from this realization, not that he wanted to.

Because the next time he proposed to Wendy Bilson Clarke, he wouldn't take no for an answer. Not like he had 40 years ago. When he'd been in kindergarten.

Why, oh why, did Roman persist? Was he simply a man who couldn't take no for an answer? But if Wendy went along with it and admitted her own deepening feelings, he'd lose interest soon enough. Men only wanted to conquer. They didn't know what to do with a woman once he'd caught her.

Did she truly believe that? Oh, it might take years for the truth to come out. It had with Dave. Surely, her ex hadn't faked it for 25 years. They'd dated for two years before he'd proposed — the second proposal of her life, if she counted young Roman Scala.

The boy had presented her with a handful of scraggly flowers he'd picked in the park. *I know I'm little now, but I'll get bigger. I want to marry you when I do!*

She'd let him down gently, but maybe not gently enough if he still remembered it 41 years later. Audrey had laughed uproariously and told her little brother to go play with his Tonka trucks and find a girl his own age.

Tears had welled in Roman's brown eyes. *But I'll love Wendy forever,* he'd said.

Forever love from a five-year-old was *not* a thing, only a sweet, funny memory. How could it mean anything more?

Wendy stood in front of the bathroom mirror in her suite and eyed her shape. She wasn't foolish enough to strip down to her skivvies and actually look at her flabby rolls. Her tunic smoothed out the silhouette a little. But, yeah, she was fat. Why wouldn't Roman acknowledge it? Why did she push him to say the words?

Then she could take them for rejection. Then she'd prove she was unlovable.

I have loved you with an everlasting love.

Her eyes widened as she met her own gaze in the mirror. Where had those words come from? They'd been a Bible verse, right? She pivoted and reached for her leather Bible, but that was no help. Fine. The search engine on her phone would fill in the gap. It did, sending her to Jeremiah 31.

Back to the leather-bound to look it up.

Long ago the Lord said to Israel…

Dave's voice intruded, reminding Wendy that she was not, in fact, Israel. The church wasn't, either. God's promises to Israel were just that. But then Granger's and Roman's voices chimed together to remind her that the principles remained.

She kept reading.

"I have loved you, my people, with an everlasting love. With unfailing love, I have drawn you to myself."

She blinked back tears. What would everlasting, unfailing love look like?

A lot like God's love, and quite a bit like Roman's.

"I will rebuild you, my virgin Israel. You will again be happy and dance merrily with your tambourines."

Wendy was no virgin. Nearly 25 years of marriage and six children birthed from her body proved that.

But Israel hadn't been virginal in the time of Jeremiah, when this had been written. They'd prostituted themselves to foreign gods. To idols. And God promised to reconstruct His nation. Basically, not a patch job but from the foundation up.

Oh, to be truly happy again! Dancing, of course, was a sin, according to Dave, but not according to God's words to Jeremiah. Hmm.

Wendy had led the homeschool co-op in crafting tambourines. They'd paraded around the church basement making a joyful noise to the Lord. They hadn't called it dancing, but maybe it had come suspiciously close.

Was this passage from Jeremiah truly a promise she could grasp?

Dave shook his head, a solemn frown on his face.

She shoved his image out of her head. He'd lost any authority to tell her what to do and how to think. She should never have ceded him that right to begin with.

There was a song they'd sung in Creekside Fellowship a few weeks ago. What was it again? Wendy ransacked her brain, trying to remember the keywords. Something about God's reckless love. It sure wasn't a song they'd have sung in her traditional church back home. The lyrics had seemed a little reckless to her. A little shocking.

There. She found it on YouTube and played it through, reading the lyrics at the same time. The singer must have come from a similar place as Wendy — though likely not obese — in feeling no worth, yet Jesus, in His kindness, in His overwhelming love, paid it all.

The words washed over Wendy as she played it through a second time. If this song were true, she'd never fully grasped God's personal love for her.

Huh. That might be the case.

Her phone rang, silencing the music in mid-word. She reached for it.

Faith?

"Hi, honey. How are things?" *And shouldn't you be in class?* But she wouldn't say that out loud. Faith had chosen her dad as the parent in charge.

"Why did you leave Dad?" Faith sniffled.

Surely Wendy hadn't heard correctly. "Pardon me?"

"Why?"

"I'm not following. Your dad had an affair with Shyanne." And others, apparently, before her, but Wendy made a point of not talking smack about Dave to their kids.

"But you're the one who left. You moved out."

"Faith, I moved out because one of us had to when we got divorced and he married Shyanne. We couldn't keep living together." *Imagine the three of them. No, don't.*

"But you left."

"I couldn't afford the house. Your father was the one with a job. With money."

"But..."

"Honey, your dad left me emotionally long before I moved out of the house. There's more than one kind of leaving."

"I just wish…"

"What, honey?"

"I just wish you were here and Shyanne wasn't."

Hadn't Wendy longed for the same thing for the past four years? She absolutely had. Until recently. "He made a decision, and he chose Shyanne over me. Some things can't be undone." Although Sheryl and Ted Johannesson had remarried after 18 years apart… but neither had been unfaithful.

"I miss you. Why did you move so far away?"

Wendy's heart cracked. "It was so hard. It still is."

"Then why?" Faith wailed.

"You know how when you fly, the flight attendants give all the safety instructions?"

"Yeah?"

"One thing they say is that in the event of emergency, you need to put on your own oxygen mask before helping someone else. I was so totally at my wit's end, I couldn't think anymore. I couldn't find my oxygen mask."

Was that Jesus? Maybe she needed to consider that a bit more.

"That was over a year ago."

"I know, sweet girl. Honestly? I'm just barely figuring out how to breathe again right now." She'd never been this honest with any of her kids before. None of them had asked. Or maybe they had, and she'd been in such a bad place she couldn't formulate an answer.

"Will you come back? I miss you."

Wendy's heart softened. "Maybe sometime, but not quite yet." An invitation for Faith to finish her senior year via correspondence from Montana begged to launch from the tip of her mama tongue, but no. She'd made the offer several times. Faith knew it was an option, but she'd clung to her decision to attend public school in Woodburn.

"Can I come visit you at Thanksgiving? And Christmas? And spring break?"

"You are always welcome here. You're my child, and I love you. I can't get enough of you."

Even though Faith had said some ugly things in the past, sticking up for her dad. Even though she'd been a typical teenager and pushed every button she could get her fingers on.

Even then.

That's how I love you.

God's voice again? No matter how many buttons Wendy had pushed, how adamantly she'd held to her own opinions, God still loved her with an everlasting, reckless, overwhelming love.

Something unfamiliar took root in Wendy's heart.

It felt like hope with a side of peace.

CHAPTER
Thirteen

"WE DID IT!" Roman leaned back and stretched before pivoting his chair toward Wendy. "The channel has officially launched." He held his palm high, and she smacked it.

"Congrats." She smiled at him. "We'll get ads rolling to it next."

"Slavedriver." He grinned back. It was nice to see her more relaxed in the past few days as they'd edited and loaded the first five videos. Five more were ready to feed in over the next week.

"Do you want success, or don't you? The odds of the general public finding you with no help are infinitesimally small."

"I know, I know. You keep telling me." He cracked his knuckles. "Okay, we have the basics set up for ads. Is it go time?"

"We could take a break first."

This was a side of Wendy he could approve of. "Sure. Let's walk up to the Christmas tree farm and see how Chris is getting on. The selling season starts in just over a week, right?"

"She opens the day after Thanksgiving." Wendy hesitated. "Sure. A walk sounds good."

They'd walked it together several times a week lately. "Bundle up. There's a crisp wind today."

Her eyebrows tipped up. "Which you know because…"

"Because I went for a run outside this morning? Bruce challenged me."

"I haven't seen much of him."

"He holes up in his room to write all morning and he's usually out of the inn all afternoon. If you came to breakfast, you'd see him then." Not that Roman particularly wanted to encourage the two of them to get to know each other, but he didn't feel as insecure about that as he might have a few weeks ago. It was hard to believe he'd been in Montana for nearly two months now.

"I keep yogurt and granola in my fridge downstairs. I'm not ready for people that early."

"Morning is the best part of the day."

"You tell yourself whatever you need to hear."

Roman chuckled. "I do. Do you?"

Wendy pulled to her feet and grimaced. "I'm trying, but it's difficult."

He hopped up. "Why is it hard?"

"It's hard because I've spent years telling myself what I thought would motivate me, but it didn't work."

Roman nodded cautiously. "Like...?"

"Like if I told myself often enough that I was fat and unlovable, it would motivate me to get skinnier and nicer."

"You're very sweet as it is."

"I notice you didn't address the other part."

"Wendy." Roman held out his arms. Immeasurable relief swept through him when she stepped into them. "Don't do that. Don't push me. Your weight is between you and God. It has nothing to do with me." Did it? No, it couldn't possibly. He wasn't part of the problem, and he wasn't part of the solution. At least, not that he knew of.

Wendy wrapped her arms around his back.

He held her close and rested his cheek against her curls. Did he dare speak his mind? But what kind of relationship could they truly have if she couldn't hear his heart? "You're doing to me what you did to yourself."

She stiffened but stayed put. "What is that?"

"You tell yourself you're fat over and over. Maybe you call it facing facts. I'm not sure. But you keep reminding me, too, as if giving me every opportunity to notice and therefore reject you. I'm not rejecting you, Wendy. I don't need you to keep putting those words in front of me. I've made my choice. My choice is to be *for* you, not against you."

"But…"

"There are no buts." He stepped back so he could see her face. "No tears, *tesoro mio*." He wiped moisture away before cupping her face between his hands. "I see *you*, Wendy Bilson Clarke. I see your caring heart. I see your talents and your willingness to serve. I see your joy in creating beauty and sharing it with others. I see you, and I like what I see. I like it a lot."

Her lower lip quivered. Roman slid his thumb across it, which seemed to make the trembling contagious, because it seemed a minor earthquake shifted the air around them. "Wendy… kiss me?"

Tears welled in her eyes.

He couldn't have staunched them all if he'd tried.

"Roman, you're the best thing that ever happened to me."

That was saying a lot, given how much she talked about her children, but he could push aside thoughts of them. He could push aside any reminder that he was nine years her junior. That she'd been married nearly a quarter of a century. None of it mattered. She was a desirable woman, and he was a man — no longer a little boy — who'd fallen deeply for her charms. "Wendy?"

Her arms came around his neck, and her fingers threaded into the hair at his nape.

He shivered at the delicious tension in the air as he lowered his head and touched his lips to hers. Fireworks exploded in his mind and in his heart. "Wendy," he groaned as he pulled her closer and covered her mouth with his.

And, oh, how she kissed him back.

No doubt, just like she'd kissed Dave hundreds and thousands of times.

Aargh, Roman wasn't going to think about her ex. The man had tossed this delightful woman aside like yesterday's socks. Dave's loss was Roman's gain.

Wendy was worth giving up his solo lifestyle for. He'd already given up the career he'd been born and bred to, though not for her sake.

She made it worth it. She was worth everything.

She pulled away first and rested her cheek against his shoulder.

"What you do to me, woman," he growled into her hair.

He felt — heard — her gulp as her hands gripped his shoulders.

"Wendy." He gentled his tone. "Thank you for this gift of trust."

"This was probably a bad idea."

"It was the best idea I've had in years," he countered. "It feels like my entire life has been waiting in anticipation of this moment."

"So dramatic." She uttered a watery chuckle.

"I'm Italian. Theatrics is part of my DNA, but it doesn't make my words any less true." She wanted drama? He could drop to one knee here and now and pledge his forever love. Ask her to marry him.

The vision made his knees quake, but he stiffened his stance. The moment was coming — please, dear God — but it wasn't here yet. Patience.

Wendy took another step back.

He caught her hands in both of his as he filled his eyes with the beauty of her. "Maybe we should go for that walk."

"Maybe we should."

But he'd much rather stay right here and kiss her again... and never stop.

Could everyone see on their faces that they'd kissed?

Wendy averted her gaze as she hurried across the lobby, zipping up her toasty jacket as she went. She could see Roman waiting outside on the stoop. Not only had he traversed several flights of stairs, he'd still arrived before her. Although, he likely hadn't stared at himself in the mirror for two full minutes, wondering what had just happened.

"Hey, Wendy!" Laura's voice.

"I'll be back in a bit. Can it keep?"

"Um, sure. Hot date?"

Laura had no idea, unless it was written across Wendy's heated cheeks. It felt like it might be.

Wendy waved over her shoulder as the automatic doors slid open at her approach. She rushed past Roman and down the circular drive. Whoa, that was more exercise than she'd had since chasing toddlers. She caught her breath as Roman caught up with her.

"Hey, did Laura threaten to bite?" His voice held more than a hint of laughter.

"No. I don't think so." Wendy took another breath, willing her heart rate to steady itself. An impossibility with Roman Scala nearby. When had he begun affecting her like this? The awareness of him had been building for weeks, but now… She nearly fanned her face, but he'd notice. He didn't need to know.

Who was she kidding? He'd kissed her. She'd returned the contact like a drowning woman seeking air. He already knew how he affected her.

Roman clasped her hand and tugged her toward the back road leading to the tree farm. And he didn't let go.

Was that really how things would go down? It's what he'd

promised; that he wasn't going anywhere. That he saw her and chose her. It was going to take some getting used to.

"There's a smell of snow in the air." Roman swung her hand.

"Snow doesn't have a smell."

He laughed. "It absolutely does."

"You're crazy."

"Indisputably, but not because of this."

"You're serious."

Roman sniffed the air. "Totally. It's... it's hard to describe. There's a specific crispness, maybe a slightly woodsy scent—"

"We're walking into 20 acres of conifers, which possibly — just maybe — might have something to do with a woodsy smell."

"This is different, though."

Wendy shook her head as she chuckled. He might be nuts, but he'd distracted her from her near panic attack over Laura. Why had she overreacted, anyway? Did it matter if Laura knew they were going for a walk together? Roman had probably told her. Besides that, Laura had claimed to be on their side after their first date weeks ago. Wendy hadn't allowed another.

Why? Still punishing herself for Dave?

Probably. She really needed to get out of her head more, but somehow being around Roman inspired even more introspection. More digging into her emotions and spiritual wellbeing, which brought pain.

Sometimes pain preceded healing.

Roman bumped his shoulder against hers. "Are you still trying to sniff it out? Some people just aren't as talented as others."

"My mind was far away."

"Drat. I hoped it was right here, beside you."

She couldn't help chuckling. "You're full of yourself."

"I'm full of *us*."

What did that even mean? But Wendy felt it, too. Oh, goodness, that kiss. She was going to obsess about it for weeks... unless they'd now happen so frequently that they'd all run together in her memory. No, a first time held a special spot.

Her first kiss with Dave had.

She shoved him unceremoniously out of her mind. In her imagination, he tumbled to the ground on his backside and looked up at her with dismay. And possibly regret.

Nope. No more Dave. He'd made his choice, and it was long past time for Wendy to accept it and move forward with her own life.

They rounded a bend. Wendy blinked and jerked to a stop, Roman beside her.

Chris stood beside her all-terrain vehicle with Bruce so near that it looked like... but it couldn't be. They barely knew each other.

Luna and Duke barked and barreled toward Wendy and Roman. Bruce shifted as he turned and waved at them. That moment — what Wendy'd thought she'd seen — must have been a trick of the angle, because now they seemed to be several feet apart. She knew all about camera angles, after all. There were ways to disguise elements like proximity and oversized bodies.

"Hey!" Bruce called.

"Hi," Roman called back. "Gorgeous day."

"Sure is." Chris clambered aboard her ATV. "Just a week until we open for tree sales! Lots to do." Duke, the beagle Jack Russel cross, leaped onto the bed of the rear rack. Chris looked ready to zip away.

"Hey, question for you two," Roman called.

Chris paused with her hand on the ignition switch. "What's that?" She sounded cautious.

"Can you smell snow?"

Chris eyed him like he'd lost his marbles, and Wendy snickered.

"Sure." Bruce nodded. "We're getting a dump of it later today, or I miss my guess."

"So, this ability is a guy thing?" Wendy kept her voice as neutral as possible, because weren't the men making it up in some kind of male bonding scam?

"I don't think so." Bruce's eyebrows scrunched. "My sister can smell it, too."

Wendy glanced at Roman. "I thought you were pulling my leg. I'm still not convinced you're not."

He bumped his shoulder on hers. "Never. I wouldn't mess with you."

"Right." Then she realized they were still holding hands. What would Chris think?

Wendy let out a slow breath. Chris would think the truth, that Wendy and Roman were exploring a relationship. Was it so terrible if people knew? No one at Maranatha was on Team Dave, but that didn't mean they were on Team Moving On.

But weren't they? They'd all been so supportive of Pam and Granger last year. They all teased Julia about Monte's attentive gaze following her wherever she went. But those two women were widowed.

Did that make a difference? Of course, it did. Marriage was for life, and divorce something to be ashamed of. Her parents had been appalled to hear of the demise of Wendy and Dave's marriage. They thought they'd raised her better than to quit.

Wendy hadn't quit. Dave had.

And God forgave. God offered a clean slate, complete with His love and blessing. Not just a reduced sentence or half-hearted attempt at erasing something deeply etched, but absolute newness.

Wendy threw back her shoulders and kept clinging to Roman's hand.

She was new in Jesus and subject to His reckless, extravagant love.

Let the whole world know.

CHAPTER

Fourteen

"I HOPE you know what you're doing," Audrey muttered.

"Good morning to you, too, sister dear." Roman set down his plate of veggie-laden scrambled eggs and three breakfast sausages.

Audrey rolled her eyes. "Don't think I haven't noticed your continued obsession with Wendy. It would be cute if you hadn't lost all perspective."

He lowered his head in a silent grace before lifting his fork and looking back at his sister. Maybe Wendy had the right of it, having breakfast in her own room. How much of that had to do with Audrey? He'd noticed that his sister scrutinized every morsel on Wendy's plate when they shared a meal... which seemed pretty rare, considering the small number of Maranatha's staff.

"Thank you for sharing your concerns."

She glared. "That's it? You'll back off?"

"No." He buttered a slice of toast. "I don't know what you have against her. Or what you have against me."

"Nothing against you." Audrey lowered her voice and glanced around.

The only other people in the dining room now were the Satterfields and maybe a dozen guests Roman hadn't met. All of them dined closer to the buffet table.

"So, you have something against Wendy." He took a bite of his toast.

"She's a mess, Roman. Surely, you can see that. She hasn't taken care of herself in years, and I'm afraid she'll drag you down with her."

"You think weight is a communicable disease?" He had another bite, thought the toast bore a distinct reminder of sawdust. "Or do you think I'll quit working out? I'm honestly not sure where you're going with this."

"Roman, don't be difficult."

"Pretend I don't understand English very well."

Audrey leaned on the table. "I just think you can do much better than Wendy. Mom and Dad would never approve of her."

Ah, now they were getting somewhere. "They don't approve of me, anyway, since I sold my share of the company to Leo. I'm 46, Audrey. If I decide to give up bachelorhood and marry Wendy, it's no one's choice but my own. And hers."

Audrey clapped her hand over her mouth as her eyes widened. "You're not serious?"

Roman laid his fork and knife on the table and stared straight at his sister. "As a heart attack."

"We don't use that term around here. Not after George."

"Don't change the subject. I've dated on and off over the years, usually when I needed a plus-one for an event or when something sounded more fun with company. I have never once in my life looked at a woman and thought I couldn't live without her." He waited a beat. "Until now."

"Romie…" Audrey whispered.

"I'd love you onboard. I'd love you to love Wendy. Not with ulterior motivations, like maybe you could fix her, but as the close friends you once were. What happened to that?"

She opened her mouth.

He held up one hand. "And don't say she gained weight. If

that is truly the only reason you don't like her now, you are far shallower than I thought possible."

"I like her."

Roman raised an eyebrow and carved a bite of his sausage.

Audrey huffed. "Why does nobody appreciate me? I care, okay? I probably care too much."

She sure had a funny way of showing it. Come to think of it, there was overlap with Wendy's self-talk. That admission a couple of days ago had taken Roman some time to work through. She'd honestly thought if she kept reminding herself she was fat that she'd be motivated to lose weight? The reasoning didn't even make sense, but here was Audrey, basically doing the same thing, except to other people.

"If Steve had listened to me, he wouldn't have died."

Roman found it hard to use his mouth to eat while also biting back all the words that vied to erupt, but if he'd ever needed self-control, it was now.

"He smoked. He drank. He ate junk. He gained weight. He got diabetes. He refused to change." Audrey closed her eyes and whispered, "He died."

"It's never quite that simple."

"It is, though. Steve's mother was diabetic and also didn't take care of herself. He should have seen the writing on the wall. What more motivation did he need?"

"I don't think... No, never mind."

"You can't start a sentence that way then quit. What?"

Roman shook his head. He'd been about to say that someone coming alongside him rather than attacking him might have given Steve motivation.

"Roman. Tell me."

"Did you love him anyway?"

"Oh, give me a break. How do you love someone bent on self-sabotage? When they basically throw all your advice back in your face?"

He pushed his plate away, all hunger having fled. "As I understand the New Testament, that's what Jesus did. Loved us when we were still sinners, so much that He died for us. He didn't nag us into submission. Just cared for our souls."

"Now you're preaching at me."

Roman couldn't win this one. "Sis, I love you. It feels like you're threatening to withhold your approval from me if I don't do as you say, but you know what? That is not how love works."

"You'd pursue Wendy even against my cautions? You can't change her, Roman. I couldn't change Steve, and you can't change Wendy."

"I'm not trying to change her."

"She'll end up like Steve if she keeps going like this."

He pushed back his chair and rose. "You don't know what's going on inside her. What her thought process is."

"And you do?"

"I'm trying to understand. I'm trying to be on her side. Supportive."

"Condoning."

Roman shook his head slowly. "Stop putting words in my mouth. If you can't say anything nice about Wendy, don't say anything at all."

"Now you sound like Mom."

"Good advice, though. I'll see you later. I've got a lot to do today."

"With Wendy." Audrey's lip curled.

"Actually, no. She's working on the inn's social media this morning. I'm meeting with Granger and Eli over at the Creekside Academy gym to go through the donations. We need to make sure every child in attendance receives a gift."

"At the Thanksgiving outreach dinner."

"That's the one."

"I still can't believe you just jumped in with both feet. This isn't even your home. Your church."

"Maybe it is now." And with that, Roman carried his plate to the bin by the buffet table then turned to the grand staircase leading to the inn's upper levels.

"Psst."

He startled and noticed Laura standing behind the reception desk. "Hi."

"Good on you."

What was she talking about? Oh, no. She'd overheard. The siblings hadn't been as quiet as he'd thought. "I thought you were Audrey's buddy."

"We're friends, but I know she's not perfect. She's going through stuff." Laura huffed a laugh. "Me, too — aren't we all? I'm trying to be there for her."

"Good. She needs a friend she can trust to have her back."

"So do you." Laura eyed him.

"You know what? I do."

"You mean Wendy."

"Not just her, but yeah." He started to turn from the desk before looking back. "Have a great day."

Not only did Wendy have Roman's back, but he had other friends here in Jewel Lake. More actual friends than ever before. Granger Durand. Eli Bryson. Bruce Leland.

Yeah, he could make Jewel Lake his permanent home.

If Wendy wanted.

On Wednesday afternoon, Wendy entered the church school's gym where Roman and Granger were already setting up tables. The academy was officially on Thanksgiving break, so they had full access to the venue. Earlier today, the men had delivered all the food packages to church households to prepare for Saturday's banquet.

The planning group didn't really need her anymore. Honestly, they hadn't last year, either. Everyone else had done all the work, and she'd simply nodded and said they were on the right track.

There was even less to do this time around, but she kept going to the meetings, probably because it was a legitimate chance to see Roman in action.

Like she needed those. Sometimes it was hard to recall they were both grownups and free to date if they wished. And... she wished. At least, when she wasn't having a panic attack about the whole world agreeing with Audrey, to say nothing of her own misgivings.

Roman had helped her to see that her negative self-talk did her no favors. That it might even drown out the still, small voice of God. God never said she needed to improve herself before He could love her. God knew it was impossible for any human being to deserve His favor. That's why Jesus died.

But, man, her self-talk had been yelling in her ear for decades now, and its volume had cranked up with Dave's rejection. Her ex had only confirmed the reasons she already knew for her self-loathing.

I have loved you with an everlasting love.

She'd played the "Reckless Love" song so many times in the past couple of weeks that she'd memorized it. Maybe it was finally seeping down into her subconscious, because it wasn't like she *wanted* to be negative.

"Wendy!" Granger called out. "Did we arrange the tables in the right formation?"

The man didn't need her approval, but she'd give it, anyway. "Looks good. I think it's about the same as last year."

"I couldn't recall for sure."

Her gaze slid to Roman who'd paused in the middle of unfolding a chair. He grinned at her, the skin around his eyes crinkling in amusement. And there were those dimples she adored, half hidden in his stubble. One of these days she'd be brave enough to trace them with her fingertips.

Not today.

"How are we doing for time?" he called.

"We need to leave in about 20 minutes."

"Okay. That gives us enough time to finish." He snapped the chair open and set it down.

"Hey, I can wrap this up myself if you guys are in a hurry." Granger pushed a dolly stacked with additional chairs closer to the tables.

"There's time." But that was why Wendy had driven into town instead of waiting for Roman to swing back to the inn to pick her up. She'd finally bought a car to replace the decrepit van she'd left in Oregon. Dave had sold it, and Adriel had guilted him into sending Wendy the money. Julia paid her decently, but a reliable vehicle hadn't been in her budget until Dave's check. Not when she'd been saving for Faith's prom dress and for her own flight back in May.

She was so not looking forward to facing Dave and Shyanne at Faith's graduation.

Maybe she should lose some weight before then. She could show Dave what he'd tossed aside.

Ugh. That was the worst possible reason, right?

She could do it for Roman.

Or... new thought. She could do it for herself.

"I'm ready to roll if you are." Roman sauntered toward her, jingling the keys to his SUV. She might finally have wheels of her own, but his vehicle was much more reliable and comfortable. Plus, it had snowed a few inches in the past 24 hours, and she'd always hated driving in those conditions. Woodburn didn't get much snow, so she could usually avoid it.

"I'm ready."

She wasn't. Not really. The clamor inside her hadn't stopped for breath all afternoon. Should she have given her daughters a heads-up that she had a boyfriend, or should she let them discover him at the airport?

The chicken in her decided to let the chips fall where they may.

If Roman had any misgivings about being sprung on Selah and Faith, he hadn't said so.

Wendy was under no illusions. The rest of her family in Oregon, including Dave, would be apprised within half an hour of the flight's arrival. Their disapproval would put Audrey's to shame.

She was so not ready for this.

Roman waved goodbye to Granger, opened the gym door, and ushered Wendy into the snowy day. "We have plenty of time, even with road conditions."

"Do you know how to drive in snow? You're from Los Angeles!"

He grinned. "And spent most of my adult life overseas. Some of those places had snow, though."

"Maybe I should drive."

Roman tugged her close to his side as they approached his SUV. "I'm driving. I promise we'll be fine. I have good tires, and even a California boy can get experience in winter driving if he makes the effort."

"If you're sure."

"I'm sure." He opened the passenger door, waited until she was seated, then leaned in and kissed her. "I think it's your general nerves talking." Then he shut the door and rounded the hood before hopping in himself.

He knew her so well and had no qualms about calling her out on it.

"I should have told the girls ahead of time."

"Too late now. They're in the air."

"I know."

"Wendy?" He cranked the engine then reached to cover her hands with one of his. "It will be okay. I'm ready for the whole world to know how I feel about you."

How she wished she could say the same.

CHAPTER

Fifteen

ROMAN ROUNDED his vehicle and opened the passenger door. "Ready?"

"I'm nervous."

He huffed a laugh. "Because of me? Don't worry. I'll charm the socks off your daughters." But he was jittery, too.

"That's what I'm afraid of," she muttered as she clambered out.

"Hey, what?" This was a new one. He beeped the locks and reached for Wendy's hand. "I can be *too* charming?"

"Sorry. I shouldn't have said that."

"Wendy?" He halted in the middle of the airport parking lot and turned to face her. "If you have concerns, don't downplay them to me. We're a team, remember? I'm here for you. I care about you." She wasn't ready to hear how much. "Tell me what's on your mind."

"It's silly. I know."

"Which didn't answer my question."

"You're as close to my daughters in age as you are to me. Oh, not Selah and Faith. They're the tail end."

"Math was never my strongest subject, but I'm pretty sure that's not true. I do recall being nine years younger than you, but I didn't know you had a child old enough to place me equidistant between the two of you. She'd be, what, 37 now?"

Wendy scrunched her eyes shut as a flush mounted in her cheeks. She tried to tug her hands free, but Roman was having none of that nonsense. "You're right. The gap is not the same. Adriel is 28. Selah is 21, and Faith 17. The boys are in between."

"You're worried I'll find a vastly younger woman more attractive than I find you? That's not going to happen, *tesoro mio*. I've met thousands of women in my life, and none of them made me want to pop the question more than the first time I proposed."

Her eyes sprang open as she stared at him. Her mouth opened. Closed.

"I have you at a loss for words." He couldn't help the smug tone. He leaned forward and touched her lips with his own. "Trust me, Wendy. I have eyes only for you, and I'm not going anywhere."

Her phone chimed with an incoming text. She pulled back to look at it. "The girls have landed and are wondering where I am."

Roman held Wendy in place. "Are we okay?"

"Sure. I'm just a little apprehensive. This is far more nerve-wracking than the first time Dave came to meet my parents."

"Your kids are a deeper part of your life than your parents."

"True. Also, I already know my parents won't approve of you."

"Your dad worked for mine years ago. They probably remember me."

"Yeah. It's not only the age gap they'll disapprove of. They think Dave is in the right, and our divorce shamed them."

"They think the adulterer is the good guy and their own daughter, the victim, is the bad guy?"

"Pretty much. Re—" She pursed her lips. "Never mind. We need to find the girls."

"What were you going to say?" He fell into step beside her, not allowing her to pull away. Thankfully, she gripped his hand like he was her anchor, and he was okay with that.

"It doesn't matter."

"Wendy. I want to know everything you think."

"Remarriage is not in my parents' dictionary, okay? But I also know that's not what's going on here, so forget I said that."

He wanted nothing more than to pull her into his arms and kiss her for the next half hour. Maybe then she would believe remarriage — hers, anyway — was 100% top of his mind. If he had his way, it would happen in the near future.

But the final crossing to the airport terminal was right in front of them. The two young women huddled together outside the building had now spotted them and were waving.

Roman leaned to whisper in Wendy's ear. "We'll talk more about this later."

She let go of his hand to embrace the daughter who'd rushed into her arms, the other one right behind. The trio rocked as they clung together.

Roman might talk a big talk, but butterflies assaulted his stomach. Did he care what Wendy's kids thought of him? Oh, yeah.

A few seconds later, the girls had their mom at arms' length as all three talked over each other.

What on earth was Roman doing, pursuing a woman with adult children? They might not be close to his own age — hadn't Wendy said Dave's new wife wasn't much older than Adriel? Next generation Clarkes were already accustomed to age-gap relationships, but Roman wasn't stupid enough to believe that he'd get a pass on that account. Society still had something against the man being considerably younger.

One of the daughters turned to him and assessed him with clear blue eyes, so much like her mom's. No smile. Hands on hips.

Roman extended his hand. "Hi. I'm Roman Scala. You must be…"

"Selah. Somehow, my mother failed to mention you." Her grip was short and firm. Threatening, almost. He got it.

Wendy had begged his forgiveness for the secret, saying she didn't want word to get to Dave, who would sway the girls' opinions before they had a chance to know Roman for themselves.

He smiled at the girl. "She's told me a lot about you and your siblings. I'm so happy to meet you at last."

Selah's eyebrows tipped up. "This is my sister Faith."

The girls looked so much alike they might have been twins, though Wendy had told him they were four years apart in age. Roman extended his hand toward Faith. "Hi. I'm Roman."

Faith's eyes warmed more than her sister's. She shook his hand then slung her arm over her mom's shoulder. "You were holding out on us!"

Maybe they shouldn't have walked hand-in-hand when the girls had spotted them, but at least that cat was out of the bag, and they didn't need to worry about how to announce they were more than friends.

Wendy gulped, her gaze flying to meet his. "Maybe? Sort of. You didn't ask."

Faith giggled. "We never dreamed! How would we randomly think to ask if you had a boyfriend? Is that what you still call it when you're ancient?"

Ouch. Roman didn't think of himself as old. Didn't think of Wendy that way, either. Compared to 17, he got it… but mental gymnastics were still going to be required. Hopefully, for the rest of his life.

If Wendy let him. And if her kids allowed them to let him.

Selah shook her head and looked away. "Dad's gonna go ballistic," she mumbled.

Both girls turned to face Wendy when she came out of her bathroom a few hours later. She'd been dreading this moment for weeks, but especially all day. The girls had been civil to Roman while they'd had dinner in Missoula and driven back to Maranatha Inn. They'd greeted Julia and Laura in the lobby and claimed exhaustion from the long trip, which was silly, since the flight was all of 90 minutes.

She'd known, though. They were waiting to get her alone before jumping on her with all four feet. She should be thankful for small mercies, that they hadn't lit into her in front of Roman or her friends.

Now, she squared her shoulders and managed a smile. She truly was delighted to see them. Hopefully the thing with Roman wouldn't overshadow her joy in their visit.

Selah, hands on her hips, led off. "What are you thinking, Mom?"

Wendy could play dumb and ask for clarification, but it wouldn't help. "I assume you're asking about my relationship with Roman."

"Duh."

"I believe I raised you to treat your elders with respect."

"Sorry. You just caught me totally off guard. Faith, too. All of our siblings are equally shocked."

Oof. They'd already been in touch? Which meant word had likely reached Dave by now.

"It's kind of new, and I thought it would be better for you to meet Roman and see for yourselves what a great man he is rather than relying on my opinion."

"Since your opinion is clearly suspect." Selah shook her head with a sigh. "Mom, I can't believe you'd do this."

"So, it's okay for your dad, but not for me?"

Faith's eyes widened. "Are you marrying this guy? Don't we get any say?"

"I'm not marrying him." Wendy gulped. "At least, not any time soon, and who knows? It might not work out, anyway. Like I said, it's still pretty new."

"It affects all of us, you know," Faith went on.

But did it really? Not so much with Wendy living in Montana.

"You've gotten okay with Shyanne."

"Puh-leeze." If Faith rolled her eyes any more dramatically, they'd spin across the floor of Wendy's suite.

"You chose to live with her and your dad."

"Because the high school is like three blocks away, and because *you* wouldn't let me attend. You forced my hand."

Wendy didn't remember it going down exactly like that, but life didn't have a rewind button. All that mattered now were the results, and that's what faced them at the moment. "I'm sorry you felt I was against you. There was a lot of turmoil. I had no idea your father's bombshell was coming—"

"Sort of how I feel right now," Selah interrupted. "Lucky us. We get two huge shocks just a few years apart. First one parent, then the other."

"I hope you can see the situation is completely different."

"Right." Selah flopped into an armchair. "Please elucidate."

Wendy perched on one of the chairs at her tiny table as Faith also settled. "First, your dad had an affair while he was married to me. That means he had—"

"We're not children." Selah's hand cut down. "We know what an affair is, Mom."

"He broke our marriage vows then threw them in the garbage disposal by divorcing me."

"Right. We know he did it first."

"He was not free, but he acted like he was. But legally, post-divorce, I *am* free to pursue a new relationship." In Wendy's imagination, her dad pursed his lips and shook his head. "However much you might like me not to say the 'sex' word, that's another key difference. Your dad did it with someone else while married to me. I have never done it with anyone other than your father."

"Not hottie Roman?" Selah's eyebrows cranked up.

That's what her daughter thought? "No. I'm still not completely thrilled with being divorced, but I totally believe in the sanctity of marriage. I believe God wants us to reserve sex for a marriage relationship, and I'm not married to anyone right now."

"He's crazy about you," Faith put in then turned to her sister at Selah's horrified look. "Well, he is! Didn't you see how he kept looking at Mom and asking what he could get her at dinner? He even held her chair for her. Dad never did that."

"I'm just… I'm not okay with this, Mom." Selah bit her lip. "You've rocked my world, and not in a good way. You don't know how rough things are at home."

Wendy braced herself. "You're away at college."

"I'm home a lot of weekends." Selah thumbed at her sister. "Faith needs me."

"I'm glad you have each other."

"If you still lived in Woodburn, *that* would be home."

If she were back in Woodburn, she wouldn't have reconnected with Roman. Wouldn't have begun to rediscover herself at all. Wendy sighed. "You know things can never go back the way they were."

"What if Dad threw Shyanne out and begged you to come back?"

Her kids couldn't possibly think that might happen… or be a good idea. It had taken distance to see how much she and Dave had taken each other for granted. Yeah, some of the fault had definitely been hers, and not only because she was fat.

I have loved you with an everlasting love.

That was Jesus. Dave's poor excuse for love had not lasted. Could Roman's? Maybe the girls were right. Not that she should accept their groveling father back — or that he'd ever beg her — but maybe she didn't deserve another shot at happiness.

Oh, she was older now. Wiser. Could clearly see where at least some of the things with Dave had gone wrong. But who was she to think she could love a second man better than she had loved the first? After all, she couldn't control anything, starting with her weight.

But, oh, the feeling of hope slipping away brought pain.

CHAPTER
Sixteen

ROMAN HADN'T SEEN Wendy all day. He'd texted her, and she'd replied that she was busy with her daughters. The three of them had gone down to Happy Trails Stables, where Faith and Selah had gone on a trail ride.

He'd have loved to tag along, not that he'd been horseback riding more than half a dozen times in his entire life. Or he could have awaited their return with Wendy. Maybe got a little kissing in.

Audrey accosted him as he stepped off the staircase in the lobby in time for the inn's turkey dinner. "There you are!"

"Hey, sis." He gave her a side hug. "How are things?" He wasn't sure he wanted to know.

"Good. I'm sorry your girlfriend ditched you for dinner tonight, though. Must hurt."

Roman stilled. What was she saying? He and Wendy hadn't discussed Thanksgiving dinner. He'd assumed he'd be her escort. Hers and her daughters'. Had he flat-out asked her? Had he needed to?

"Wendy's girls met Granger's family at dinner last year," Audrey went on. "Granger's granddaughter asked if they could sit together again. I'm sure you knew that..."

No. No, he hadn't. He flashed a smile at his sister that he didn't feel at all. Inside, his gut clenched. Wendy wouldn't... couldn't... would she?

By his sister's smirk, Wendy would. Or, at least, she had with a little encouragement.

Audrey linked her arm through his. "You're with Laura, Chris, and me. We've also got the Satterfields and Eli and Harper at our table."

"What about Bruce?"

Audrey frowned as she looked at him. "What about him? He flew to Denver for the weekend with his brother's family. Didn't he tell you? I thought you guys hung out some."

"Oh." Roman had wondered about Bruce's frequent visits to the Christmas tree farm, but maybe there was nothing to see there. Maybe a guy with hearts in his own eyes imagined them dancing in other people's eyes, too. "No, I haven't seen much of him the past few weeks."

"Too busy with Wendy." Audrey shook her head. "Little bro, I have to tell you—"

"Save it." Behind him, the elevator chimed before the door rolled open and Wendy, Selah, and Faith exited. Roman shook off his sister's hand and stepped toward the Clarke women. "Happy Thanksgiving, Wendy. I hope you all had a great day." He nodded at the girls in turn, hoping his smile held.

"We did, thank you." Wendy didn't quite meet his gaze. "I hope you don't mind, but we're sitting with the Durand-Everett clan this evening at dinner. The girls connected last year."

Oh, he minded, all right, but he wasn't about to throw a temper tantrum like the toddler version of himself, no matter how tempting. "Audrey just informed me."

Why hadn't Wendy? He'd thought they'd made great strides recently. Wendy had started to relax and accept him into her life as more than an old — or too young — friend. She would not have kissed him the way she had if her own feelings did not run deep. She hadn't been trifling with him.

Selah tugged at Wendy's arm. "I see Melissa and Sidney over there!"

"Excuse us, please." Wendy stepped to the side.

"Talk to you later?" Roman couldn't keep the hope out of his voice.

She flashed a fleeting smile in his direction. "Of course!"

Audrey's hand rested on Roman's as he watched the three of them walk away. "That's how it will always be, Romie. She's a mother first. You'd only get the dregs like—" Her voice chopped off in mid-sentence.

He turned to his sister with narrowed eyes. "What else were you going to say?"

"Leave it."

"No. You had more on the brain. Spit it out."

Audrey huffed a sigh. "Okay, fine. I'm thinking that's how Dave felt, like all he got was the leftovers from Wendy. Every bit of effort and focus went to her kids."

Roman didn't know whether to laugh, cry, punch his sister, get on his knees in front of Wendy, or what, but somewhere, deep inside, his sister's words resonated. Truth lingered there. They might have been spoken in spite, or jealousy, or whatever, but they weren't completely unfounded.

It had been easy to fall for Wendy here, far from any other parts of their lives. Well, except for Audrey, who'd done her best to keep Roman grounded. He'd thought she was only being spiteful, following the nagging pattern that had almost certainly contributed to her own marriage's demise. But what if it was more? What if his sister could see the bigger picture and was warning him out of sibling love?

His head hurt. Why couldn't he retreat to his room now to think and pray this through? He'd been asking God, hadn't he? Had Roman been so sure of what he was doing that he hadn't even noticed if God put roadblocks in his way?

But no. The lobby milled with dinner guests. Pam, Granger, and Vance Satterfield arranged the meal on the warming buffet, while Laura showed an older couple to their places. Each table held a cinnamon stick candle holder wrapped with white lace and studded with glass jewels.

Roman gulped as he recalled the day Wendy's workshop had made similar creations. She was so talented.

His gaze slanted toward where she stood close to the exit with Granger's daughter, Melissa Everett, and her two children, whom he'd met a couple of times. Sidney Everett had hero worship in her eyes as she chatted with Faith Clarke. Wendy focused entirely on Melissa, sparing no glance Roman's direction.

Audrey couldn't possibly be right about Wendy. On the other hand, shouldn't her children come first before a new man in her life? Yes? No? How should he know?

Pam eyed Wendy as they took seats side-by-side. "I thought you'd be with Roman," she whispered.

Wendy forced a smile at her friend. "The girls wanted to sit with your family," she whispered back.

"But..."

"It's okay. Really."

Pam tipped her eyebrows up. "It shouldn't be. Not if you and Roman are serious."

Were they? Wendy wasn't sure. Oh, she had a pretty good idea what Roman thought would happen, but he was an unencumbered man in his 40s. Things were different for Wendy. Age. Stage. Size. Probably more reasons existed why she should stay away from him and his enticing kisses.

It seemed like they lived in a bubble at Maranatha Inn, far from her parents, her ex, her kids, and his most-certainly-disapproving parents. Audrey tried to poke the bubble at times, but she hadn't quite managed to pop it all on her own.

But Selah and Faith had contacted their siblings, and every single one of them had texted or phoned within 20 minutes of each other, wishing her a happy Thanksgiving, asking about this new man in her life, and berating her for keeping him a secret.

Dave's text was the cherry on top: *Make sure you know what you're doing, Gwendolyn.*

Was her ex threatening her? Commiserating with her? Chiding her? She didn't know, and she wasn't asking. Dave retained zero right to have an opinion at all, not after the way he'd treated her.

Which didn't mean he was wrong.

Pastor Marshall Smith intoned a longwinded prayer of gratitude in lieu of grace for the meal.

Wendy tried to listen, tried to be thankful for her many gifts and mercies and new life in Christ, but focus remained difficult when she could see the back of Roman's head a couple of tables over.

Yeah, yeah, her eyes should be closed, but she wasn't feeling it. Thanksgiving was a farce. She felt chains tightening around her ankles and wrists. Around her neck, maybe.

She couldn't even wish she'd met Roman before Dave, because she had. But what starry-eyed bride would think about her friend's barely teenaged brother at a time like that? None, that's who.

Finally, Pastor Marshall uttered a hearty, "amen," echoed by many around the tables. With relief, no doubt.

Pam looked ready to bounce out of her seat, but Granger slid his arm around the back of her chair and caressed her shoulder while Julia, as hostess, gave instructions for the buffet.

Wendy loved to see Pam so happy. Loved to see Granger show his adoration for his bride of seven months. He'd managed to pull Pam into his family. Surely it wasn't impossible for Wendy to integrate Roman into hers.

But there were big differences. Pam literally had no one else. Melissa's mother — Granger's ex — phoned occasionally from Georgia and had visited briefly in the summer, but she wasn't really a part of Melissa's family's life. For all practical purposes, Granger and Pam were the only grandparents.

Wendy knew Pam had had trouble opening herself to new love, though. She hadn't felt worthy. She hadn't wanted to find reasons for gratitude amid the loss of her family and had clung to her hurts.

Was Wendy doing the same? It would be so much easier if Dave were killed in a crash the way Pam's first husband had been. Then she'd know she was free to move on, and their children wouldn't have divided loyalties.

She scrunched her eyes shut for a moment. *I'm sorry, Lord. I shouldn't wish Dave dead. I know that's not a godly thought. Please forgive me.*

On the other hand, she wasn't completely wrong. It *would* be so much easier. Her path wasn't destined for simplicity, though. That much seemed plain.

"Shall we?" Granger rose and pulled back Pam's chair as she stood.

Was it their table's turn already? Wendy scanned the dwindling line at the buffet. Seemed so. If Roman sat beside her, he'd pull out her chair like Granger had done for Pam. Dave had never done that, not even in their romantic early days, but that had been an era of exaggerated gender equality. Men simply weren't as gallant as a hundred years before.

Back when women were possessions and not allowed to vote. Maybe chivalry *was* outdated if it came entangled with the bonds of yesteryear.

And then she caught the smile on Pam's face as she received a quick kiss from Granger. Caught the soft light in his eyes as he took in his beloved.

Wendy turned away, blinking back her lurking tears. No, chivalry wasn't outdated. Possession hopefully was, but not kindness and service.

Roman looked at her much the same way, as though she were something precious, even though she was fat. He chided her for using that word so often. His reasons seemed valid, that smack-talking oneself was no better than smack-talking someone else. Would she ever keep telling a friend how worthless she was?

No. Never. Wendy wasn't that mean spirited. Except when directed at herself.

"Mom? Coming?" Selah eyed her with concern.

"Um, yes." Wendy pushed to her feet and followed the rest of her table to the buffet as Julia called another table to come next. Maybe she'd have less mashed potatoes and gravy and more salad. Some people loved salad. Wendy could try.

"Hey, beautiful," Roman's voice warmed her ear.

She managed not to whirl into him in her surprise. "Hi."

"I wish we were sitting together tonight," he murmured.

"Me, too." And despite her misgivings, she spoke absolute truth. Being with Roman always settled her and gave her heart a reason to hope.

"Want to go for a walk later? Do you think your girls would mind sparing you for an hour or so?"

Wendy reached for a plate from the stack at the end of the buffet. Would the girls mind? Almost certainly, yes, but was she duty-bound to humor them? No, they didn't have authority over her.

It was kind of like Granger pulling out Pam's chair, though. It was serving someone you loved and making their lives easier or better.

But was it the same? Even Faith was nearly an adult now, certainly old enough to understand moving forward after life dealt a setback. It turned out Faith hadn't only been testing her mother when she begged to finish at public high school, but the medical schools she was busily applying to preferred a state-issued diploma.

And Wendy hadn't even known of her daughter's aspirations.

She loaded her plate, forcing herself to keep the dressing and the potatoes and the green beans amandine to a minimum. Salad. That would take up half her plate.

Ugh.

No! It was good for her! If she didn't drown it in fatty dressing.

Why was life so hard?

She felt Roman behind her in the line. His arm brushed hers when he reached for a scoop of vegetables. She heard his breathing.

Life wasn't so terrible, not when there was a man like him who saw her on the inside, saw her as a desirable woman in spite of her curves.

No more smack talk, Wendy Clarke.

She leaned back less than an inch and was not at all surprised that her shoulder brushed against his chest. "Ten o'clock in the lobby?"

He pressed back. "I'll be waiting."

CHAPTER
Seventeen

"YOUR SISTER TOLD us disturbing news about you."

Roman clenched his phone and felt his ire rise as he stared at the moon out his window. "Oh?"

"She said you were dating Wendy Clarke. Surely that's not the same Wendy Bilson who used to hang out with Audrey when they were teens?"

Lord, help me. "One and the same, Dad."

"She's a lot older than you."

"I'm aware of that."

"Your mother and I hoped to have grandchildren one day."

Roman forced a chuckle. "I thought you might have given up on that by now. I'm 46, after all."

"Men can sire children well into their old age."

He heard the unspoken 'unlike women.' "That may well be true, but that card isn't in the deck I've been dealt."

His father huffed. "Get a new deck."

"Dad? With all due respect, this is my life, and I'm making my own decisions."

"You made that very clear when you sold your birthright for a bowl of pottage."

Good to know Dad remembered some of the old Bible stories. "It's not quite the same thing."

"No, Emil told me how much Leo paid you. Shouldn't that payout have been mine?"

Ah. Now Dad was getting down to the crux of his complaints. And it certainly wasn't because Roman's parents were hurting for money. "There were no such strings attached when you handed over your half of the company."

"I never dreamed you'd betray me."

Roman couldn't help his astonished laugh. "Betrayal? Really?"

In the background, he heard his mother speaking in rapid Italian. Then a scuffle before her voice came over the airwaves.

"Roman, this is how you repay us? With a woman who is much too old for you? And one who is fat, Audrey says."

"Audrey should mind her own business."

Mom gasped. "She is your *sorella*! Your sister. She cares for you."

"Why am I not allowed to make my own decision with whom I fall in love?"

"Enzo! Talk sense into your son." Grappling as the phone at the other end switched hands again.

"Respect your mother, Roman."

Roman managed to hold in his sigh. "I do respect my mother. And I respect you, Dad. I'm grateful to be your son." Although less so at the moment. "But I'm no longer your little boy. I'm responsible for my own decisions, which I am doing my best to make with God's guidance."

"You don't even have a proper job."

His parents were all over the map with their accusations tonight. So much for the bubble he'd existed inside with Wendy as they explored their growing feelings. He should have known Audrey would tattle and make sure they fell for her spin on the situation. Did that mean he should have phoned first to let them know about Wendy? But Audrey probably had been feeding them information long before Roman had a clue how deep he was getting. For the entire past year, she'd likely told their parents about poor Wendy and how she'd let herself go. There would have been no way to counteract that after the fact.

Roman braced himself. "I'm building a job here in social media marketing. Wendy excels at that, too. She's good at a lot of things. I think, if you give her an honest chance, you'll like who she has become."

Dad must have covered the phone's pickup, because the rapid-fire conversation in Italian was muffled and not completely comprehensible. Roman did pick up words like 'fat' and 'divorced.'

His parents hadn't responded well to Audrey and Steve's divorce, either. Dad had sided with Steve, most likely because Steve had wormed his way deep into the inner workings of the import company, and replacing him would have been a hassle. A fear that had found fruition when Steve's health failed, and he'd stepped out of his role a few months before his death.

Divorce was rarely something to celebrate. Some of Roman's classmates had been married and divorced several times. It seemed they'd entered relationships fully expecting to end them when the joyride ended.

Not for Roman. He wasn't a halfway kind of guy. When he married, he'd be all-in, determined to succeed where so many failed. Anything worth having or experiencing was worth the inevitable difficult times.

But it took two to make a marriage succeed. He had only to look at Wendy to remember that she'd felt the same about her ex, that she'd been resolute in holding things together even as Dave abandoned his own vows.

It was enough to make Roman's head hurt. And the barely intelligible conversation ongoing in his parents' house right now wasn't helping.

He glanced at his watch. Nearly go time. "Dad? Mom? Thanks so much for calling."

His father came back on the line. "Roman?"

"Happy Thanksgiving! I hope you had a great day with Uncle Emil and Aunt Martina. I need to go now, but I appreciate hearing from you."

"Your mother says we need to come to Montana."

Roman's world quaked. This was exactly what he did *not* need. "Sure! You're welcome anytime. You can call the front desk to reserve a room for your visit. Are you thinking of coming for Christmas, maybe?" That would give him time to get things back on track with Wendy. Maybe even propose to her. Might be too soon for that, but also? Maybe not.

More Italian in the background. Roman had been away from home too many years to easily follow the speed of the conversation.

"Soon."

Ugh. Hopefully that didn't mean as imminent as it sounded. Roman felt like his relationship already teetered, and his father, especially, would take great delight in knocking it the rest of the way over. Mom might add a gleeful shove. And Audrey would watch with a smug smile on her face.

Why had he lingered anywhere near a family member? The globe was a big place, and he'd lived in more than a dozen countries over the past decades. He hadn't needed to come to Montana. But... if he hadn't, he wouldn't have reconnected with Wendy.

"Send Audrey and me the details once you've made plans. Talk to you soon." And Roman clicked to end the call.

He had a bit more of an understanding now of the pressures Wendy faced from her own family.

Her daughters had not been okay with Wendy's choice to meet

Roman for a walk, but at least they hadn't demanded to come along.

Wendy felt torn. Shouldn't she respect her kids' opinions? But they weren't giving Roman half a chance. They'd made up their mind in the first five seconds, and that had been that. It hadn't been anything Roman had done or not done, other than hold Wendy's hand. He'd been a perfect gentleman, polite and friendly to the girls and attentive to Wendy.

She stepped off the elevator as Laura hit the switch to dim the lobby lights. Laura winked and tilted her head toward where Roman stood in front of the bow window, looking out at the night sky.

Wendy paused for a moment to admire the view, though she was far too warm with her parka, beanie, and mitts on.

He must have heard the elevator chime, or else he felt her watching him, because he turned. An appreciative smile spread across his face. He came toward her, hands outstretched. "Wendy."

In front of Laura? Oh, why not? Wendy grasped his hands. "Hey," she said softly.

"Hey." He gave her a swift hug then turned toward the doors.

"I'm locking up, you know." Laura stood behind the desk, powering down the computer.

"Yep, I remember the door code." Roman held Wendy's hand as they crossed the area.

"Have fun, kids. Don't do anything I wouldn't do."

"Thanks for the warning, Laura."

Roman's voice carried more humor than Wendy was capable of. She still linked Laura to Roman's sister, expecting her to spout Audrey's nonsense. It had been a while, come to think of it. Now Laura seemed supportive. Julia and Pam, too. Wendy had seen little of Chris lately, so who knew what the arborist thought? But Chris had never been as forceful as Audrey, even back in Bible college. She'd chosen a solitary career and seemed even more introverted than back in the day.

Wendy had always thrived on people. Now she could see some unhealthy patterns around it, like having unrealistic expectations of approval, followed by being crushed when praise didn't flow. Like a beat-up puppy, she kept coming back for more, hoping it would be better this time. When would she learn not to take her worth from others?

The November night air froze all other thoughts. "Oh, it's cold!" she gasped.

"Kissing will keep us warm." Roman's breath on her cheek heated her for just a second.

She started down the circular drive. "Roman, are we a good idea?"

His gloved hand captured hers. "I sure think so. Why do you ask?"

"My kids are so unhappy with me. All six of them." Maybe she should have given them clues ahead of time. Dropped Roman's name in conversation a few times, but would that have helped? She didn't see how any other way might have been better. Also, wait. He was uncharacteristically quiet. "Roman?"

He sighed. "I just got off the phone with my parents. They gave me an earful. I'm ungrateful and a lot of other things."

"Are you, though?"

"Dad's still furious about me selling out to Leo. Compared me to Esau in the Bible."

"Selling his birthright to his brother."

"Yeah. And here I thought when Dad signed the company over to me, that it was actually mine. Turns out, he still planned to keep his hands on the reins. I've ruined his good name, and a whole lot more."

"I'm sorry." But it wasn't the same thing as being upset because of whom he dated.

"And they apparently hadn't given up on having grandchildren."

"Oh." Wendy heaved a sigh. "I'm sorry." Again. At least, her parents couldn't throw that line at her. "I understand if you want — need — to step back."

"What? No!" Roman's hand tightened on hers. "Just, navigating everyone's expectations is harder than I thought."

She huffed a laugh. "Even Dave texted to ask me if I knew what I was doing."

Roman gave her a sidelong look. "How did you respond?"

"I didn't answer. It's none of his business."

"Whew."

"You couldn't possibly think anything he said to me would sway me? He lost that right a long time ago."

"No. It's just… everything feels so topsy turvy right now. I want your daughters to like me. To accept me. I want to hang out with the three of you this weekend so they can get to know me and hopefully give a good report to the others."

Ahh. He felt neglected, which was fair, because she *had* neglected him. "I'm trying to spend quality time with them."

"I can't be part of quality?" He turned to face her, capturing both her hands.

They were most of the way down the drive by now, out of sight of the inn. Not that anyone was likely watching. And what did it matter if they were? Wendy was 55 years old, not 15. She didn't need to answer to anyone else, but it always felt like she did… or should.

"You're right. You can." She let out a breath. "What would you like to do with us tomorrow? I know Saturday will be busy for all of us with the outreach event, and the girls are flying home Sunday afternoon."

"Do you want to do something in Missoula tomorrow? Or we could just have a games afternoon or evening. Or a movie. However much interaction you think is best."

Wendy hesitated. If she and Roman were to have a future, then he was right. Selah and Faith needed to know him and like him. Then they could call their siblings off. Dave's opinion didn't matter. At some point she'd need to talk to her parents, too… or she could assign Adriel that task. Adriel's in-laws lived in Seattle, not too far from Wendy's parents.

"Games?" she suggested. "We can meet in my suite about mid-afternoon, or there's more room in the staff lounge." Which he had access to, thanks to working together on his YouTube channel.

"How about all of it? We can start with games then order in pizza and maybe finish up with a movie and popcorn."

"My girls are into romcoms, for the record."

"I can handle that."

It seemed Roman could handle anything life pitched his way. He was exactly the kind of anchor Wendy needed in her life.

Except... she should be depending on God for that, not a man.

Her thoughts stopped right there because Roman kissed her.

CHAPTER
Eighteen

WENDY WOKE TO A PINGING SOUND. Probably a text from Roman. They'd had such a lovely walk last night. She smiled and stretched before she reached for her phone… and scowled at the sight of Julia's name.

Julia: *You didn't tell me your kids were coming! But they're here.*

Wendy frowned. Weren't Selah and Faith asleep on rollaway cots in her tiny main room? Surely, Julia didn't mean the other four. This must be a prank of some sort.

Wendy: *What are you talking about?*

Julia: *Haha! Shall I send them downstairs?*

Wendy gave her head a shake as she tiptoed to her bedroom door and peered out. As she'd believed, her two daughters were asleep.

Wendy: *Give me a minute. You woke me up.*

It was only 6:15 am. She threw on some clothes, brushed her hair, then paused in the doorway. Laura wouldn't hesitate to play a joke on her, but that didn't fit Julia's personality.

But none of the other Clarke kids could possibly be at Maranatha Inn unless they'd driven all night. Plus, Adriel and Silas were both married with little ones. No, this had to be a setup.

But what if it wasn't?

It had to be.

She took the elevator to the lobby and exited to find her other four kids flopped into the love seats in front of the fireplace. Ezra looked sound asleep.

Not a prank.

Adriel jumped up at her mother's approach. "Surprise!"

Wendy engulfed her eldest daughter in her arms. "It is most definitely a huge surprise to see you. Where are Liam and the girls?"

"At home. This is a quick trip."

"I see." And Wendy did see. "I assume your sisters put you up to this."

Adriel had the grace to look guilty. "You could say that."

"In that case, I only think it's fair that you wake them up." Wendy turned to her sons. Silas and Theo embraced her while Adriel kicked Ezra's foot to waken him. Then Wendy got a hug from her youngest boy.

Wendy averted her gaze from Julia's as she led the way back to the elevator. There was no space for seven people in her tiny apartment. Well, maybe, if they sat on the girls' cots. That had to be preferable to the staff lounge where Audrey or Laura might come through at any moment.

She sent Adriel in first. The boys didn't need to be in the room until their sisters were decent. She listened to the hushed voices. No shrieks or squeals. Therefore, no surprise.

Just as she thought. This had all the markings of an intervention. Nice her kids cared this much... but was it, really?

She turned to her second-born in the corridor. "Anything you want to say to me about this unexpected visit?"

Silas grimaced. "Let's wait."

Yay. Intervention it was. Wendy pressed her hands together and closed her eyes. *Lord? I could really use some wisdom here.*

Adriel flung the door open. "Come on in."

Wendy glared at Selah and Faith. Both girls had taken a minute to brush their hair but still wore their pajamas. Nothing worse than their brothers had seen a thousand times. Her kids exchanged subdued greetings. Right, they saw each other all the time. Even Ezra was home to Woodburn on his days off from the construction site in Portland.

Her three sons sat on Faith's cot while the girls settled on Selah's.

Wendy rested her hands on her hips and looked the six of them over. "Okay, who's in charge here? Because I'm not stupid enough to think this was a chance visit. So, let's hear it."

Faith picked at her fingernails with a clear 'not it' gesture.

Adriel and Selah exchanged looks. Finally, Adriel sighed. "Mom, we're concerned about you."

"Uh huh." Wendy refused to make this any easier on her brood.

"We understand you're dating a man way younger than you are. We weren't prepared to hear about you dating at all, let alone that!"

"The divorce from your father has been final for four years."

"Right, but..." Adriel cast a helpless glance at Silas, who took over.

"You always told us marriage was for life."

"And I still believe that, but both parties need to hold their vows tightly for that to happen. Your father—"

"Yes, we know what he did," Silas interrupted. "But does that give you the right to copy him?"

Wendy felt her eyes bulge. "I'm not copying him. I'm not the one who had an affair while still married. I'm not the one who filed for divorce. I'm not the one who moved my new love interest right into the very home I'd shared with my spouse."

"We know, Mom." Silas sighed. "But—"

"There isn't a 'but' you can put on that, son."

"What if Dad was sorry? What if he wanted you back?"

Wendy had clung to that mirage for far too long. She'd seen Sheryl and Ted remarry after 18 years of divorce, but their history had been quite different than Wendy and Dave's. And now?

She straightened her spine and searched her kids' faces. All eyes, even Faith's, were on hers. "No. He's shown no sign of remorse and, even if he did, how could I ever trust him again? What we had is over. I'm sorry you kids feel trapped in the middle."

"Dad doesn't want that, anyway," Faith mumbled.

Just as Wendy thought.

"I'm done trying to please your father. Done trying to please anyone but God."

The boys eyed each other. "How about this Roman guy?" Theo asked.

Something snapped into place in Wendy's mind. Roman had not once presumed to tell her what she should think or do. He seemed pleased with her regardless of her weight or what she wore or what she did or said. Dave had wanted to offer permission for her to help out with the homeschool co-op. He'd had opinions on everything, opinions she'd been required to value and treat as though they were laws.

Dave loved control, but Roman loved Wendy. Oh, he hadn't said the words, but the sentiment remained evident in every word, every touch, every smile. He loved her for who she was with no thought of changing her or controlling her.

"Roman Scala is a fine man. I assume you all want to meet him, and I'll make sure that happens. Maybe we can all go out for breakfast." It wasn't fair to spring four unregistered guests on the inn's breakfast buffet, nor was Wendy ready to expose her kids to Audrey or Laura just yet. "I don't know where you guys plan to sleep tonight."

They exchanged another look. Had they honed that silent speech when they were little?

"We're driving back tonight," Silas said.

"But you must have driven straight through *last* night!"

"We traded off driving every couple of hours, and the rest of us slept." Theo shrugged. "We're good."

Wendy's perimenopausal self would never put up with that

kind of nonsense, but hey, her kids were under 30. If they said they'd be fine, they'd be fine.

"Excuse me." She went into her bedroom, closed the door, and sat down on the edge of her bed. Text Roman, or call? Either way, pray first.

At least Roman had a little warning. Wendy'd had none. He showered, trimmed his beard, and brushed his teeth, all while constantly praying. How was he going to impress Wendy's other four children if he'd failed so badly with the two he'd already met? Selah and Faith had called in reinforcements.

In the same way, Audrey had tattled on him to their parents. Did everyone think they needed to stage an intervention?

He pulled on his parka, his hand stilling on the zipper. What he and Wendy should do was elope. No one else's opinion mattered. Not his parents' or hers. Not his sister's. Not her kids'. Definitely not Dave's.

Why did everyone feel the need to stick their nose in his and Wendy's business? *Because they love you.* He snorted. Yeah... no. It wasn't that, at least not in every case. Maybe for Wendy's children, but they'd also been brainwashed by their father.

Everything had been going so well in the past week or two. Wendy seemed more comfortable with herself, more confident. How big a setback would this weekend offer? He didn't even know when his own parents would show up, but hopefully not for a while.

Yeah, elopement looked better and better. He loved Wendy, not that she'd seemed ready to hear those words yet. But... maybe now. Maybe she, too, could see that was the best option. Let everyone deal with their marriage after the fact rather than try to break them up beforehand.

He had no doubt that Wendy Bilson Clarke was the woman for him. He'd never met anyone who captured his heart the way she had. He refused to allow anyone between them. Not her family. Not his.

Roman gave himself a firm nod in the mirror before grabbing his wallet, phone, and keys and heading down to the lobby. With any luck, he'd beat the Clarke crew there.

Luck did not favor him. Three young men looked over as he stepped off the staircase, men he recognized from the photos Wendy had shown him. There was no point pretending they weren't waiting for him, so he strode over and extended his hand. "Hi. I'm Roman Scala."

"Silas Clarke." The shortest one of the three gripped his hand in a show of strength that nearly forced a chuckle from Roman. "My brothers, Ezra and Theo."

Roman looked each in the eye as he shook their hands. Wow, they all offered a threatening grip. "It's nice to meet you. Your mom has talked about you a lot."

"Oh?" Ezra shifted from one foot to the other. "She failed to mention you at all."

"I understand." Roman nodded.

Theo's eyebrows shot up, but just then the elevator door opened, and Wendy and her three daughters stepped out. The younger two looked somewhat abashed. No doubt their mom had given them a talking-to about calling in the troops.

Roman walked to Wendy and kissed her cheek. "You look lovely this morning." Then he turned to her family. "We're going downtown for breakfast at the Golden Grill. You can follow my Jeep, or you can find it via GPS. It's just a few minutes away." He reached for Wendy's hand. "Let's go."

Her hand convulsed in his. It seemed a miracle that she didn't pull away, but maybe she'd come to the same conclusion he had. A show of unity was required... unless she'd break things off with him on account of her children. If that had been her thought, she wouldn't have called him this morning and poured her frustration into his ear. She'd have gone silent, maybe texting later to cancel their date. As it was, he'd hold her to that family time if at all possible.

Imagine Roman Scala, stepdad to six adult children. And somehow, he was set to become a step-grandfather, too. Bring it.

He nodded to Selah and Faith. "You're welcome to ride with your mom and me, if you like."

Silas shrugged. "We brought my car, so only one of you can come with me."

The two linked arms. "We'll go with Mom then."

"Perfect." Roman smiled at the two of them. They weren't trying to be mean or belittle him. Probably. They were young, and they cared about their mother. Just because their siblings had shown up in solidarity didn't mean this would end badly.

Just because his parents also felt the need to interfere didn't mean that, either.

Why couldn't he and Wendy be respected by both of their families?

A question for later. Right now, he needed to quietly prove to six skeptical young adults that he had their mother's best interest at heart. That he'd go to any length to protect her right to make her own choices.

Even if she decided against him.

CHAPTER
Nineteen

THE GOLDEN GRILL'S OWNER, Estelle, looked alive with curiosity as she pushed two tables together with help from Theo. They might have avoided the speculation of their friends at Maranatha Inn by coming downtown for breakfast, but Estelle wasn't known for discretion.

Wendy straightened her shoulders as Roman seated her near center then took the chair next to her. Selah slipped in beside her with Faith across, leaving the three boys facing Wendy and Roman. Wendy wasn't sure if it was good or bad that Adriel sat next to Roman. She and Silas seemed to be the ringleaders as they always had been as kids. They were the oldest, after all. If Wendy didn't miss her guess, Theo and Ezra had mostly come along for the ride. They wouldn't want to be left out of this family conference.

Estelle passed out menus while everyone but Faith ordered coffee.

Roman opened his menu as he glanced around. "Breakfast is on me, by the way. Please order whatever you'd like. I've never been here for breakfast before, so I don't have any specific recommendations, but I haven't ever had a meal here I didn't enjoy."

Estelle beamed as she set a bowl of creamers and sugar packets on the table.

Wendy stared at the photo showcasing a stack of pancakes. Nope. Not in front of this judgmental crew, but indulging in private eventually became visible to everyone else. Still, what was the most slimming option? The vegetarian omelet seemed bland… and like giving in to other people's expectations. Why did she always have to overthink food choices?

Roman nudged her elbow and angled his menu toward her. "That looks good. I'm hungry!"

Hmm. Canadian bacon with loaded scrambled eggs might be a decent choice. "I'll have that as well." At some point, she needed to sit down and have an honest, nonjudgmental talk with herself about choosing wisely and sticking to a plan.

Wendy would not be having that talk with Audrey, for all the other woman had a degree in nutrition. She didn't need judgy eyes.

Maybe she did. She squirmed, and Roman casually slid his arm around the back of her chair, lightly rubbing her shoulder. How could he remain calm in the face of this onslaught? Because the four young adults sitting across from them had not missed his gesture. Theo's eyebrows shot into his tousled hairline as he gave Wendy a pointed look.

Maybe it had been a mistake to keep her growing relationship with Roman from her kids, but what if it hadn't worked out? Then she'd just have looked silly. Irresponsible. Unable to keep *any* man, not just their father. No, she'd had to keep her feelings private, but the cat was well out of the bag now. She'd never dreamed her offspring would show up en masse to assess for themselves. Maybe that was a good thing? Maybe it proved they cared. Yes. She'd take it that way until or unless evidence proved otherwise.

She twisted her fingers together in her lap and sent a prayer for guidance heavenward. Just for a moment, she gained strength from the warm, gentle pressure of Roman's arm across her shoulders and the light touch of his hand on her upper arm. Felt a sense of calm settle over her heart.

Not only was she not doing something bad, but something good. Roman was good, with a genuine faith, not merely a mask hiding his real self.

Wendy wanted her kids' approval. Of course, she did, but this wasn't their life to live. It was hers, and God had brought Roman into it when she most definitely hadn't been looking for love.

Love? Hope sprouted in her heart, a tiny green thing taking root. It brought clarity. It brought confidence. It brought her chin up.

"I'm really thankful for all of you kids," she blurted.

Six heads came up. Six pairs of eyes focused on hers, even Adriel's, though she had to lean forward to see past Roman.

"I believe you made that overnight trip because you love me and care about me, and I'm really thankful for that, too."

Silas shifted in his chair, bumping Theo's arm. The brothers glanced at each other before turning back to her.

Wendy let out a slow breath. "I've felt unneeded — unwanted — for the past few years, and it is doing my heart good to have you here."

Faith grimaced. "That's probably on me."

The unwanted bit? "Partly." Wendy wasn't about to mince words. "But it's also on me."

"How so?" Adriel sounded genuinely curious.

"I don't want to make excuses or linger in the past, okay? But I always supported your father. In some ways, I was his mouthpiece."

Adriel nodded thoughtfully.

Silas huffed a laugh. "Yup." He mimicked Wendy's tone. "Dad's not happy with your grades, son."

Wendy shook her head. "I hid behind his authority, I guess. And it backfired, because I made myself insignificant." Which was quite a feat, come to think of it, as wide as she was. Maybe she didn't need to discuss that part with her children. At least, not this minute. "Your father didn't honor me to you kids. Not in a way that showed his love or pride in me." Why hadn't she seen that at the time? But she hadn't.

The youngest two, Faith and Ezra, exchanged a look, both slowly nodding.

"I didn't want to compete with him for your love. I guess I was afraid you'd choose him."

Adriel leaned on the table. "You kind of forced us to do that."

"I can see that now. I'm sorry."

"You basically abandoned us to Dad," Selah accused.

Wendy bit her lip. "I'm sorry."

Roman's hand warmed her shoulder, his presence constant and quiet. This man. How did a woman like her deserve... nope. That's not how it was.

Wendy looked around at her children. Did she dare entrust them with the bigger truth? They were all adults. Even Faith, mostly. "It may look like I ran away when Julia called, but there was more to the decision. I didn't have a job or any purpose once you moved out, Faith."

Her daughter winced.

"And your father..." She let out a long breath. "He didn't figure he needed to keep paying for the apartment for just me. When Julia offered purpose and accommodation, I felt wanted here. Needed. Appreciated. Plus, it gave me time to figure out my new life." The one she hadn't wanted.

"I'm sorry, Mom. I didn't know... didn't realize." Faith's lower lip trembled as her eyes filled with tears.

"I know, sweetheart. From your point of view – all of you – I did abandon you. I've missed so much of your lives in the past... well, year, especially, but longer than that, really. I was too busy licking my wounds to figure out how to readjust as a parent."

Licking her wounds... and eating doughnuts. Maybe entering a better space with her kids would help with her personal choices, too. That tiny green sprig of hope in her heart unfurled a minuscule leaf.

Silas raised his chin as he studied her then flicked a glance at Roman. "Are you going to move back to Woodburn so we can get together more easily? Teri and I have missed you. Missed having you in our little guy's life."

"I've missed squishing that baby more than you can imagine." Wendy's voice caught. "And your girls, Adriel. It's felt like cutting off my arms not to be there for the little ones."

"So... is that a yes?" Theo, too, eyed Roman. "You'll come home, Mom?"

They knew Roman would be a big part of that decision. Could she move away from him to be reunited with her family? Oh, not with Dave. Her parents were also unlikely to come around, but maybe God would perform a miracle with them.

But... Roman. She couldn't give him up, and he was starting to build a business here. As yet, fledgling, but they'd started to see an uptick in views and subscriptions to his channel.

"I can't answer that question right now." Wendy studied her children's precious faces. "It's taken removal from my former life to get any clarity at all, and I'm not sure I'm strong enough to return. Also, Roman is here, and he's important to me."

"Thanks," he murmured for her ears alone.

"My friends here have my back. They knew me before I met your dad, and they've all helped in the healing process." Even Audrey, in her own way. "I don't know what the future holds, but I promise to stay in closer touch. I'll visit. You visit, too! And maybe some of you might find work in Jewel Lake or Missoula. I'd welcome you nearby."

Estelle began setting plates in front of Adriel's end of the table.

How much had the woman overheard? And how much did Wendy care?

Because for the first time ever, she didn't. Care, that was.

"You're brave," Roman whispered to Wendy as he linked hands with her. The conversation over the meal had shifted to sports and a family friend's purchase of an oceanside inn. He'd sat beside Wendy and listened in, trying to get a feel for each of her children's personalities and opinions. Six at once proved a little overwhelming.

They exited the Golden Grill to a brisk, icy wind, and crossed the street to the vehicles.

"That's the cutest park," Adriel gushed. "My girls would love playing there."

"Come for Christmas?" Wendy suggested. "I can see what rooms are available."

"Liam's parents are expecting us in Seattle."

Roman's heart hurt for Wendy. "Maybe over New Year's."

Adriel's brows furrowed as she studied him. "Maybe. I'll talk to Liam and see what he has for time off."

That inner fist pump had better stay deep inside. He nodded at Adriel. "I'd love to meet your family."

"You're sticking around, then?"

"For the holidays? Of course. This is where I live now." Although he should maybe start looking for a rental in town. Or should he put his money where his mouth was and buy a place like Granger had done last fall?

Adriel tipped her head toward Wendy. "I meant sticking with my mother."

His fingers tightened around Wendy's. "As long as she'll have me. Forever would be fine by me."

Wendy gripped back, and his heart soared. Yes! They were on the same page.

Silas glanced past his sister. "Do you have any kids, Roman?"

"Me? No. I've never married or been in that sort of relationship."

"Why?"

It sounded too weird and sappy to say he'd been waiting for Wendy, especially when their age gap came into account. Roman shook his head. "Never met anyone worth giving up my lifestyle for. I traveled a lot, moving from country to country every couple of years or so, working for my family's import company."

"I'd love to live overseas. To travel." Theo sounded wistful. "I haven't been anywhere interesting."

"It gets old, and the interesting becomes commonplace."

The younger man laughed. "I'd have to experience that to believe you. No offense."

"None taken. But I could put in a good word for you with my cousin Leo. I sold my share of the company to him last summer. I can't promise he'd make room for you, but asking can't hurt."

"You'd do that?"

"Just say the word."

"I might." Theo nodded. "Thanks, man. I'll pick your brain later."

"Sure. I'll give you my contact info."

"Cool."

One down, five to go.

"Look! That pond is frozen right over!" Faith yelled, pointing at the kids playing on the ice. "Come on!" She linked arms with Selah and Adriel, and the three of them dashed across the icy grass then slid across the pond, shrieking all the way.

Their brothers leaned against a climbing dome, laughing as they watched their sisters.

Wendy pressed against Roman. "Thanks."

"For what?" He slid his arm around her waist and tugged her close.

"For being so patient and kind to my children."

He turned to face her. "It's my honor and privilege."

"But you didn't have to."

"Sure, I did. How better can I honor you than to honor the ones you love?"

She studied his face. "I don't deserve you."

"I think we've been over this before. Love isn't about deserving. It's a choice... and a gift from God." Had he ever said the words to her? He didn't think so. This might not be the best moment. On the other hand, when better? He cupped her face between his hands. "Wendy, I love you. You mean the world to me, and I'm so thankful God brought us back together all these years later."

She bit her lip as she studied him. She seemed to have forgotten the presence of her children nearby, but Roman hadn't.

"May I kiss you now?"

Her sideways glance proved she wasn't as in the moment as he'd guessed. But then she looked back into his eyes. "Please do. I love you, too, Roman."

His heart swelled at her words as he searched her eyes, trying to convey what was impossible for words. Then he kissed her. Passionately... but briefly. "More later," he whispered.

Much, much more. And hopefully, not too much later.

CHAPTER
Twenty

THANKFULLY, when they arrived back at Maranatha, Roman suggested a walk up to the Christmas tree farm.

The man was so thoughtful. He could see that Wendy needed help figuring out how to spend an entire day with her visiting family.

"This is amazing." Selah twirled on the road. "I love the smell of trees."

Hadn't Wendy brought her and Faith here last year when they visited? Maybe not. She'd been so busy preparing for the outreach on Saturday evening. This year, they had things well under control in advance, so the pressure seemed less. She'd still have plenty of time to stress about it all tomorrow during their final prep and the event itself.

Today, on the first day of tree sales, a dozen vehicles parked along the road. Voices and laughter rang out, punctuated by the buzz of Chris's chainsaw.

"We won't be in the way, will we?" Wendy whispered to Roman.

"I can't see how." He squeezed her hand. "There are 20 acres of trees and not so many buyers that we're interfering. Makes me wonder if Chris needs a hand, though."

"She'll never ask."

"I gathered that. What's her story?"

Wendy shook her head. "Besides being introverted and super self-sufficient?" So the opposite of Wendy. "She was just like that in Bible college, too, but now she's... more."

Roman chuckled. "I think that can describe any of us from years gone by. We don't change all that much, at least not in personality. We just become *more* of whatever that was."

Was Wendy the same? Probably. She'd been a people-pleaser then, too, always wondering what others thought of her and trying to align with their perceived expectations. She'd been a model student and attempted to be the very best of best friends. And even then, she'd been hurt when her friends chose each other over her.

Like Audrey. They'd been so close through middle school and high school, dreaming of going off to Gilead Bible College together. It hadn't taken long for Audrey to connect with Laura, leaving Wendy on the sidelines. Julia had always been the welcoming one. She definitely hadn't changed, just deepened her gift of genuine hospitality. She'd ensured that Wendy and Chris, the other outlier, had felt included.

"Maybe you're right," Wendy murmured to Roman, half listening as Adriel and Silas argued the pros and cons of fir trees versus spruce. Which smelled better? Which had better boughs for decorating? Which needles stayed intact longest?

Chris stopped her ATV beside Wendy's gang. "Hi, guys! I don't think I've met all of you."

She'd chatted with Faith and Selah yesterday morning, so Wendy introduced her friend to her older children. Laughing, Chris answered Silas and Adriel's questions about the merits of each tree species.

Silas elbowed Adriel. "Hey, we could strap two trees to my roof rack and take a bit of Montana back with us. Teri would be happy not to have to deal with getting a tree. What say you?"

Adriel wrinkled her nose and shook her head. "My girls are

older than Tommy. Liam and I are already building traditions around the tree with them, so I need to pass."

Silas turned to Theo. "How about you?"

Theo held up both hands. "Nope. Not me. I have a three-foot artificial that's good enough for me."

Adriel stared at her middle brother. "That's not even a tree. It's barely a shrub."

He shrugged. "I don't have more decorations, and I'm not home much."

Roman leaned to Wendy's ear. "Sounds like a typical bachelor."

She managed to hold her giggle inside. "I guess."

"We all have the decorations Mom made for us every year of our lives," Adriel insisted. "You can get a bigger tree and buy a box of glass balls to fill it in."

"You made decorations?" Roman whispered. "I have to see them. I bet they're gorgeous."

"Just crafty little things."

"Made with love."

Well, of course. Maybe she should make something for Roman to commemorate their first Christmas. Would they still be together in a month, or would he tire of her? But he showed no signs of that. If anything, he proved more and more each day that he was here for the long haul. Like… a lifetime.

Silas video-called his wife as he wandered off, showing Teri the tree options he'd found. Guess he'd given up trying to drag a sibling into the mix, but Wendy's heart warmed to know he cared enough to support Maranatha and, by extension, his mom.

Finally, he jogged down to the parking lot, drove back, and tied his selection to the roof rack before they all trooped back to the inn.

Bless Pam. She brought a slow cooker full of soup and a basket of sourdough rolls to the staff lounge downstairs, and the Clarke kids dug in. Pam stayed for a few minutes to make them feel welcome.

Wendy's suite simply wasn't large enough for eight people to hang out, so the staff lounge was perfect. Julia stopped in for a bit and offered the three youngest summer jobs. Ezra declined, saying he was happy in his Portland construction job, but Selah and Faith told Julia they'd consider coming on the housekeeping staff for the busy months.

Laura hung out for a bit, chatting with Adriel about toddlers, as her granddaughter was a similar age as Adriel's girls. Laura missed little Ruby, and Wendy could sympathize for sure.

After Laura left, they broke out a few decks of cards and began a *Hand and Foot* marathon. Adriel took immediate charge, assigning Theo as Roman's teammate and Faith as Wendy's. Wendy was fine with that, as it allowed her to stay seated beside Roman.

"Your kids are cutthroat," he murmured to her when Selah and Adriel squealed and high-fived across the table over catching the other three teams with unplayed 'feet.'

"They are." Wendy's heart had filled to overflowing spending this day with her children. They might have made the journey to assess Roman, but he seemed to have passed the test. At any rate, they treated him as one of the crew, just as ganged-up-upon as the others.

The elevator doors opened, and Audrey stepped out. She stopped and surveyed the scene, an inscrutable expression on her face.

Wendy pressed her knee against Roman's as he stiffened. Her other friends had been nothing but kind and welcoming, but Audrey? Audrey had her own agenda.

The hand complete, Roman rose. "Hey, guys, I'd like to introduce my sister, Audrey. Or maybe you've already met her?"

Audrey came nearer, her gaze roving the group. Wendy straightened her shoulders. No way was she letting Roman's sister sever the bonding they'd achieved today.

"Hey, Aunt Audrey," Adriel said easily. "It's been a long time."

It really had been, but Wendy and her friends had always

encouraged their kids to treat their friend group as extended family.

"It has. I hear you have two daughters, Adriel. Congratulations."

"Thank you! Liam is a busy dad today with me away."

"I bet he is." Audrey's gaze swept back and forth over the boys. "I'm sorry. I can't place which of you is which."

Roman cleared his throat and pointed them out in turn. "Silas. Theo. Ezra."

Wendy's sons stood. "Hi, Aunt Audrey," Silas said, and the other two nodded toward her.

"Why don't you join us?" Adriel offered. "Selah and I have creamed everyone in *Hand and Foot*. We're ready for a break."

"Hey, Si and I are close," Ezra protested. "You just don't want to give us a chance to catch up."

Adriel smirked. "Busted. But we can also be polite." She waved her siblings away from the table.

"Round two in a bit," Silas warned.

They settled into the sofas and looked expectantly at Audrey.

Great. This was going to be awkward.

"I'm going to swing by Super One for a couple of bags of salad then pick up the pizza we ordered." Roman jingled his SUV keys a few hours later. "Any other requests?"

"Yeah, can I come with?"

Roman looked at Theo. "Sure. I'd love to have you."

"Maybe a case of pop," Adriel said.

"Deal. Anything else?" Roman raised his eyebrows at Wendy.

She shook her head. "No, but thank you."

"Anything for you." He didn't care if he sounded sappy to her

191

kids. They needed to understand that his first loyalty was to Wendy. Well, second, next to God. "Be back in a bit."

Theo followed him out to the Jeep, and they buckled in. "Why does your sister not like my mother?"

Roman gave the young man a side-eyed look as he backed out of the parking lot. It had been that obvious, huh? He'd thought Audrey had been quite polite, all things considered, though she hadn't stayed in the lounge for long. "Audrey has her own stuff she's dealing with, and she projects it on others." Hopefully that was safe enough.

Theo shook his head. "And here I once thought that being an adult meant having your life together."

Roman laughed. "I wish that were true. But... nope. Adults are just older than kids. More life experience sadly doesn't equate to maturity."

"What kind of stuff? For your sister, I mean."

"She's always been a bit of a control freak." Maybe more than a bit. "Her answer to life problems is to double down and let nothing slip."

"So, she looks at my mother and thinks she's too weak."

"It seems she does. But your mom isn't weak."

Theo sighed. "I know. My dad put her through the wringer. She used to be so bubbly and fun, but he crushed her spirit, I think."

"The divorce hit her hard," Roman replied cautiously.

Theo turned in his seat and stared so long that Roman had no choice but to glance his way.

"My siblings and I have been talking."

Roman managed not to grin, because that was so totally not a surprise.

"If you hurt our mother, you'll have us to answer to. All six of us."

"I have no intention of hurting your mother."

"Neither did Dad. At least, not at first."

Roman nodded. "I'm sure that's true. I haven't met your

father, so I never observed them together. The last time I saw her before coming to Montana was at Audrey's wedding. Your mom came from Oregon with two little kids and round with pregnancy."

"That would have been me, I guess. I'm kid number three."

"Your dad didn't accompany her. He didn't keep the kids to make it easier for her. I don't know. He might have offered, and she insisted on bringing them. I haven't asked, and it's honestly none of my business."

"Uh huh." Theo eyed him. "You're a lot younger than she is."

No point pretending otherwise. Roman turned toward Jewel Lake's downtown core. "Nine years."

"That's a lot. That'd be like me dating a high school sophomore."

Roman forced a chuckle. "Sort of, yes, but not at all the same thing."

"Oh?"

"At your age, it's a significant percentage of your life. Even more of the fictional girl's life. At least, I assume she's fictional?"

Theo scowled. "No way would I even look twice at a girl that age. Or a divorced woman in her mid-30s."

"I get it. Might sound simplistic, but the older you get, the less the age difference matters. Did I come to Maranatha thinking to kindle something with one of my sister's friends, even the one I'd known when I was a little kid? It totally wasn't on my radar." Roman parked in the Super One lot and turned off the Jeep. "But sometimes, life doesn't turn out the way you expect it to. Are you a Christian?"

"Yes. Of course."

No 'of course' about it, but Roman didn't go there. "Then you know that walking with Jesus requires faith. It requires being open to His leading. When you want His will more than anything else, sometimes surprising things happen."

"Huh. I guess."

"Meeting your mom again was one of those surprises. My

sister told me Wendy was at Maranatha over a year ago. The surprise came when I found myself drawn to her. Don't think I didn't try to talk myself out of pursuing her. I was as aware of our age difference as every onlooker has been. It seemed presumptuous at first, but... it doesn't anymore."

Theo jumped out of the Jeep.

Roman did the same, beeped the locks, then strode toward the supermarket beside Wendy's middle son. "I want you to know I love your mother." He gulped. Man, he hated putting himself out there. Being vulnerable. "At some point, I plan to ask her to marry me. What will you and your siblings say to that?"

Theo narrowed his eyes. "Does it matter?"

To Roman? Not so much, but he wasn't the only one impacted. "It definitely matters to your mom."

The young man stopped outside the Super One. "Does it matter to you that your sister isn't onboard?"

"Less so, if I'm honest. She's not my offspring, and it really doesn't affect her the same way it affects you and your brothers and sisters." Did Theo have to remind Roman that his own parents were coming to Montana to express their own displeasure? All Roman could tackle was one problem at a time. Thankfully, nothing more was required.

"I've seen how you support her," Theo said at last. "How you're always making sure her interests are taken care of. If my dad ever did that, I don't remember noticing. So, yeah, go for it, I guess. But it's weird. I just want to make myself clear."

Roman lightly punched Theo's shoulder. Maybe someday he'd offer a man-hug but today wasn't that day. "Thanks. I don't take your approval lightly. You won't regret it."

"I'd better not." And Theo turned to the store.

Roman was getting good at keeping all those fist pumps inside his head.

CHAPTER
Twenty-One

ROMAN HAD STOOD beside Wendy and her two youngest as they waved goodbye to the other four yesterday evening. Then he'd hugged Wendy goodnight and climbed the stairs to his own room on the third floor, where he'd spent half the night awake, tossing and turning, before finally giving up and settling into the armchair with his Bible.

The sky was still dark. November was like that in the north. Short days. Long nights.

His thoughts drifted to Christmas. What should he buy Wendy for a gift? Was it too soon for a diamond? She'd healed quite a lot in the past two months, and the visit with her kids yesterday had been cathartic. She'd beamed when Adriel hugged Roman goodbye. When the boys shook his hand, each with a confirmation that it had been good to meet him in person. He had their blessing, or whatever he might choose to call it.

His sister? Not so much, but Audrey had seemed more thoughtful than combative when she stopped by for a brief visit. Maybe she was coming around. And then there were his parents and their threatened visit.

Roman was riding on a high, though. If he could win over Wendy's six kids, she could do the same with his parents.

God was in it.

He lifted his gaze from the Bible he'd yet to crack open and stared into the flame of the gas fireplace in his room.

God was in it.

Yes, Roman truly believed that was the case. Therefore, he didn't need to worry about Enzo and Bianca Scala's response to Wendy. Their visit was a mere formality so, yes, he could look to the future with a clear mind.

Thursday had been Thanksgiving, and he'd been truly thankful, even though he hadn't sat by Wendy's side at the feast. Yesterday, he'd earned that spot with her family. Today was the church outreach dinner, and tomorrow was the first Sunday of advent.

The Sunday of hope, a time of expectation, not in a wishful thinking "I hope it doesn't snow" kind of way, but a deep anticipation of the fulfillment of God's promises to send a Savior. The Israelite people had been experiencing a long, dark night in their collective history. A November night... with the promise of a coming dawn.

As Julia liked to remind anyone who would listen, the word maranatha meant advent. Literally, 'Come, Lord Jesus.' The decorations on the trees and mantles and windows and, well, on nearly every inch of the inn were rife with reminders of the ultimate meaning of Christmas.

A baby come to be king. A baby who was already king, but who'd temporarily given up the throne to make sure humanity had the opportunity to be reborn into citizenship of that eternal kingdom.

It was mind-boggling, honestly.

It put Roman's love for Wendy into perspective. Yes, it mattered to him, to Wendy, and to those who surrounded them, but not compared to the big picture.

Hope. Such an interesting word, at least in a biblical sense. So confident, so full of faith and focus. Hope looked past the trials of today to the ultimate fulfillment of God's promises. This expectation had been given to God's people as they faced hardship and exile. What prophet had it been again? Isaiah.

Roman opened the Bible and thumbed through the first few pages of Isaiah until he came to chapter 9. There it was!

Nevertheless, that time of darkness and despair will not go on forever. The land of Zebulun and Naphtali will be humbled, but there will be a time in the future when Galilee of the Gentiles, which lies along the road that runs between the Jordan and the sea, will be filled with glory. The people who walk in darkness will see a great light. For those who live in a land of deep darkness, a light will shine.

Ah, the specificity of it! A gleam of light, like the first rays of dawn piercing a deep, dark, seemingly endless night. Imagine being faced with the unimaginable horror of becoming prisoners of war in a country known for its brutality. Then imagine the prophet's words. How the people must have come to cling to that faint glimmer.

But not just a single ray, but a great light breaking forth!

Their God would not forget them or abandon them, though it might seem like that for a time. Some surely gave up all hope and had been plunged into the depths of despair. But some must have clung to Isaiah's words and looked for that great light to come.

The light of the world is Jesus.

The old hymn played in his mind.

The whole world was lost in the darkness of sin; the Light of the world is Jesus. Like sunshine at noonday His glory shone in; the Light of the world is Jesus.

The lyrics didn't mention hope by name, but the song overflowed with that theme.

Roman went back over the first seven verses of Isaiah nine, which closed the Messianic prophecy by saying, *The passionate commitment of the Lord of Heaven's Armies will make this happen!*

It was as though it had already happened... but it hadn't. Not yet.

Wasn't that the theme of advent? Reflecting on what had already taken place in the birth, life, and death of Jesus... and then turning toward the future, toward the 'not yet,' and believing that the promises of eternal life would also come true by God's passionate commitment, in His own time.

The faint hint of dawn had begun to peer in through Roman's window when his phone vibrated with a gentle hum. If he hadn't been awake, the sound wouldn't have roused him from night mode. He reached for it and frowned at Eli's name.

"Hello?"

"Roman. It's Eli."

"Good morning?"

"I wasn't expecting to catch you." Eli coughed. "But, man, I've been up all night, sicker than a dog. There is no way I can attend tonight's banquet, let alone speak."

Roman clenched the phone. He could hear his friend's raw, gravelly voice. "I'm so sorry. You sound terrible."

"Thanks." The chuckle turned into a coughing fit that went on and on. "I need to ask you if you'll cover for me tonight."

"Cover for you? You mean… preach?" With 12 hours notice?

"It's not really preaching. Ten minutes tops. Even five would be enough."

"I've seen the video of last year's event. You spoke for at least 20 minutes."

"Yeah." Cough. "I get wordy sometimes, but you wouldn't need to. Can I count on you?"

"I'm no preacher. Ask Marshall?" After all, Marshall Smith was the senior pastor.

"He can't. He's really struggling with his health right now."

"Granger?" Yeah, Roman knew he was grasping at straws, but why him?

"He's got everything else on his plate already with being the MC and playing Santa."

"Why me?" But Roman could feel his resolve slipping.

"Because I've asked God, and He showed me you've got something to say about hope."

"Right, bring the big gun into it."

Another chuckle that turned into another cough. "Sorry-not-sorry, because it's true."

But hadn't Roman spent the past few hours delving into Christian hope? He just hadn't realized he was preparing to preach. No matter what Eli called it, that's what it was. He took a deep breath. "Okay."

Wendy emerged from her bedroom the next morning to find her two daughters still crashed on the narrow cots that took up most of her main room's floor space. Usually, she'd fix herself breakfast in her suite, but she wasn't quite ready to face the girls, especially if they hadn't had enough sleep.

She could do breakfast upstairs. It wouldn't be the end of the world. And, besides, Roman might be present. That was worth it right there. She couldn't help the smile spreading across her face. Didn't want to help it.

Roman loved her.

He'd spent the entire day with her and her kids... and won them over. Today, they'd help out at the Christmas tree farm for a while — Wendy couldn't believe Chris had actually asked for assistance — before the final prep for the outreach event tonight. She had all the papers cut and directions duplicated for the origami angel craft she'd be leading.

Wendy slipped out of her suite and headed to the dining hall. The breakfast cook, Jelly, set out a luscious buffet every morning in a heated serving table, but Wendy headed for the other counter where granola, yogurt, and berries would be her friend. Oh. Her eye caught on the cranberry orange muffins. A couple of those would be good. Maybe she'd skip the granola.

She poured herself a coffee and hesitated with her spoon in the sugar bowl. A dish sat beside it with alternative sweeteners. She could try one of those, whatever a monk-fruit-erythritol blend was. Maybe two packets. She'd survive. Finally, she turned to the tables, where a smattering of guests and staff sat.

Wendy frowned. Roman wasn't here, but Laura waved her over. Her friendly smile was better than sitting alone, for sure, so Wendy set her food down in front of the chair around the corner. "Good morning."

"Hey! Don't usually see you here for breakfast." Laura's plate was empty except for a few crumbs, but her coffee cup was full. Probably a refill.

"I didn't want to wake up the girls."

"Ah." Laura winked. "If that's your excuse."

"Not an excuse." Not much, anyway.

"Roman was in here a bit ago, but he went back upstairs."

"Oh. Well, he's not why I came." If that were true, her mood shouldn't sink like a granite boulder in a lake.

Laura smirked. "How did yesterday go?"

Wendy ducked her head and offered a quick prayer of thankfulness... even if her morning started with Laura rather than Roman. "It went really well, actually. Surprisingly so."

"Good. I'm glad your kids took the bull by the horns and came out to see for themselves instead of stewing back home."

"I am, too. I only wish they could have brought the littles, but I get why two overnight trips back-to-back would have been too hard for toddlers."

Laura nodded. "I'm flying home for Christmas. I've been away from Ruby for too long, and I don't want her to forget me."

"I'm sure you miss her parents, too." Wendy winked.

"Well, duh. But Michael and Katie don't change so much every week as a toddler."

"I know." Wendy mixed her berries into the yogurt and had a bite. "Trust me, I know."

"I imagine you feel more torn than I do, though. I only promised Julia a few months at first, as we all did. She could easily run this inn without me if I decided to move back to Maine."

Wendy's spoon stilled in mid-air. "Are you considering that?"

"Maybe? I don't know. I don't do anything here that couldn't easily be done by someone else. Julia could hire a local to run the front desk on her days off."

"I guess she could. I'd miss you, though." Truth, to Wendy's surprise.

"Thanks. I'd miss all of you, too. But you've got Roman here. I have no real good reason to stay."

Wendy studied her friend. "You're right that I feel torn. I never intended to make this my permanent home. Accepting Julia's invitation last year then staying was easier than facing Dave and Shyanne back home. It was easier not to make my kids choose between spending time with me or with their dad."

Laura nodded. "Dave's a jerk. You know that, right?"

Wendy winced. "I know. But he's still my kids' father."

"You're much nicer than I would be in your situation. Thankfully, Michael isn't Gord's son, so he doesn't have divided loyalties. That made it possible to cut ties completely."

"Have you ever told Michael about his biological father?" Because Laura had never confided in her girlfriends. Unless one or more had been sworn to secrecy, and Wendy was the only one in the dark? Maybe, but she couldn't see it.

Laura's lips tightened as her eyes narrowed. "Nope. I'm grateful he hasn't insisted. He went through a stage, years ago, when he badgered me. And Katie asked me for details when Ruby was born. Said it might be necessary to know the other half of Michael's medical background."

"Valid." Wendy took a sip of her coffee and frowned. That sweetener tasted… okay, much to her surprise. Could it really be better for her than sugar?

"Not valid. If Ruby ever has a medical need, I'll consider it then, but it would have to be life-threatening."

Wendy couldn't imagine keeping a secret of that magnitude. "Do you have peace about that decision?"

"Close enough." Laura looked up as Audrey paused beside their table. "Hey, girlfriend."

Wendy gave Audrey a cautious smile. "Good morning, Audrey. Heading out for the day?" Because Audrey was wearing a parka and had her purse slung over her shoulder.

Audrey gave the two of them a tight smile. "I don't know what's with the people in our lives. First Wendy's kids show up unannounced, and today it's my parents. Except not completely unannounced, I guess. They gave me a few hours' notice of when to meet their plane in Missoula."

"Your... parents?" A block of ice form in Wendy's stomach. "Wow, I haven't seen them in a lot of years."

Audrey lifted an eyebrow. "I think their impromptu visit is thanks to you, just like your kids' visit was. You wield a lot of power, Wendy."

"Hey, Audrey, play nice." Laura smacked her friend's arm.

The other woman sighed. "Right. I know. Sorry. It's just that nothing I've ever done brought my parents across several states. They don't care that much about me, but Roman? He just has to sneeze, and they come running."

Laura looked between Audrey and Wendy. "But he lived over-seas for years."

"And they visited him. Dad did, at least."

How could Wendy surreptitiously check her phone for a message from Roman? Because it didn't feel right hearing about this from Audrey and not from him.

Unless he didn't know, either.

CHAPTER
Twenty-Two

ROMAN LEANED his elbows on the desk in his room and rubbed his temples as he scanned the notes he'd tapped into his tablet. How could he take all these diverse thoughts and turn them into a cohesive talk? There were so many things he could say, but which of them would speak the clearest to those who needed that message of hope?

The dinner demonstrated Creekside Fellowship's open door to the community, with tickets gifted to single moms and families and singles down on their luck. People who needed to know that Jesus loved them, and so did their neighbors. That Creekside wasn't an elite club for perfect people.

Ha.

Roman had only attended there for a couple of months now, but he already knew the people weren't perfect. After all, he was one of the regulars, as was his sister. Pretty sure the veneer on others wore equally thin. But that didn't mean they didn't try to follow Jesus and His teachings. The Bible's mandate was clear: to extend love and mercy and grace to the widows, the foreigners, and the needy.

Creekside's Thanksgiving outreach dinner was only one example of doing that and, over the past few hours, he'd come to be honored and grateful he could play a part beyond canvassing for donations for the Santa gifts.

He glanced at the time on his phone. Whoa. Nearly 9:30 already? Where had the hours gone?

Roman rose and stretched. He'd grabbed a coffee and a couple of muffins when breakfast first opened in the dining hall, but that had been hours ago now. He should take a break, find more food, and see what Wendy and the girls were doing. She'd definitely be up by now.

Roman: *Good morning, beautiful! I hope you slept well.*

Then he pocketed his phone and headed downstairs. Pickings were slim as Jelly had begun cleaning up the buffet warmer, but he filled a plate with the scraps before feeling his phone vibrate. He carried his food to a table and checked the device.

Wendy: *Good morning. I hear your parents are coming?*

Oh. His gut sank. He'd purposefully kept that to himself. Yesterday had been all about Wendy's children, and he hadn't wanted to muddy the waters. Besides, there was always the chance his parents were blustering.

But wait... how did Wendy hear?

Roman: *They've threatened to visit sometime, yes.*

Hopefully, that would suffice to set her mind at rest. He took a bite of his scrambled eggs before his phone buzzed again.

Wendy: *Today?*

He frowned. What did she mean, today? Had he missed something? He double-checked texts. Nothing. Email? None from his parents in the long queue he'd been ignoring, but one from his sister sat nearly at the top.

His frown deepened. Why would Audrey email him rather than text? He tapped it open, and there it was. Their parents' flight details with an arrival time of mid-afternoon and Audrey's assurance she had it covered since she knew he was busy with the event.

She didn't even know how busy he was, because he hadn't told anyone about Eli's early-morning phone call.

Today. His parents were already on their way. Had Audrey secured tickets for them for the outreach event? His gut soured. How harshly would Dad judge Roman's sermon? Because, yes, for all Eli's downplaying of the role, Roman hadn't been born yesterday. A talk, a speech, a sermon... the term didn't matter. Roman would stand in front of a couple of hundred people and offer a message of hope.

He hadn't replied to Wendy yet, but what could he say? He felt utterly gobsmacked. And annoyed. More than annoyed. He wasn't a high-school kid whose daddy needed to oversee his homework. He wasn't a newbie employee whose boss needed to sign off on his files. He was a grown man with a history of good judgment calls behind him.

Roman: *I didn't know until you mentioned it. I thought it was a vague threat, but I see Audrey emailed me to say she was picking them up this afternoon. No clue why she'd email rather than text, but there you have it.*

Wendy: *You didn't know?*

Roman: *That's what I said.*

And he didn't appreciate being cross-examined by his girl-friend, like she agreed with his parents that his assessment was faulty. He scrubbed at his temples. Now he had a headache, and the hunger he'd felt had fled. He got up, scraped his plate, and added it to the bin.

Wendy: *I'm sorry. I didn't mean to make it sound like I doubted you.*

Yeah, he was a heel. He'd overreacted. Lack of sleep did that to a guy. Even as he thought it, he mentally kicked himself. He couldn't put the blame there. He couldn't put it on his focus on writing his message, either.

Roman: *I'm sorry, too. Where are you at? Something unrelated happened I'd like to talk about.*

Wendy: *In my room, but the girls are still asleep. Meet in the lobby or the staff lounge?*

Roman: *Lobby is great. I'm in the dining hall now getting a coffee refill.*

No need to mention the aborted attempt at second breakfast.

Wendy: *See you in a few.*

He filled his coffee cup before crossing the lobby to the sitting area beyond the reception desk.

Julia looked up. "Good morning, Roman!"

"Hi. How are things?"

"Good. It's been a busy weekend with so many guests plus preparing for the event tonight. Your team has done an excellent job of planning everything."

Was this where he mentioned the changes? No, not until he'd spoken with Wendy. "We always need to be prepared for the unexpected, though."

Julia gave him a questioning look, but he shrugged. He wasn't normally a pessimist, but he knew firsthand that things could go wrong. And did.

"True." She looked about to say more, but the elevator dinged, and they both turned toward it as Wendy exited.

Roman set his coffee cup on the counter before crossing toward her and holding out his arms. She stepped into his hug, a definite win after the odd exchange a bit ago.

"I'll leave you two to it." Julia chuckled.

Wendy couldn't let herself get too comfortable in Roman's arms. Every time she did, a curve ball smacked her like she had a target taped to the middle of her back. She led the way to the lounge area beside the fireplace and took a seat in an armchair.

Roman's eyebrows curved up, but he made no comment as he settled into the end of the love seat nearest her. He probably thought they'd snuggle as they talked, but Wendy needed to see his face. It seemed impossible he hadn't known his parents were coming today but, as far as she knew, he hadn't lied to her any other time. Why would he now?

He set his coffee cup on the side table and leaned forward, elbows on his knees. "I didn't sleep much last night."

Here it came. He'd decided she was too much baggage, after all. Or that she was too fat to please him or his parents.

She bit her lip. "I didn't, either. Lots going on inside my head."

"Me, too." He shot her a smile. "Most of it good. Yesterday turned out awesome."

Wendy studied his face. "Most of it? What part wasn't?"

Roman's brows drew together. "I didn't mean it that way."

"When did you find out your parents were coming?"

"The threat itself is several days old. The actual fact? About an hour ago."

Right. The man was glued to his phone, checking it every time it beeped or buzzed or chirped. Was she to believe he'd ignored it completely?

He shook his head. "My parents didn't tell me. They apparently arranged things with Audrey, who emailed me instead of texting. And... I was busy this morning."

"Busy?" Wendy tried to keep the skepticism out of her voice. Likely failed. It just sounded too much like Dave's deflection that she should have recognized years before she did.

"Busy." Roman held her gaze.

She was the first to look away. Okay, fine. She couldn't prove otherwise.

"I didn't sleep. Finally, I got up and opened my Bible."

Something Dave would never have done... or pretended to. Wendy waited.

"I was thinking about the hope that ancient Israel had in their coming Messiah. Thinking about how dark it was outside right then, and how that must have been how Israel felt when they heard Isaiah's prophecy that a great light would come."

He told a convincing story, but that's what he was good at. A fledgling YouTuber, but a marketing professional.

"Then my phone vibrated. It was on night mode, so it didn't ring. I only noticed because I was awake, and it was in my hand. And it was Eli calling."

Wendy blinked. Bringing Creekside's youth pastor into it was a new level of storytelling. Might Roman be telling the truth? He wouldn't lie. She was getting him confused with Dave.

"Eli's sick, Wendy. He could hardly utter a sentence without coughing for longer than he'd spoken."

"Oh, no!" Wendy straightened in her chair. And to think she hadn't believed Roman. This was more than anyone in their right mind would make up to get out of accountability. "But... we need him for the outreach event! He's speaking."

Roman huffed a laugh. "Not anymore. Apparently, I am. So, I turned my phone off completely and dug deeper into the Word, trying to discern what God wants me to share tonight. I must admit I was startled when I realized the time, texted you, and received your reply."

"You honestly didn't know." She didn't even try to make that a question.

He met her gaze. "Not a clue. But they're not here to judge you... at least, no more than they're here to judge me."

"Nice try." She shook her head. "We all know Audrey doesn't love me. They wouldn't be questioning your common sense if it weren't for me."

"You're wrong, you know." Roman chuckled. "My father has been disputing my intelligence for the past six months, if not longer. He was furious with me for selling out to my cousin, and that decision had nothing to do with you."

"True." Wendy tried to relax, but the thought of standing tall against Enzo and Bianca Scala's scrutiny made her weak at the knees while sending an entire herd of butterflies stampeding through her stomach. She looked down. "It's just... I don't know. They'll approve of you more if you forget about me."

"Wendy."

His tone was so tender, the touch on her knee so gentle, that she couldn't help looking up. She bit her lip. "Yes?"

"I'm not breaking up with you. Not now. Not ever. If we ever go our separate ways, it will be on you, and you will have trouble convincing me you mean it."

She gulped back a sob. "But your family."

"My family doesn't dictate my life. Your kids… they're different. They needed to be onboard and, after yesterday, I believe they are. Unless they told you otherwise?"

"They like you," she whispered.

"Whew." He heaved a sigh. "You had me worried for a minute, but I thought the day went well. I like all of them, too, and I'm happy they love you enough to make sure I'm worthy of your attention."

Wendy ran those words through her mind several times. "I guess that means I should be happy Audrey and your parents love *you* enough to make sure I'm worthy of *your* attention. But I already know I've failed the test with Audrey."

"Audrey is fighting demons of her own that have nothing to do with you or me."

She peeked at Roman. "I wish I could believe that's all it is."

"Stick with me, sweetheart. You'll see."

"You're not worried in the least about your parents' visit?" If only Wendy could be half as calm about it as he seemed to be.

"I didn't say that, but it's not because they stand a chance of swaying my love for you. That is solid. On the other hand, I'd love to have their blessing."

"I would, too." It felt so long since anyone had approved of her. But that was a falsehood, wasn't it? Roman did. Julia. Pam and Granger. Chris. Even Laura. Pastor Eli. The women who took every workshop she offered seemed to think she walked on water.

Yes, some people disapproved. Dave… whose opinion no longer mattered. Audrey… who had her own issues, as Roman mentioned. Her own parents, who were bogged down in a patriarchal backwater.

Wendy stiffened her back and raised her chin. She'd phone her parents tomorrow after the girls left and tell them about Roman. She wouldn't wallow in their condemnation any longer. Dave's infidelity and the divorce were on Dave, not her. Her parents should have supported her — not financially, but emotionally.

Roman's fingers grasped hers on her lap. "Are we okay?" He sounded so concerned.

If you want us to be.

No. She wouldn't cast it back on him that way. He might be nine years younger, but he owned his actions and reactions in a way she hadn't ever done. Until now.

"We are."

"I love you, Wendy."

She gulped back a sudden sob. "I love you, too."

"And as much as I hate to do it, I need to get back to that sermon prep." He glanced at his watch. "We still on to help at the Christmas tree farm at noon?"

"Do you have time?"

"Of course. We promised Chris, and it will be good to spend some time in the fresh air. You good?"

"I'm good."

And she was.

CHAPTER
Twenty-Three

HELPING Chris at the Christmas tree farm had been the perfect distraction to keep Wendy from obsessing about meeting Roman's parents. Oh, she'd been in and out of their house on a regular basis decades ago, but she hadn't seen them often since her parents' move from SoCal. They'd come to Audrey's graduation from Gilead Bible College, and she'd also spent time with them at Audrey's wedding. She hadn't made it to Steve's funeral.

Meeting them as their son's lady friend was a whole lot different than as their daughter's chum. The stakes were higher.

But Roman said he chose her over his parents, which seemed crazy... until she realized she was doing the same thing. Her parents had disapproved of everything Wendy had done since Dave's infidelity had come to light. Probably before that, but she hadn't noticed. She'd bounced along in her perfect little bubble, acting as though the whole world were a happy place.

That bubble had certainly shattered with a vengeance.

She shook her head.

"What's wrong, Mom?" Selah asked.

They were driving over to the church for final setup for this evening. If the Scalas wanted to judge her, they'd have to fit it in around her schedule. Too bad her girls would have to witness their mother's humiliation. Again.

"I'm nervous about tonight." Not a lie.

"About the dinner?" Selah swiveled in her seat. "Everything is under control. It was amazing last year. Of course, it will be excellent again."

"It's not that simple. There are always new things that can go wrong."

"Your team — ouch!" Selah turned to the backseat. "Why did you smack my shoulder?"

Faith snorted. "Because you're so dense."

"I am not!"

"You are so. Mom's nervous about Roman's parents, not the dinner. The dinner is in the bag. They... are not."

At least one of her kids was astute. Wendy kind of wished Faith hadn't been, though. Why, because she liked pretending her life was perfect? Her kids knew otherwise.

"Faith is right."

"Why didn't you just say so?" Selah rolled her eyes.

"You don't need to worry," Faith added. "Selah and I will take care of them."

Selah chuckled and rubbed her hands together. "Sounds ominous, but I'm on board."

"Which is worrisome in itself." Wendy managed to crack a smile.

"Nah, you don't need to panic. Selah and I know how to behave. At least, I do. We'll charm their socks right off them. Wait and see."

"You're not setting me at ease." Wendy turned the car onto Agate Street. Only a dozen blocks to the church now.

"Faith's right," Selah put in.

"Self high five!" Faith crowed. "It's not every day that my mom *and* my big sister acknowledge my brilliance."

"I wouldn't go that far."

Wendy smiled for real this time. "I'm so glad you two are here this weekend."

"Me, too, and I'm glad we didn't come with the sibs and be squished in a vehicle for over nine hours each way. Flying is way better."

"Totally," Selah agreed. "Also, Silas's taste in music is the worst, and they came in his car, so I'm sure he dibsed it."

Wendy parked beside the gym entrance. Several cars were already here, including Granger's. Not Audrey's, thankfully. And Roman would be coming a bit later. His sermon prep took precedence over final tweaks on the decorating front. He'd been at the tree farm, too, but seemed distracted.

Tomorrow. Tomorrow they'd analyze the weekend. Tomorrow she'd phone her parents. Today was to bring hope to the downtrodden of Jewel Lake.

She turned to Faith as she turned off the ignition. "Grab the origami box?" She'd decided on a simple craft even fairly young kids could do at their tables in just a few minutes.

"Got it."

"It's cold," Selah grumbled as she exited the car. "Nasty winter wind."

"Yeah, give me an Oregon winter anytime." Faith tucked the box on her hip.

"It gets cold there, too," Wendy protested. "The ocean effect doesn't reach Woodburn."

"Montana is colder." Selah hunched her shoulders and scurried toward the entrance.

Wendy pulled the box of spare tablecloths and centerpieces from the trunk before locking the car and following the girls. The other team members had set the tables yesterday while Wendy was busy with her family, but one could never be too careful or prepare for too many contingencies. One tip of a gravy boat, and they'd need fresh linens.

Wendy stopped in the kitchen first, where Pam was hard at

work. Apparently, some of the vehicles in the parking lot belonged to church members dropping off food.

"Everything good?"

Pam flashed her a smile. "So far! Everyone responded to my queries and said they'd be on time with their drop-offs. They reported no trouble with the recipes."

"Excellent." Wendy smiled at Kathryn Cavanagh, who set a slow cooker on the counter and plugged it in.

"Hi, Wendy!" Kathryn grinned. "Green bean casserole for the win. I made another just like it for my family's Thanksgiving dinner on Thursday, and everyone raved over it. Pam said the recipe came from your collection."

"Great. I'm glad to hear that." Wendy remembered arguing with Pam last year about simplifying the recipe and leaving out the almonds to minimize possible allergens. "Always a favorite with my kids, too."

"Mmm, yes." Selah propped an elbow on Wendy's shoulder and peered past her. "Is there anything I can do to help, Aunt Pam?"

"Yes, please." Pam tapped her notebook where it lay on the counter. "Can you check off items as people bring them, and put them where they need to go? I have some last-minute prep of my own."

"Sure." Selah came around Wendy and scanned the notebook page. "I've got this."

Pam winked at Wendy, and Wendy grinned back.

She loved how her girls got along with her friends and considered them honorary aunts. "Okay, I'm off to check on the other areas now."

Wendy pivoted back into the cavernous space where Granger had a folding chair sitting on a spare table. "What's up?"

"This one had a loose screw. I'll check them all. We'd hate for a chair to give way and land a guest on the floor."

It was on the tip of her tongue to suggest he get someone else to do that, since his bum knee made it difficult for him to get up and down, but he was a grownup, and if he wanted to handle it himself, he could.

Faith, however, wandered over to Granger. "What are we looking for?"

Good kid. Maybe she'd been raised right, after all.

Wendy glanced over to the trio of Christmas trees in the corner, the floor beneath heaped with brightly wrapped gifts with flamboyant bows. She and Roman had been instrumental in making sure every invited guest had a present with their name on it. There were a few extra, too, just in case.

The podium with its microphone stood ready next to Laura's electronic keyboard. Faith had set the origami box on a table nearby, so Wendy hurried over to lay out her papers on the table itself and stow the cardboard box beneath it.

But then she heard Audrey's voice behind her. "Mom, Dad, I'd like you to meet Pam's husband, Granger Durand."

Wendy froze, her back still to the gymnasium. Time stood still except for the annoying insects buzzing around her head.

"Nice to meet you, Mr. and Mrs. Scala." Granger's deep voice.

Where was Roman? He was supposed to be at her side for this. Wendy closed her eyes, took a deep breath, cast a prayer heavenward, and turned to face Roman's parents. Without him.

Roman had seen Audrey's car turn in at the church while he was still several blocks away. He'd stepped on the gas, but his parents and sister had already entered the gym before he parked. No doubt, Audrey had done her best to make it look like he was the tardy one, not that she'd arrived earlier than she'd told him.

He opened the door just as his mother bore down on Wendy, who stood beside the Christmas trees at the other end of the huge room. As he watched, the deer-in-the-headlights panic in Wendy's eyes dispersed and her shoulders firmed.

Good girl.

Wendy smiled at Mom. "Mrs. Scala! I heard you were coming for a visit. How was your flight?"

Roman needn't have worried, but the same might not have been true two days ago.

Mom stopped a few feet away from Wendy. He couldn't see his mother's face, but he'd bet Wendy's warm welcome had caught her unaware.

Dad and Audrey stood beside Granger and Faith, but all four were turned to the women at the other end of the room. Roman strode up the side of the space, ignoring his father for the moment. That might come back to bite his backside but so be it. His first priority was Wendy. He came in beside her and slipped his arm around her shoulders with a gentle squeeze.

"Hey, Mom. What a surprise."

She had the grace to look guilty. "Audrey said you were busy and not to bother you with our plans. After all, you already knew we were coming."

He kept his smile firmly in place. "I didn't know it would be today! But Wendy and I are glad you're here."

Perhaps Wendy leaned into him just a touch. He'd take it.

"That's... nice."

Dad and Audrey flanked Mom now. Dad looked between Roman and Wendy.

"Happy Thanksgiving, Mr. Scala." Wendy stretched out her hand.

"Uh, you, too." Dad shook it.

A win for the history books. Roman tried to catch Audrey's eye, but she seemed to be staring right past his head as though the Christmas trees were the most remarkable things she'd ever seen. He'd deal with her later.

"Audrey's right that we're plenty busy here until after the

outreach event. Did she get you tickets, or do the three of you have other plans for dinner?"

His sister's chin came up. "We have tickets here."

He needed to sit her down and explain a few things. Going behind his back like this was unacceptable. "Great. There's a terrific meal coming together in the kitchen as we speak. You met Granger — he's the MC tonight as well as Santa. Laura's singing a couple of solos as well as leading carols for the guests. Wendy's leading a craft, and I'll be preaching."

Dad did a double take. "Preaching? You?"

"I thought that was Eli." Audrey couldn't avoid his eyes now.

"It was, but he's sick. I've been in prep mode all day." Roman looked between his family members. "That's why I didn't see Audrey's email until much later in the day. A text would have gotten my attention sooner."

"Oh. Sorry."

She didn't sound it. Again… later.

"You are preaching, Romie?" Mom rested her hand on Roman's chest. "*Grazie a Dio!*"

Praise God? Well, okay, then. "I am. Since tomorrow is the first Sunday of Advent, we're focusing on hope tonight as well. And I've found plenty of reasons to hope recently, both in my Christian life, and in my relationship with Wendy."

Audrey looked away.

His sister's loss if she couldn't accept Wendy and him together. Her approval didn't matter, though it would be nice to have. She and Wendy had once been such close friends, but cracks had appeared in that relationship long before he came on the scene. It had nothing to do with him.

Audrey simply couldn't accept Wendy as she was. She seemed to struggle with Chris, as well, but Chris didn't spend a lot of time down at the inn, so it wasn't as obvious. Also, Roman wasn't in love with Chris. That honor — such as it was — belonged to Wendy.

The gym doors opened, and cold air blasted in, accompanying two women carrying roasting pans.

Roman turned back to his parents. "The doors don't open to guests for another hour. Audrey can get you settled at Maranatha Inn, or you could spend a bit of time exploring downtown Jewel Lake. Either way, I'm sorry, but I have duties here in preparation for our event." He allowed a little air between him and Wendy but took her hand in his.

Dad's gaze narrowed, but Roman wasn't about to allow that to affect his day. He'd made a choice.

A choice for Wendy.

A choice for hope.

CHAPTER
Twenty-Four

WOW, what a day it had been. So many highs and lows, but the main event had been a success. Families in need had enjoyed a sumptuous feast and had taken home Christmas gifts from the local community. Hopefully, each guest had felt seen and cherished.

Wendy turned the key in her car's ignition. "You two were amazing tonight."

"Not as amazing as Roman." Faith had called shotgun for the drive back to Maranatha Inn.

"Right?" Selah responded. "Who knew he had a preacher in him?"

Wendy's heart swelled with pride. "He did an amazing job for someone with 12 hours to prepare."

"Yeah." Faith tucked her mittened hands in her armpits. "I know we always did the Advent readings when we were kids, but this thing about hope struck a little deeper this time."

Selah jabbed her sister's shoulder. "You're finally growing up."

Faith made a face. "I miss being a kid and all the excitement of waiting for Christmas."

"Me, too." Selah sighed.

"Me, three," Wendy added. "But there is a circle of life. One day you will have kids of your own, and you can teach them the way we taught you. On the other hand, you're old enough now to take responsibility for your own Advent devotions. I know I got all of you kids to download the YouVersion Bible app years ago. Are you using it?"

"Uh…" Faith bit her lip. "I keep forgetting."

"It's not too late to do an Advent group reading plan on the app." Selah sounded thoughtful. "I could start one and invite you and the sibs."

Wendy couldn't have stopped the wide smile even if she'd wanted to. Was this what hope felt like? That her kids had the potential to become mature in their individual walks with Christ? "Count me in."

"Yeah? Okay, I'll do it." Selah tapped the back of Faith's seat a few times. "Do you think Roman would like an invitation, too?"

Wendy nearly swerved off the road. Then her eyes filled with tears, and she had even more trouble driving for a few seconds. "I'm sure he'd be honored, but I'll leave it up to you."

Faith glanced over her shoulder at her sister. "Good idea. I think it's safe to say that we all like Roman. I mean, it's still weird to think of you dating somebody other than Dad—"

"Let alone a guy so much younger!" Selah interrupted.

"That, too," agreed Faith. "You caught us by surprise Wednesday afternoon, and we didn't know how to react or what to think."

"I'm sorry?"

"Awkward," Selah affirmed. "But we get it. Can't believe the sibs just jumped in Silas's car and showed up here, though."

"I was just as shocked to see them all as you were to see Roman with me."

"That was kind of the point." Faith smirked. "But it was a good day. Adriel is usually too busy with her kids to hang out with Selah and me."

"Yeah," Selah agreed. "Now, if we can only get Roman's

parents to like all of us, the weekend will have been a total success."

"They don't have to like *all* of us, just Mom."

"Hey, we're a package deal. They can't have Mom without all six of us and all our baggage."

Uh oh. Wendy hadn't even thought of all that. She turned off Agate Bay Road, her headlights flashing past the Happy Trails Stables sign. "You girls didn't get a chance to ride this year."

"Maybe next time." Faith turned to Selah. "Are we going to work at Maranatha over the summer like Aunt Julia invited us? We could ride often on our days off."

"I'm not sure. I grad in April, and I'm trying to find a job in my field. But maybe."

Chambermaiding sure wouldn't put Selah's degree in interior architecture to good use. Other than that, Wendy would love to have both girls here next summer. Maybe someday she'd move back to Oregon. She felt in a better place than when she'd made the move northeast 15 months ago, but her future still felt up in the air. Would things work out with Roman? That was the question.

Although hadn't he answered that question this morning? She recalled his words as though he'd said them ten seconds ago.

I'm not breaking up with you. Not now. Not ever. If we go our separate ways, it will be on you, and you will have trouble convincing me you mean it.

Wendy needed to hold onto the belief that he meant those words, that his parents — or hers — couldn't sway him away from that commitment. What would a life with him look like?

She parked her car in the staff lot beside Audrey's, and her girls piled out.

Audrey. How could Wendy reconcile with Audrey? Was it only possible if Wendy asked Audrey for help getting skinny and fit? But that didn't seem like a good basis for friendship. That was coach and client... and what would happen when Wendy failed?

Because she would. If getting and staying trim was simple, then obesity wouldn't be endemic in America.

The alternative sweetener hadn't been terrible. Passing on dessert at dinner had been relatively easy since she'd taken that opportunity to pass out the supplies for the origami craft around the tables.

Maybe she should find a coach that wasn't Audrey. Someone less judgy. Less invested. How would she even begin looking, when she had no idea what she needed? Some days it would be a firm kick in the rear. Other times, perhaps a sympathetic hug. Someone who would pray with her. Did coaches like that even exist? Maybe Julia would have some ideas. Wendy could trust Julia.

She grimaced as she grabbed her box from the backseat, locked the car, and headed toward the inn. The girls had already disappeared inside.

But it was a crisp, beautiful night. Wendy paused and looked up at the night sky, though the beams from the streetlights blocked most of the stars. "God? I don't want to keep hating myself. I don't want to live defined by my negative thoughts. Can you help me find the right person to hire?" Not that she had a lot of money to put to coaching, but maybe investing in herself was a positive first step.

She chuckled, thinking of the weekend's theme. "I need hope, Lord. The kind that isn't dreamy, wishful thinking, but is grounded in Your word and in Your love. I need the real deal."

I have loved you with an everlasting love. With unfailing love, I have drawn you to myself.

Her heart settled, just a little. "Thanks for that, Lord. I need wisdom. I need strength. I also need to make friends with Enzo and Bianca Scala... and Audrey. Please cover me with your favor and keep me close to You."

Still, she lingered in the cold and dark. A minute to herself in such a crazy busy weekend was like a little taste of heaven.

Roman looked up as Selah and Faith entered the lobby, laughing and jostling each other. They stopped by the reception desk to drag Laura into whatever thing they found animating.

Those two. He couldn't help grinning at their exuberance, even as he wondered where their mother was. She'd been helping Pam tidy up the kitchen when his parents had dragged him back to the inn. Was it his imagination, or did Wendy have a bit more energy than she used to? Maybe all those walks together were paying off. He knew he enjoyed the moments spent together, chatting about anything and everything. She'd asked about some of the countries he'd lived, and he'd regaled her with stories. Someday, maybe he'd take her to see his favorite places, and not just as his channel's official videographer.

Faith finally looked past Laura, her face lighting up when she noticed him by the fireplace. "Roman! I was just telling Laura and Selah how much I loved your talk tonight. You nailed it."

He blinked. "Talk? That's what we're calling sermons these days?"

She wrinkled her nose. "Whatever."

Just own it. "Either way, thank you." He wanted to mention the time constraints and the stresses of the day, but no. He'd worked hard on pulling his thoughts together cohesively, and playing it down wasn't helpful to anyone.

Selah came around the end of the counter toward him. "It's not often I agree with my kid sis, but with this? She's right. I was proud to be your…" Her face scrunched. "Whatever I am to you. It's something, right?"

Roman laughed. "It's something, all right, but I don't know what. Not yet."

Faith glanced over her shoulder toward the doors and lowered her voice. "But sometime?"

"I sure hope so."

"Me, too. Mom's changed a lot since you came into her life."

"For the better," Selah hurried to add.

"She didn't need to change." Well, except to stop cutting herself down all the time.

"And that's why it worked. She's more confident."

"I don't think I can take credit for that. She needed some distance from your father."

"And from us." Faith unzipped her jacket as she flopped into the love seat across from him. "That's on me. It's hard being a teen when your family explodes."

"It didn't explode." Selah perched on the arm of the armchair, scowling at her sister.

Faith rolled her eyes. "You weren't there, okay? Just Ezra and me, and he was in twelfth, busily pretending his foundation wasn't eroding beneath his feet."

"It must have been hard." Roman was thankful for the insight. For the trust in him Faith showed. "But your mom held onto God through it all. The trials made her stronger."

Selah nodded. "True. She reminded me of a Bible verse from Jeremiah 29 yesterday. 'For I know the plans I have for you,' says the Lord. 'They are plans for good and not for disaster, to give you a future and a hope.'"

Faith straightened in her seat. "Am I the only one who hears Dad's voice saying that promise was for Israel at a specific time in history?"

"Like Dad gets to inform our theology anymore. He hasn't been to church in years that I know of."

"True." Faith's gaze went to the entry doors. "There's Mom now. I wonder what took her so long."

"You should have carried her stuff."

"*You* should have." Faith glared at Selah.

Roman rose and headed around the reception desk.

"You go, Roman," Laura whispered.

He laughed and shook his head. What a fishbowl. A guy

232

wasn't allowed to have a single thought without everyone weighing in.

"Hey, beautiful." He kissed Wendy's cheek as he took the box from her arms.

"Hi." She smiled up at him. "Are the girls pestering you?"

"Nah. They're just keeping me company. I like them."

"We like you, too!" Selah hollered.

Laura snickered. "Oh, look, it's 10:00. Time to close up. I'll get out of your hair now." She crossed the space, locked the doors, and dimmed the lobby lights. "Come on, girls. Let's give them a few minutes without us."

Faith pulled her legs up into the love seat. "I don't know. I'm pretty comfy."

That kid. Roman set the box beside the elevator and pressed the button. It opened immediately, and he gestured with a sweeping bow. "Your carriage awaits."

Selah grabbed her sister's arm, and they followed Laura into the enclosure.

"Don't do anything I wouldn't do." Laura winked as the doors slid shut.

Wendy chuckled. "That was mastery right there."

"Laura, you mean? I owe her."

"No more than I do." Wendy took Roman's hand and pulled him toward the fireplace. "Your parents are settled for the night?"

Right. His parents. "I think so. Audrey got them a room at the east end of the fourth floor. She might still be up there with them." Which meant she could walk through the lobby at any time. Whatever. Let her.

Roman tugged Wendy down beside him and settled his arm around her. "So... I'm not fishing for a compliment."

She laughed, and his heart warmed at how carefree it sounded, considering the multiple stresses of the weekend. "You did a great job speaking, if that's what you need to hear. It's true."

"I said I wasn't fishing." He mocked a growl and bumped her cheek with his nose.

"Oh, I thought that was reverse-speak. My boys are good at it." Wendy giggled.

"It's not that. It's… Eli is still sick."

Wendy's brows pulled down in a frown. "Is it serious?"

"Probably not, but Harper says she's keeping a close eye on him. It's… well… he was also supposed to preach tomorrow morning."

Wendy turned to look at him. "Uh huuuh."

"So… Pastor Marshall asked if I'd repeat the talk in the morning. There's not a huge audience overlap."

"I think this is when it goes from being a speech to being a sermon."

Roman couldn't help the chuckle. "That's likely true."

"I'm proud of you." She snuggled in against him. "I won't mind being reminded of all the things you said again tomorrow."

"Thanks. I appreciate that sentiment. Hopefully, others will agree."

She touched his jaw. "They'll understand. It's not like Eli put you on the spot on purpose. Did he?"

"No. I'm sure he didn't."

"Maybe a new career as a preacher is in your future."

"I doubt that, but public speaking isn't as horrific as I dreaded when I was a teen. I've spoken in enough board meetings and conventions that it's not too bad. There's even a bit of a thrill to it."

"I don't mind it a lot, either. For me it was homeschool groups and, more recently, the workshops. Being prepared helps, and knowing your subject well."

"I've been learning a lot about biblical hope the past few weeks, so I guess that counts." Roman lifted his hand to her cheek. "You've helped teach me."

"Me?"

"You. Definitely you."

CHAPTER
Twenty-Five

"GOOD MORNING, MOM." Roman kissed her cheek then turned to shake his father's hand. "Good morning, Dad. I hope you both slept well."

"This is a lovely inn, and the bed was quite comfortable. Didn't you think so, Enzo?"

Dad grunted what was likely agreement.

"Breakfast is over this way." Roman gestured toward the buffet. "The options are similar to what you'll find in many of the higher-end hotels. Is Audrey meeting us?"

Mom frowned. "She said she'd come in about a half hour. She wanted us to wait for her."

"I'm sorry I asked you for earlier, then, but I need to head down to the church shortly to prepare for the morning service."

"I can't believe you're a preacher now." Dad shook his head.

"Just filling in. I doubt it will be a regular thing." Though Roman wasn't blind to the fact that Pastor Marshall had been inching back from some of the duties he'd handled for years, from what Eli had said. Eli had been picking up the slack with help from some of the congregants, but Creekside Fellowship couldn't keep going like this indefinitely. Roman hadn't attended any one church long enough to be this invested since he'd been a teen in SoCal. How had it happened now? He'd only been here for a couple of months.

He followed his parents to the buffet.

Loretta Satterfield looked up from her place in line in front of them. "Roman! I hear you did a lovely job filling in for Eli last night. Bless you, sugar." Eli's mother-in-law's Southern accent came through loud and clear.

"Thank you."

"Are these your parents? I see a strong resemblance."

"Yes. Mom, Dad, I'd like you to meet Loretta Satterfield. She and her husband, Vance, visit often from Atlanta. Loretta, meet my parents, Enzo and Bianca Scala."

Loretta gathered Mom's outstretched hand in both of hers. "It's so lovely to meet you. You have raised two exceptional children, although I'm not into Audrey's fitness craze." Loretta chuckled. "But she is adorable, and it's been so nice to get to know Roman on our most recent visits."

Adorable Audrey? Roman blinked. That was a new one. Apparently, his sister could be charming if she put her mind to it.

"Thank you. We are proud of our children."

Roman noted Dad didn't comment, just shot a look in Roman's direction. He'd lost Dad's approval when he sold his shares to Leo, and there'd be no coming back from that except by God's grace.

"And Wendy is so sweet. I'm sure you both must just love her."

Mom sent a panicked glance Roman's way.

He smiled at Loretta, doing his best to keep smugness off his face. "They have fond memories of Wendy as a teenager, but they have yet to get to know the adult Wendy." That's why they were here. Except Dad didn't actually want to get to know Wendy. He wanted to convince Roman to drop his ridiculous infatuation. Dad's words, not his.

It must be hard being a parent when your kids didn't follow the path you'd laid out.

Wendy felt the same about her kids. Roman would never know what it would be like. Would he ever regret not having his own? He didn't think so. It had never been a driving force in his life, unlike what Laura had said about her ex.

Loretta picked up a plate and scanned the offerings on the warming buffet, and Roman's parents fell in behind her.

He followed along as Loretta invited them to join her and Vance, who'd come down earlier. He took all the trays over to the cart while Loretta introduced her husband to his parents. When he took his seat, he ducked his head for a quick prayer.

"Good morning, Roman." Vance glanced over as he closed his Bible and set it aside. "How nice your parents could join you this weekend."

Roman managed a smile. "It was quite a surprise, for sure."

"Our weekend isn't turning out like we'd expected, either," Loretta put in. "We usually spend a lot of time with Harper and Eli when we're here, but with his illness, we'll be keeping our distance for a while."

"Are you headed back to Atlanta soon?" Roman spread jam on his whole-grain toast.

"Wednesday," Loretta confirmed. "I'm sure he'll be feeling better long before then."

"I hope so." Roman hated to think what else the church leadership might ask him to do if not.

"And you're filling in for him again this morning," Vance went on. "You've set Eli's mind at rest with that. Harper's, too."

"I don't mind, especially since I can reuse the same script I wrote for last night."

"Which we didn't get to hear, so I'm glad for the opportunity."

The Satterfields had donated generously to the outreach event but hadn't felt they should take up valuable chairs that should be used for locals in need.

Roman dug into his breakfast. "I hope I don't disappoint."

"I doubt it. God will use your words to further His kingdom."

Wait, what had just come out of Roman's mouth? Similar self-deprecation he chided Wendy for. Maybe not identical, but how was it difficult to own that he'd done a decent job yesterday and would again today? It wasn't pride unless he discounted God's part in the preparation and delivery.

He nodded at Vance. "Thank you for the reminder that it's all about God and not about me."

Loretta leaned forward. "I saw some of the origami angels from the craft Wendy led last night. Do you think she'd show me how to do that, too? They are so darling, and I can imagine an entire banner of them in our foyer back home."

"A heavenly host of angels." Vance chuckled.

"Exactly!" Loretta beamed. "I've never been particularly crafty. Not like Wendy. She is so talented and makes everything seem so doable. Easy, even."

"Have you attended any of her Saturday workshops?" Roman asked.

She nodded enthusiastically. "Every time we're here over a weekend. Now don't you take that lovely lady away from Maranatha Inn, you hear me? We need her here."

Roman stilled. It seemed the universe paused with him. His parents stared at Loretta then their gazes swung to Roman in slo-mo. He managed a breath. "How long Wendy stays here will be up to her."

"Oh, I thought…" Loretta glanced at his parents.

Here went nothing. "If things continue as I hope they do, where we live and what we do will be a joint decision. I know she misses her kids in Oregon, but she also loves it here. She's a valuable member of Julia's team, and she's been a huge help launching my YouTube channel. But, if she wants to leave Jewel Lake, we can film *Roaming with Roman* anywhere."

"Maybe you two will move to Los Angeles!" Loretta beamed. "I'm sure your parents would love to have you nearby."

Dad's jaw twitched, while Mom's eyes widened... and not in a good way.

Roman shook his head. "I don't see SoCal as an option, though both Wendy and I were raised there. I spent too much of my adult life in urban centers, and I love the slower pace and connection with nature found in smaller towns and rural areas. But, never say never."

He glanced at his watch. "Sorry to eat and run, but I'm due down at the church in 20 minutes." He turned to his parents. "Take your time. I'm sure Audrey will join you here shortly, and I'll see you at the church, okay?"

Wendy loved the way Creekside Fellowship embraced the season of Advent. The pastors and leadership team took heart preparation for Jesus seriously. And it was even better today with her girls flanking her, belting out the old Christmas carols that spoke of hope.

"O holy night, the stars are brightly shining. It is the night of our dear Savior's birth. Long lay the world in sin and error pining, till He appeared, and the soul felt its worth. A thrill of hope, the weary world rejoices..."

And Wendy experienced that thrill of hope. It had been several years since she'd entered Advent with anything close to expectation. Even before Dave's infidelity had come to light, the Advent season felt like a required gauntlet of activities and duties to perform. The luster had worn thin. The window of time after the divorce and before she'd come to Jewel Lake had been difficult. She, Ezra, and Faith had only fit in the two-bedroom apartment because Wendy slept on the pullout sofa. No wonder Ezra had abandoned her when he finished school and began working full-time. No wonder Faith had been fixated on moving to her dad's — the former family home — after her brother left.

But now, healing was occurring. Some, at least. Between Wendy and her kids, between Wendy and God. She'd felt abandoned by Him while her world crumbled around her. Why hadn't He prevented it? Why hadn't Wendy's efforts to keep Dave happy been successful? She'd blamed everything on her weight... and she'd blamed her weight on the way God made her.

By now, the congregation was singing "O Little Town of Bethlehem." *The hopes and fears of all the years are met in thee tonight.*

She'd always thought 'thee' referred to Jesus in that carol, but that wasn't actually what it said. Bethlehem was the focal point, the place where the Israelite nation's hopes and fears collided at that point in history. In Jesus's birth.

The fears? Ah, yes. The dear Savior's birth had been an opportunity for the evil one. If he could only destroy that Child before His life's mission was completed, evil would triumph.

But Jesus had conquered it.

You couldn't celebrate Christmas without Easter. Without recognizing the 33 years Jesus lived as a human on this planet... and the way evil had nearly prevailed, or so it seemed.

A thrill of hope, indeed.

Wendy took her seat between her daughters, her heart full as Laura mounted the steps to the platform. Laura had chosen to sing "Hope has a Name," the newer song that Julia had made them all listen to months ago now. The music and lyrics sent goosebumps over Wendy's skin with its bold, triumphant declaration that Emmanuel was the name of hope. The Messiah had broken through the silence of Israel's 400 years with no prophecies. Emmanuel had come to set captives free and shine a light through the darkness.

That's what Roman had shared last night at the outreach event. He'd talked about Jesus being the light of the world, like flipping a light switch on in a room or cave fully consumed with darkness. Didn't people sitting in darkness need the hope of a brilliant light to come?

Laura's solo came to a close in a sanctuary so saturated with awed stillness that Wendy could have heard a pin drop as her friend stepped off the platform.

Then her heart did a little thrill of its own as Roman entered from the other side and took his place behind the podium.

"Today, on the first Sunday of advent, we look back in history. The people of Israel had been promised a Messiah, a Savior, from time immemorial. The prophets had recorded tantalizing snippets of information here and there, but it was hard to merge all the bits into a whole. No one knew for sure what parts of the revelations would occur soon, and which were in their distant future. Only now, looking back, can we begin to discern, but all the details are still not fully clear."

Roman looked around the sanctuary, his gaze meshing with Wendy's for just a few seconds. She was so very proud of him.

"Isaiah recorded over 200 messianic prophecies. Today, I'd like to focus on the first seven verses of chapter nine, and verse two, in particular. 'The people who walk in darkness will see a great light. For those who live in a land of deep darkness, a light will shine.' I'd like you to close your eyes for a moment and feel the despair of these people who had shunned God over and over. Experience the total darkness in their souls. Feel the weight of impending doom, the horrors of crushing tyranny. Feel their misery, their desperation, their anguish."

Wendy didn't have to reach too far into her imagination to capture these emotions. No, her feelings of despair weren't the same as the heaviness described in Isaiah. She also didn't need Dave's voice in her head reminding her of the differences. But she had certainly experienced enough to get a solid glimpse.

A thrill of hope! A weary world rejoices!

The hope-filled promises written by Isaiah and others must have been a guiding light to the faithful few back in their day. And now? Wendy sensed it, too.

Hope that one day, Jesus would make everything in her life new and refreshed, like a lush garden after a summer rain. That the roots and tendrils of hope would flourish and blossom and bear fruit.

It was absolutely Jesus.

But Roman played a big part in it, too, as he continued to preach a message of hope to Creekside Fellowship. And to her heart.

CHAPTER
Twenty-Six

WENDY HUGGED SELAH THEN FAITH. "I'm so glad you girls came for the weekend."

"Even though we called in the troops?" Faith grimaced.

"Even so. Friday was a special family day. I needed that." She didn't dare tell her kids how much, though she'd already hinted at it.

"So, about Roman..." Selah swung her carryon out of the trunk. "If he asks you, go for it."

Wendy feigned ignorance. "If he asks me what?"

"To marry him, silly." Faith rolled her eyes. "The six of us had a group video call, and everyone agrees. Even Silas."

Wendy gulped as she closed the trunk. How could they spring this on her at the airport as they were leaving? At least she'd found an actual parking spot and wasn't idling at the curb in front of departures. "You're serious?"

"About our agreement, or our assessment of Roman?"

"Yes."

Selah grabbed her mom's arms and looked her in the eye. "We're serious about both."

"Group hug!" Faith crowed, encircling them both. "You should know Dad said something the other day that made me think he regretted how things turned out."

Wendy set her chin.

"I know, I know. He's the one who had the affair," Selah said. "I don't think Shyanne makes him as happy as he thought she would."

Faith muttered something under her breath.

Wendy chose not to ask for clarification. Probably best she didn't know.

"Maybe hearing some other man finds you attractive and desirable made him think he gave up too soon."

"That's on him." But really, Dave thought he had a right to jealousy? Wendy could go on a rant about the hypocrisy of that, but not to her kids.

"Anyway, Roman. We like him. We like how he treats you." Faith hugged her. "We also like how he treats us. He's the real deal."

Wendy gulped back emotion. "He really is. I never expected this. I wasn't looking for it."

"We know. He was a bit of a shock to us last Wednesday, too."

"Sorry about that. I should have handled things better."

Selah laughed. "There was no way to soften that one, but we're happy for you."

Faith glanced at her watch. "I hate to be the one to break up this emotional moment, but we've got a plane to catch."

"Go on, you two." Wendy released them. "Let me know when you're home."

"Will do. And... Mom?" Selah paused. "Don't let his snooty parents get in the way. You're a grownup. You don't need to make them happy."

"Thanks, but that doesn't go for you. I still get a say in whom you get serious with."

"Yeah, yeah. Rex was a bad idea. I'm over him." Selah offered another swift hug. "Gotta go. Love you, Mom." She jogged off after Faith, her carryon rattling over the uneven sidewalk.

Wendy watched them go. She'd envisioned her and Roman dropping the girls off together then going out for dinner, but with his parents visiting, she'd excused him. He'd reluctantly agreed, complaining he'd rather spend time with her than with them.

The girls disappeared around the corner, and Wendy got back into her car. It had not been the weekend she'd expected, for sure. On Wednesday, she'd only hoped Selah and Faith could accept Roman's presence in their mother's life.

She hadn't expected her other four to show up Friday. Or for Roman's parents to arrive. Or for Roman to be asked to preach twice.

Or for Dave to express an opinion on her love life. She scowled as she recalled how she'd found out about Shyanne. It took a lot of nerve on Dave's part to assume his viewpoint mattered now.

She'd felt completely abandoned for so long. Maybe she should be thankful to discover how many people cared about her and Roman. Her kids wouldn't have made the overnight journey if they didn't have her best interests at heart. And Roman's parents? Same. They cared about their son. As they should. But they should do so without interfering.

The only remaining people who might think they had a right to voice an opinion were her own parents. Wendy hadn't asked her kids if their grandparents knew. Dave might have told them. They liked their ex-son-in-law better than they liked their own daughter. Maybe Wendy had done *too* good a job of saying only positive things about Dave over the years. Hmm.

She drove out of the parking lot and turned toward Jewel Lake. Roman had invited her to dinner at the Rendezvous with his family tonight. But she had enough time right now to place a call or two. This newer car had Bluetooth, unlike the old van she'd abandoned in Oregon. She hadn't used it much, so she pulled to the side of the road to put the call through before continuing on.

"Hello? Is that you, Wendy?"

Her mother sounded old. Wendy's heart squeezed. "Yes, it's me. I just dropped Selah and Faith off at the airport and I'm driving back to the inn. It's been a while since we talked, so I thought I'd call."

"Yes, it's been a long time."

"The phone lines go both ways, you know."

"But you're always so busy. We knew that if you had time to catch up, you'd call."

Wendy bit her tongue. Her mom was an expert at playing the guilt card. "Well, I'm here now. How are you and Dad doing?"

"Okay. The doctor changed up his heart medications, and he's doing better."

It really had been too long. Wendy hadn't known there'd been issues that needed improvement. "I'm glad to hear that."

"And you? Did you have a good Thanksgiving with the girls?"

"I did." Here went nothing. "Remember Audrey's family from the Rossmoor years? Her brother, Roman, has been at Maranatha this fall, and their parents also came for Thanksgiving."

"I remember them." Mom sounded guarded. Did that mean she'd heard, or that she had negative memories?

"So..." Wendy gulped. "I just wanted you and Dad to know that I'm dating Roman."

Silence for long enough that Wendy checked to make sure she hadn't driven into a dead zone without cell coverage. No, the call was still connected.

"But he is so young."

"Not anymore." *Trust me. Roman is a fully grown, gorgeous, thoughtful, kind man.*

"But... Dave..."

"Mom, let's not go back there. Dave cheated. Dave divorced me. Dave remarried. Dave is history."

"I don't like this."

Blunt honesty was never a problem with Wendy's mother. "I don't like what Dave did, either. It hurt an awful lot for a long time, but God has given me hope for a future, and I'm so grateful to Him for that."

"You know what your father and I think."

"I'm sure I do. I love you, and I respect you, but I'm 55 years old, and I'm seeking God's will for the remainder of my life. I just wanted you to know what that might look like."

A semi roared by, shaking her little car. Maybe talking while she drove was a bad idea.

"God wants us to be content with what we have."

Wendy shook her head, not that her mother could see. "God wants us to be content — delighted, even — with the gifts He has given us. I think that means we shouldn't turn down those gifts. I hope you'll come to accept Roman, because I believe his presence in my life is a blessing from above. He has a strong faith. His example and his leadership and his prayers lift me up. I'm so thankful for him."

Mom sighed. "But he is so young."

"Forty-six isn't *that* young." The nine-year gap had certainly given Wendy pause at first, too, but they were well past the age where that difference actually mattered.

"I suppose. I must go now, or dinner won't be on the table by five when your father expects it."

Of course, that took precedence. "I'm glad I caught you for a few minutes. Give Dad my love."

"All right." But Mom sounded reluctant.

Wendy tapped to end the call and glanced at the clock. She had time for one more phone call.

Roman settled at the round table in the Rendezvous with Wendy on one side of him and his mother on the other. Technically, this was a four-person table, but the staff had squeezed in an extra chair. Hopefully, Wendy wouldn't feel too self-conscious about that. For himself, he was only glad to be close beside her. They'd had so little time alone together this weekend, and the dearth wasn't about to end just because her daughters had flown back to Portland a couple of hours ago.

His parents were staying for several more days, no doubt hopeful to put an end to this thing between him and Wendy. As though they had the power or the right to do so.

After they'd placed their order, Wendy turned to Audrey on the other side of her. "I've been thinking…"

"Oh?" Audrey raised her eyebrows. "About what?"

Wendy's fingers clenched in her lap, and her cheeks flushed. "Have you ever heard of Trim Healthy Mama?"

"I can't say that I have."

"I… I've been looking into different programs."

Roman blinked. She had? They really hadn't spent enough time together in the past few days.

"This one — I came across it and asked Julia. She said she knew a Christian coach over in Idaho. I gave Sierra — that's her name — a call this afternoon."

Mom leaned in. "I've heard of THM. Your Aunt Martina lost some weight with that."

"Good for her." Audrey rolled her eyes. "She needed to."

"Yes, she says her doctor is happier with her blood sugar, and she feels better."

Roman glanced at Wendy. Good for her being proactive on the topic. At least, if she was tackling it for her own sake and not because she thought his parents would like her better. Or that she thought it would take the wind out of Audrey's sails.

"What's it about?" Audrey's fingers flew across her phone. "Hmm. Like keto… but not."

"Yes." Wendy's shoulders straightened. "But they let you eat certain carbs. They say women need carbs for hormone balance."

Audrey glanced up with a skeptical face.

"Hey, carbs are good," Roman put in. "What's the similarity to keto?"

"Well, they don't eat sugar or most processed food." Wendy glanced between Roman and Audrey. "I found those sweetener packets at breakfast a couple of weeks ago. They're not bad in coffee."

"The monk-fruit-erythritol ones?" Audrey's frown deepened, like she didn't know what to do with Wendy's revelations.

Roman didn't know either, but he could cheer Wendy on for taking charge. It seemed Mom approved of the conversation, and who knew about Dad?

"Yes, those."

"I agree they're not terrible."

Roman blinked. Audrey agreed with something Wendy had said? Red-letter day, right there.

Wendy carried on. "The carbs they include are fruit and brown rice and sweet potatoes and things like that."

Audrey bit her lip. "Complex carbs. Just be careful not to ingest too many calories."

"This program doesn't count calories." Wendy shot him a sidelong look. "I kind of freaked out when I saw the list of guidelines there, so that was one bit of good news. The program makes sense, sort of, and there are tons of testimonials, but…"

He covered her hands with his. "But what?"

"I'm not very good at that sort of thing."

Roman wouldn't press her for details. Not in present company.

"I could save you money and coach you myself." Audrey set her phone down.

He opened his mouth but snapped it shut again. Wendy had to make her own choices, and he'd support her however he could. But Audrey wasn't—

"Are you a Trim Healthy coach?" Wendy asked.

"No, but it doesn't look too hard. I could adapt their system, I'm sure."

"I want a coach certified with their program. Actually, that's what I *need*. And, no offense, but it will be hard enough with a stranger."

Audrey managed to bite back a response, something Roman wouldn't have thought possible.

"Your Aunt Martina has a lovely coach in Rossmoor."

Bless Mom, anyway. If Wendy only needed to show willingness to lose weight to get his mother to like her... was that what Wendy was doing? It didn't sound like it. He knew her shape bothered her, and he'd done his best not to get dragged into conversations with her about it. Maybe that's why she'd made this contact without mentioning it to him first.

And maybe that was okay. He'd walk the path with her regardless.

Even if she ditched sugar? He gulped. Man, he liked his desserts, but wouldn't it be rude to eat pie or cookies in front of her? Or even to eat it in secret so as not to tempt her? This might require some soul-searching of his own.

The server placed their plates in front of them. Now Wendy's order of a dinner salad with grilled chicken made a bit more sense. She was trying to make healthy choices.

"Wendy, you know it will be hard, and most people fail." Audrey's voice sounded patronizing, like she was speaking to a small child.

"I can do hard things." Wendy's response was soft and not at all confident.

This weekend had overflowed with way too many activities, too many people, and too many opinions. Roman's brain reeled for a few seconds before a clear thought emerged. "You know that success is simply trying one more time than you fail. We fail at tons of things in life, but eventually we overcome if we keep starting over."

"I taught you that, boy." Dad entered the conversation for the first time.

"Yeah, you did." Roman grinned at his father.

Wendy straightened in her seat one more time. "I can start again."

"I still think I should be the one—"

254

"Sis…" Roman broke in.

Wendy's hand now squeezed comfort onto his. "I appreciate your support, Audrey, but I feel that would complicate our relationship too much. I need someone encouraging who isn't as invested as you might be."

"But…" Audrey's gaze darted around the table. "I guess I see your point. It's just…"

Silence around the table. It had been a while since Roman had seen his sister at a loss for words.

"Okay, I'm over controlling! I get that. Excuse me." Audrey dashed from the table.

"What just happened?" Roman asked into the stunned silence.

"I'm not sure," Wendy murmured.

"Audrey… she has her own struggles." Mom glanced toward the restrooms where his sister had disappeared.

With her weight? That was a new one. Audrey had been obsessed with her body and working out as long as Roman could remember. If she'd ever gained five pounds, he couldn't pinpoint when in her life it had been. Not that he'd been around much.

Dad leaned over. "So… Roman. Leo says your video channel has good content. He says you are good at it."

Leo watched his channel? "Cool, but it's Wendy who makes the videos look as good as they do. She's a great videographer with a talent for pulling it all together."

"The subject matter makes it easy." Wendy smiled at him.

Amazing how much more relaxed it was at the table without his sister, even with Dad's entry to the conversation. But was Audrey okay? Roman couldn't very well barge into the women's restroom to find out.

Mom had a few more bites of her meal before laying her napkin on the table. "Let me check on Audrey."

"Please do." Wendy bit her lip and looked at Mom. "I didn't mean to upset her."

"You did nothing wrong." Mom glanced between Wendy and Roman. "Nothing. I will see to her."

CHAPTER
Twenty-Seven

"THAT WAS... INTENSE." Wendy sat in front of the fireplace in the lobby late that night and managed a few deep breaths. It would take time to come down from the intense emotional swings of the day. The entire weekend, really.

"I think it went pretty well, all things considered." Roman pulled her close to his side. "I hadn't realized you were looking at coaching."

"I was praying, and I felt God nudging me to text Julia and ask her. Sure enough, she knew someone." How had she doubted God could do that?

"I'm proud of you."

"I'm trying, Roman. It's hard, but I'm trying."

His hand slid up and down her upper arm. "You're amazing; that's what you are. I think you won my parents over."

"I'm not so sure, but they were kinder than I expected. I phoned my parents on the drive back from the airport. I probably forgot to tell you. It's been crazy."

"What did they have to say? Only good things, I hope."

Wendy huffed a laugh. "I never thought yours would be easier than mine. I've been so conditioned to honor my parents that it's hard to know when that stops. Or... if it ever should." Wendy didn't want to think about her own kids choosing to go their own way, regardless of their age when that might happen.

"I might be wrong, but I don't think you've rejected them. I doubt you've been rude. I'm sure you were polite and kind. I've never seen you any other way."

She blinked back a tear.

His arm tightened over her shoulders. "Besides, blind obedience is for children, not adults. You're a mom. I'm sure you've said, 'because I told you to' to your kids."

Wendy chuckled. "Far oftener than I thought I would, but not so much in recent years."

"Because they're old enough to understand and then weigh actual explanations."

"Hmm. I see what you're getting at. And you're right."

"Pardon me?"

"I said you're right."

"Can I hear that again, please?"

"Oh, you!" She smacked his arm lightly.

Roman caught her hand and pressed it tight as he leaned over to kiss her. "I'm not an expert at parenting, as you well know, but I'm an expert at having parents, and maybe I've learned a few things. Babies aren't asked for their opinions. They don't have choices. Their parents pick them up and move them around and that's that. But then they begin walking and talking, and with that comes the ability to disobey."

"About the first word many of them learn to say is 'No!'"

"As I suspected." He winked. "But you tell them to stop something like — I dunno, running out into traffic, and you expect instant obedience since you'd rather your kid wasn't run over, right?"

"I grabbed Theo's arm and practically dislocated his shoulder, but the bus missed him by inches. That's a memory I'd rather not relive."

"Sorry. I didn't know."

"But you guessed. And you're right that as they get older, they get more explanations and fewer things flat-out forbidden."

"Until they're teenagers and take stupidity to a whole new level." Roman eyed her. "Unless your kids were particular angels."

"Their friends weren't too bad an influence."

"Anyway, just saying that the relationship between parents and kids morphs as the years go by, and that's what it should do. So, no, I don't think it is dishonoring to our parents to choose to love each other, regardless of their current opinions. I'd be willing to bet they'll all come around, but even if they don't, it changes nothing for me."

She bit her lip and looked down. "Thanks for that. And you're right. I've had such a difficult relationship with my parents because they're old-school authoritarian. Dad rules the roost and applauded Dave for doing the same. That's just how it was."

Roman grunted. "I don't see how they could still be in favor of Dave after all this."

Right? "Mom mentioned him this afternoon."

"Are you kidding me?" Roman muttered. "After all that's happened?"

"I shut her down pretty quickly on that topic. But they do have one thing against you besides that you're not Dave."

"Let me guess. I'm too young."

"How did you guess?" Wendy managed a chuckle. She'd thought the same at first, so she could hardly fault her mom for going there. Now? It was a mildly amusing objection. "And it's not Dave, so much. It's that divorce is taboo in their world."

"I'm not a particular fan of it, myself. But I'm also not in favor of abuse, whether it be sexual, emotional, or spiritual." Roman kissed the side of her head. "It seems to me that God is in the business of forgiveness and new beginnings."

"Jeremiah 29:11," Wendy mused. "A plan for good and not for disaster, to give you a future and a hope."

"Exactly like that. We've all sinned. All done wrong. The Bible makes it clear that we deserve death, but instead we're given grace. Mercy. Wild, crazy, reckless love."

"He's come to set the captives free." She'd been one of those. Oh, not literally. It wasn't like Dave had forbidden her from leaving the house.

"Yeah, that song Laura sang illustrates the hope Jesus gives us. Everything changes when we have hope."

"Thanks for that reminder." Wendy stretched to kiss his lips. How long had it been since Dave had tried to lead her closer to Christ? More to the point, had he ever? Or had he just passively gone along with her?

Silence stretched for a few minutes, and Wendy simply reveled in being held. She felt safe. Comforted. Loved.

"Question for you..." Roman said at last.

"Hmm?"

"I don't want to overstep."

Uh oh. That didn't sound like a good topic introduction. "Go ahead."

"You mentioned hiring a coach. I hope the timing wasn't because you thought my parents or I would approve of you more if you did so."

Tears prickled Wendy's eyes. "Maybe a little."

"I love you, Wendy. You don't have to change for that to be true."

"But your parents..."

"If they can't see your heart, they're not really looking at you. A number on a scale is a terrible way to determine someone's worth."

"That's true." She still wasn't used to hearing it. "My decision wasn't just about them or Audrey. The timing maybe was, but I've been thinking about it for a while. I've felt... I don't know. Mired, maybe? Stuck. I didn't know how to proceed, and it seemed daunting to try to figure it out on my own. But then it seemed like God told me to open up to Julia, so I texted her." Wendy managed a little laugh. "She didn't even question why I didn't ask Audrey."

"Wendy, my love, I'm proud of you. Just be you, sweetheart. Thinner? Only if you want. But don't ever let your heart shrink. I love your hopeful heart."

As for Wendy, she loved everything about Roman Scala.

"I can't believe you talked Pam into this."

Roman grinned. Surprising Wendy was one of his favorite things to do. Maybe because he liked how she rewarded him. "It wasn't hard."

"I'm not sure I believe you. Pam has plenty of opinions of her own." Wendy examined the options on the inn's buffet table.

"Hey." He nudged her. "Have I ever lied to you?"

"Not that I know of." She chuckled. "And there's no sugar in any of this?"

"That's what Pam said." He scooped brown rice onto his plate. It might not be a staple in the Asian countries he'd lived in, but he could get on board for Wendy's sake. "She read the guidelines from your coach and said she could make adjustments no one else would even notice."

"I can't believe you talked to her."

"Why wouldn't I? She's on your side. Everyone is."

Wendy bit her lip, and he nudged her again. "Dish up, Wendy. Everything here is on your plan. Even the stir fry sauce."

"I don't love vegetables all that much, but I'm learning."

"I know, love." He chuckled. He'd cooked a couple of meals lately for her in her suite, not that he was a skilled chef. He'd eaten most meals out in his adult life. Other times, he'd hired a local cook, a perk of the job with the import company.

"Okay." She exhaled and dished rice onto her plate. "It's hard to believe this is a supposedly slimming meal. And you don't need that."

"Thanks for noticing," he murmured in her ear. "But healthy is for everyone." There was a lineup behind them now, so he ladled a scoop of chicken and veggies in a sweet-and-sour sauce on his and then hers before leading the way to the table where they usually sat.

"Is she really going to make THM food for every single dinner from now on?" Wendy poked her fork through the food on her plate.

"She said she can offer options. Besides, keto is pretty popular right now, so being able to advertise the health benefits will bring in diners. She might have asked me to do a segment on *Roaming with Roman*."

Wendy took a bite, and her eyes widened. "This is better than I expected. I can't really tell it's supposed to be healthy... except for all the vegetables."

"Then I've done my job!" Pam dropped into the chair across from Wendy and set a small tin on the table.

"I can't believe you'd go to all this trouble just for me."

"I like a new challenge, and I like you." Pam shrugged with a grin. "And I overheard Roman telling you it will be a great angle for the inn as a whole."

Roman watched as his sister approached the buffet from the lobby. Had she always taken such small servings? He really hadn't paid that much attention, but Mom's words had stuck with him. Audrey had issues of her own. Food issues, if he had to guess, not that he knew much about eating disorders. Might need to do some research. Might need to talk to his sister, though she'd probably shut him down right quick.

"One more thing." Pam pushed the tin toward Wendy.

He dragged his attention back to their table.

"Oh?"

"Don't sound so nervous." Pam laughed. "I made some non-bake chocolate cookies that are on-plan for you. I think they turned out pretty well, but I'd love to hear your opinion."

Wendy eyed the container. "How many are in there?"

"Two dozen."

"You trust me with that many?"

"Wendy." Pam's eyes were full of compassion. "You are the strongest woman I know."

Tears pooled in Wendy's eyes. Roman could practically see her rewiring her brain minute by minute. "Thank you," she whispered.

"I might want one or two." He pried the lid off the tin and looked inside before tipping it toward Wendy. "These look and smell amazing, Pam. Thanks."

"I'll finish my stir fry before trying one."

"See? That's strength!" Pam winked then looked up. "Hey, Audrey."

Audrey pulled out a chair and glanced around the table. "Hi. This looks delicious, Pam."

"Thanks! I'm learning new tricks to help Wendy out."

"That's nice." She cut her eyes toward the open tin. "Cookies, too, I see. You're all in."

Roman had never heard his sister sound so... flat. Had she really counted on being the one who coached Wendy out of her dilemma? Or was there more going on?

"Well, not *all* in. It's coming up on Christmas, and there will be the usual festive cookies and desserts. But I figured I could try a few non-traditional recipes for Wendy. Turns out there are other people who prefer less sugar in their diets."

Audrey had a few bites before pushing her plate away a little.

Was she going to finish that? Not that he was going to ask.

"What are you and Granger up to for Christmas?" Audrey asked.

"The usual. I'll be working a lot, and Melissa and the kids will be over on Christmas Day. It should be good. How about you?"

Audrey glanced at Roman. "My parents invited me home, but

I doubt I'll go. Like you said, we're pretty busy here over the holidays, and there's nothing there for me anymore. I sold everything when Julia called. I have nothing pulling me back."

Roman chuckled. "Palm trees? Ocean breezes? Absence of blizzards?"

She shrugged. "I prefer it here. What about you? You were only planning to come until the end of the year."

Roman reached over and clasped Wendy's hand. "Things have changed, but no, I'm not planning on leaving for Christmas. Wendy's got workshops every Saturday, and I'm enjoying helping out at the Christmas tree farm. And there's my channel."

"We could invite our parents here." Audrey stirred her fork around her half-eaten meal and pushed it further away.

Roman considered his sister's words. "We could."

What would Christmas look like here at Maranatha Inn? Julia already had the entire place decorated to the hilt. To be honest, there'd been a tree in the lobby when he arrived in September. That corner had grown into a small, twinkling forest. Several more trees had sprouted up beside the fireplace, those with a muted woodland theme.

The aromas of peppermint and ginger wafted lightly throughout the space, while carols old and new looped through the sound system.

And Wendy was here, which meant there was no place on the planet — and he'd seen plenty of them — he'd rather be this Christmastime.

Here. At Maranatha. With Wendy.

CHAPTER
Twenty-Eight

"I CAN'T BELIEVE you're all here for Christmas." Her heart almost full, Wendy looked around the cozy staff lounge at her four youngest. "If only Adriel and Silas and their families could have been here, too."

"I've got time before my new job starts." Theo gave a firm nod and a wide grin to Roman. "I can't thank you enough, man."

Roman's hand squeezed Wendy's. "I'm glad I could help. Where is Leo sending you first?"

"I'll be spending a while in SoCal for training. Then, Bangkok, where the weather is balmy, and it doesn't snow." Theo linked his hands and stretched forward until his knuckles cracked.

Ezra elbowed his brother. "You're the one who wanted to ski the Snow Bowl while we were here."

Theo shrugged. "It's fine for a vacation, but I'm tired of dealing with it."

Selah snorted. "Like Portland gets snow."

"It gets some! And fog and rain are even more depressing."

"You should try Seattle," Wendy said. "It was quite a shock to me when I moved there with your grandparents after L.A."

"No wonder Liam wanted to live in Woodburn after growing

up in Seattle," Faith mused. "I know Adriel would rather have come here for Christmas than to her in-laws' place."

"I'd rather, too." Wendy's heart constricted. "But I'll take what I can get. I don't want to spend all my time this next week wishing for more blessings than I already have with the four of you here."

"Don't I count?" Roman murmured in her ear.

Her face immediately flushed. "Of course, you do." Since that tumultuous, upside-down Thanksgiving weekend, things between them had settled down... and heated up. Oh, how she loved this man! Someday... but no. No wishing for extra blessings, remember?

Selah's phone trilled, and she reached for it.

Was Wendy going to have to put a box at the door for phones? It seemed her kids were always on their devices. Certainly not the way she'd raised them.

Selah glanced around. "So, um, it's Adriel looking for a video chat. Can we pop that on the big screen, Roman?"

Oh! That was a plenty good enough reason.

"Sure." He rose, grabbed the remote off the bookcase, and turned on the TV. "Mirror your cell?"

"On it."

Wendy worked with tech. She shouldn't still be amazed by how it all worked these days, but hey, she'd raised her kids on VHS tapes, even though the format had already been mostly replaced by DVDs in their childhood. And now everyone streamed everything. It took some getting used to.

Selah set her phone to capture the staff lounge just as Adriel's face appeared on the screen.

How Wendy missed her firstborn. Missed those two little girls leaning over their mommy's shoulders.

"Hi, Gamma! See, there's Gamma!"

"Hi, you sweet things! Are you at your grandma's house?" Liam's parents, of course.

"At Nana's house."

Wendy blinked. Nana? That was the name her kids had called her parents. She studied the background of the screen for a few seconds. She didn't know what Liam's childhood home looked like, but this one did look familiar.

Just then the screen morphed, adding Silas and Teri to a section. "Hi, Mom! Hey, Roman. Hey, sibs."

Wendy's hand covered her mouth. "You kids!"

Faith arranged her own phone in front of Wendy and Roman, and they also appeared on the screen. Ugh. Too big. But she didn't dare argue.

"Sorry we can't be there in person, Mom." Silas said. "But we wanted to get together for a few minutes and wish you a merry Christmas Eve."

"It just got merrier. Thank you!"

"So, um… Mom?" Adriel again. "Someone here wants to talk to you."

The girls. Wendy's heart warmed, but if it heated much more, she was going to spontaneously combust. Darn perimenopause, anyway. Although maybe she'd moved past that into the full thing.

Adriel shifted aside, and Wendy's parents filled that segment of the screen.

Wendy stared. "Mom! Dad! What a surprise." Of course, she knew that Adriel often popped in on her grandparents when she and Liam visited Seattle, but there'd been a lot of silence punctuated by a few brief, stilted conversations in the past weeks.

"Hi, Wendy." Mom's gaze didn't meet the camera.

Wendy understood. It was difficult for many people to look at the camera lens rather than the screen where those they were speaking to were visible.

"Theo. Selah. Ezra. Faith. It's been a long time since we've seen all of you."

Wendy refused the feeling of guilt that threatened to over-whelm her emotions.

Faith bounced in her seat. "You'll have to come to my high school graduation in May! I'll send you an invite."

Dad cleared his throat. "We'd like that." Then he bit his lip before continuing on. "Roman Scala. You don't look a bit like how I remember you."

Roman chuckled. "I'm sure I don't. You may have gained a few gray hairs in those 35 years yourself."

"So have you."

Roman inclined his head. "True enough."

Dad turned away as Adriel said something unintelligible in the background. Then he faced the webcam again with a resolute expression on his face. "We had a long talk with Adriel last night."

"Oh? That's great." It *was* great. Right? But it also seemed foreboding. Surely Adriel wouldn't put her grandparents on a group video call so they could cut her down in front of everyone.

"She explained a few things about your marriage to Dave. We, uh… we didn't know. We should have tried to help. To understand."

What exactly had Adriel said? Wendy willed her face to remain impassive. If she was supposed to reply to that, she had no idea what to say.

"You know we believe in the sanctity of marriage."

Wendy nodded and clenched Roman's hand as though her life depended on it. Maybe it did.

"We also know the Bible allows for divorce in certain circumstances. Remarriage is harder."

Once again, Adriel said something in the background.

Wendy fought the urge to scrunch her eyes shut or to run away and hide, but she was bigger than life on the video call, and everyone would see.

Dad heaved a mighty sigh. "We still don't love this, Wendy, but Adriel can be pretty convincing. She said we needed to come to terms with this thing." Dad made a vague sideways flopping gesture.

Wendy hazarded a guess he meant her and Roman.

"Or we'd regret it."

The protest from Adriel was audible this time.

Dad's face softened. "No, it wasn't a threat, but she's right, all the same. We already regret so much. We feel like we let you down when you needed us most, Wendy. Can you forgive us?"

Her heart swelled. "Oh, Dad. Of course, I forgive you."

"And Roman... Adriel says you are a fine Christian man who loves our daughter. So..." Dad looked helplessly at his wife.

Mom took over. "Not to put ideas in anyone's head—" Adriel's giggle came through the call "—but we give our blessing. Not that you need it."

If Wendy'd thought her heart would burst earlier, now it seemed the fragments would be glitter strewn across the universe. Glitter that got in everything and could never be completely obliterated. Not that she wanted this joy to fade. Not now. Not ever.

Roman cleared his throat. "Thank you, Mrs. Bilson. Mr. Bilson." His voice choked up. "I can't tell you how much this means to me."

"Or to me. Thank you." Tears dribbled out of Wendy's eyes, but she made no move to wipe them away. It would be a lost cause, because an entire torrent rivaling Niagara Falls awaited.

Movement at the end of the corridor to the staff suites caught Wendy's eye, and she turned to see Audrey standing there, arms wrapped tightly around her middle, with a look of longing on her face.

"Audrey! Come say hi to my parents."

"I couldn't interrupt." She made as though to retreat.

"No, really."

Audrey closed her eyes for a second before her shoulders braced. "Okay. Where's a connected camera?"

Roman rose — Wendy felt an immediate chill from where he'd been pressed against her side — and carried Faith's phone to his sister. A second later, the two of them were in focus on the TV.

"You remember Audrey, I'm sure."

VALERIE COMER

Audrey gave a little wave. "Hi, Mr. and Mrs. Bilson. It's been a long time."

"It really has." Mom stared. "You're looking good, Audrey. Older, of course."

"That seems to happen as the years go by."

"And how are your parents doing?"

Roman and Audrey looked at each other before turning back to the call. "Fairly well, I think. They were here at Thanksgiving."

"That must have been nice."

It had ended better than it had begun, that was for sure. Roman and his dad had cleared the air some about the import business, and Bianca had complimented Wendy on the 'darling' angel origami craft, then oohed over the cinnamon stick center-pieces. A semblance of acceptance had been present by the time they'd left.

"Well, we don't want to intrude on your Christmas Eve, and Adriel and the girls need to return to Liam's parents' place."

"I'm so grateful for this call." Oh. She wasn't onscreen. She rose, made her way to Roman, and took the phone before repeating. "Thank you. It means so much to me."

"And to me." Roman leaned over her shoulder, his face beside hers.

She leaned back into him, not that it took much. "And to all my kids. You guys sure know how to make Christmas special. Thanks." Her voice choked.

Roman pressed a kiss to her temple before taking the phone from her hands and returning it to Faith.

Wendy touched the side of her face. Had her parents seen that? How could they have missed it? But they'd already given their blessing. They had to know where things between her and Roman were going. Some day. Wendy willed herself to be patient.

"Adriel? Silas?"

Her oldest two turned back to their cameras. "Did you get the ornaments I sent?"

Silas grinned as his wife leaned closer. "The paper quilled

272

snowflake! It's so gorgeous. I can't believe the amount of work that must have gone into it. It's holding pride of place on our tree."

"Thanks, Mom." Silas offered a crooked smile. "It's great."

"Agree!" Adriel put in with a nod. "Did you make six of those?"

Wendy really needed to start making them for the grandchildren, too. They'd all entered the world after it became a dark place for her, and she'd done little to celebrate Christmas. The hope of Advent had been dim in those years, but not anymore. "I made eight." She picked up a little box from the bookcase and opened it.

Faith squealed and tilted the phone toward it. "Mom! Those are *stunning*! But there are six here, and you already sent Silas and Adriel theirs."

Wendy reached in, lifted the top one out, and turned to Roman. "This one is for you, to commemorate our first Christmas together."

He held out his hand, and she laid it in his palm. He turned it over and over, but when he turned to look at her, his eyes were filled with love... and maybe a little moisture. "Thank you, Wendy. This means everything to me."

Selah handed snowflakes to her siblings but held up the extra. "And the last one?"

"For me. Because I deserve to have pretty things, too. And because the snowflake reminds me of hope. Winter is a time of being dormant, of waiting patiently. Sort of like a longer version of Advent. The world — the northern part, anyway — lies under this insulative blanket, quietly resting and waiting for new life." She looked up at Roman. "But when the time of waiting is over, there's new life. Things become alive again. Maybe I'm doing a poor job of explaining this."

"Oh, Mom. That's beautiful." Faith crushed her in a hug.

Roman kept his arm around Wendy's waist and leaned in to kiss her after Faith released her. "Even more special. Like you."

"I love that, Mom." Adriel waved at the camera. "I'm sorry I've got to go now, but we'll have to do this again soon."

"Definitely," Silas agreed. In the background, baby Tommy wailed. "We need to go, too."

"We'll do it again," Roman said. "Promise."

Oh, how Wendy loved how much her kids liked Roman. The faces on the big screen winked out one by one.

Selah turned the mirroring off on her cell phone and grinned at Wendy. "Surprised?"

"Yes. Especially with your grandparents. I had no idea Adriel would do that." Or that she'd succeed.

"You know Adriel." Faith rolled her eyes. "She doesn't take no for an answer. She's kind of a bully that way."

"It's the firstborn in her." Theo shrugged. "She can't help being bossy, but at least this time she used her talent for good, not evil."

Wendy turned to Roman's sister, who still stood off to the side with what might have been a wistful expression on her face. "Audrey, we're putting on Home Alone in a minute. The kids offered to make hot chocolate and popcorn. Join us?"

Audrey's smile faltered. "Only if you're sure I won't be interrupting."

"Not a chance. We're friends, remember? And I'm dating your brother."

"So, you are. Okay."

"Don't worry, Selah brought some sugar-free hot chocolate mix from Portland, and I'm good with that."

This time Audrey managed a chuckle. "Perfect."

CHAPTER
Twenty~Nine

IT WAS ONLY a few days later, but Wendy's kids were leaving soon. Ezra needed to be back at work Monday morning. Adriel and Liam had returned to Woodburn after Christmas in Seattle. Tonight was the night.

And Roman couldn't quell the churning in his gut. What if Wendy said no? She wouldn't. But maybe she'd think it was too early. As far as he was concerned, it had been a long time coming.

He trimmed his beard and hoped he'd remembered enough of the details from 41 years ago. That had been the only other time he'd proposed marriage, and his beloved had gently refused... as she should have turned down a five-year-old.

Replicating the day was impossible, partly because he refused to wait until spring when he might find wildflowers. A casual bouquet from Petals would have to do. The florist had argued with him. A proposal bouquet needed roses: red ones for love and passion, white ones for purity and new beginnings, and pink ones for admiration and elegance.

He'd stood his ground. Purple pansies. Yellow jasmine. White snowdrops. He'd allowed a few fronds of greenery and a cheery yellow ribbon, since it didn't seem the florist would ring through his purchase without. It did look pretty, and the colors roughly matched the scraggly wildflowers he recalled from four decades back.

Roman patted his tuxedo pocket. Yes, the box was in place.

Forty-one years ago, he'd likely been wearing shorts, a dirty T-shirt, and bare feet. He'd do the same if it were summer. Well, maybe a clean T-shirt.

But then he wouldn't have asked Wendy to video New Year's Eve for his channel. Wouldn't have done it up big. Public.

This could backfire.

It wouldn't.

But it could.

"Lord? I know You're in this." He prayed through the tumult until calm arrived.

Go time.

Wendy set her camera on a tripod, since the script Roman had sent her seemed to indicate the same backdrop throughout. He'd do some talking, then Julia, then back to him. Her kids and Audrey, Chris, and Laura, would be visiting around the fireplace in the background. They'd have party horns and sparklers for the appropriate moment.

Selah had insisted her mom wear the pretty pink dress she'd bought for Pam and Granger's wedding, citing that they'd have the real party after the filming. Thankfully, the dress hung a little looser than it had in spring. Wendy had survived five weeks sugar-free, or nearly so.

Go her.

"Everyone ready?" she called. "Where's Roman?"

Theo checked his watch. "He should be down soon."

Wendy eyed her four younger children. "You kids clean up nice."

"So do you." Faith laughed. "That color suits you."

"Thanks."

Julia bustled in from the other room. "Nearly ready here? Pam and Granger popped in, and I invited them to join us."

Ezra rose. "Do we need to pull in another couple of chairs?"

"That might be good. Just check your camera angle, Wendy, if you don't mind."

"Not at all." Wendy kind of wished she could be in the video, but she had a job to do. Cinematography didn't happen in a vacuum.

You're good at your job. Think of all the subscribers to Roman's channel. All the positive comments.

Yeah, yeah. She'd still rather be part of the party than recording it.

"Happy New Year!" Pam gave Wendy a hug.

"You, too! Wow, everyone's so dressed up."

"Julia told us to, since we're having a party. Plus, we never disobey the boss."

Everyone laughed.

Chris came in from outside, stamping snow off her boots. She shed her jacket, revealing a pant suit far more feminine than anything she usually wore.

Wendy left the tripod to approach her friend. "Chris, it's so good to see you. Have you recuperated from selling all those trees?"

Chris smiled. "It's been lovely to have a quiet week."

Take a chance. "Is Bruce coming back in January?"

The smile froze. "I don't know."

"I thought you two had gotten to know each other pretty well this fall." And maybe found love, not that Wendy would say those words out loud. Chris wasn't the sort of person you could tease like that.

"Some. He enjoyed helping with the trees and hanging out with the dogs."

"Roman!" Faith yelled.

Wendy turned to see him descend the last few steps while Faith stuck her fingers in her mouth and wolf-whistled. Wendy cringed. How had she failed to teach her youngest child manners?

Roman winked at Faith.

Maybe it was okay.

Roman looked over at her, and his gaze warmed. "Nearly ready?"

Wendy turned, flustered. "I think everyone's here. Chris, there's a spot on the hearth beside Selah."

Chris nodded. "Okay."

Wendy took her place behind the camera and fiddled with the settings a little more. There was plenty of natural light from the bow window, and the woodland-themed trees had just enough sparkle on the other side of the fireplace. With flames crackling and faint music playing, the ambience seemed complete.

"Okay. I'm ready."

Roman kissed her cheek. "You sure?"

How odd of him to ask. "Of course."

"All right. Everyone to your places. Julia?"

"Coming." Julia came around the back and stood beside Roman. "I approach from here, right?"

"Yes. The taped X on the floor marks the spot."

"That tape better not leave a residue."

Wendy chuckled. "It won't. Okay, let's get going. I'll start recording now with the group around the fireplace. Then, Roman, step onto the X and say your piece. I'm okay editing the segments to make them flow together if needed. Ready? And go."

But Roman was already off script. He leaned over the back of the love seat, talking to Ezra.

"Just start filming," Julia breathed. "You said you can edit, right?"

"Yeah, I can." Wendy frowned. It wasn't like Roman to mess with his own script. That was one of the things she liked about him. He made a plan and followed it through. His casual professionalism came through in every video. Maybe he'd had another idea and thought he'd told her. Either way, Julia was right. Editing was a thing.

"Camera rolling… three, two, one." She pressed the button and squinted through the viewfinder. All was well. She stepped back.

Roman turned to the camera holding a… bouquet?

Wendy blinked. The man was way off script.

Selah, seated on the hearth facing the camera, tipped up her phone, showing something to Chris, beside her. They both smiled at the device.

That sort of distraction was not what Roman was going for in his channel.

Wendy fumed silently. Her kids knew better than this.

"Happy New Year's Eve from Maranatha Inn in Jewel Lake, Montana," Roman began. "As you can see, we're still in full festive mode here." He looked back, and everyone waved. Everyone except Selah, who was still on her phone. Aargh. That kid!

"As you can see, today's episode is a little different than our usual fare." He grinned, holding the bouquet in front of him for all the world like a bridesmaid. "I'd like to introduce all of you to my videographer, Wendy." He held out his hand.

Wendy's eyes widened as she pressed her palm to her heart. *Me?* she mouthed.

He nodded, his smile lighting his eyes and creasing his cheeks to reveal a hint of his dimple.

Wendy took a deep breath and came around in front of the camera. The kids must know. That had to be the only reason Selah had done her hair and makeup while Faith had fussed over her dress.

Roman slipped his arm around her, still facing the camera. "This woman is Wendy Bilson Clarke. Not only is she the genius behind the camera, but she's the love of my life."

Wendy inhaled sharply. Hopefully that sound wouldn't be recorded.

Roman turned toward her. "Once upon a time, there was a little boy who adored his big sister's best friend. She was always kind to him and even kissed his booboos a time or two."

Wendy blinked and sucked in her lips. No, that was a bad look for the camera, but neutralizing her face was painfully difficult. She gazed into Roman's warm eyes, and the panic eased just a little.

"One day, this little boy picked a few wildflowers in the park and presented them to his sister's friend. With all the swagger any five-year-old could muster, he asked her to marry him. Oh, he knew he might be a little too young just yet…"

Laughter from around the fireplace as he pressed the simple, commemorative bouquet into Wendy's hand.

"She was also rather young, for that matter, but he recognized a gentle spirit when he saw one." Roman grinned. "She turned him down. I can't imagine why."

Okay, the tears would not be staunched. Wendy gripped the flowers with one hand to free up the other to wipe under her eyes. That mascara had better be waterproof.

"That little boy was me. The sister's best friend was Wendy. And on that momentous day I told her I'd love her forever. Here I am to make good on that promise. Gwendolyn Marie Bilson Clarke, I love you with everything in me. Will you marry me?"

And with that question, Roman dropped to one knee and opened a tiny velvet box toward her.

Wendy's hands flew to cover her suddenly enflamed cheeks, the flowers tumbling unceremoniously to the floor. "Oh, no!"

"No?" Roman's smile froze.

"I dropped the flowers. I'm sorry."

"That's okay, sweetheart. Will you marry me?"

"Yes!" Then she burst into tears and turned from the camera.

Roman's arms came around her, and he cradled her head against his shoulder. "Wendy, are you all right? I didn't mean for you to cry."

"I'm crying because I'm so happy."

"Me, too."

She tilted her face back. "You're crying?"

"Maybe a little." But he took the opportunity to kiss her.

Long. Deep. Passionately. In front of her kids. In front of the camera. In front of the entire world, most likely. And she didn't mind a bit. "I love you, Roman Scala. Whoever would have guessed this was where we would end up all those years ago?"

"Oh, sweetheart, this isn't where we've landed. It's only a launching pad for a beautiful future together."

"The ring, Mom!" Faith called out. "We want to see the ring!"

Oh! Wendy hadn't even looked at it herself.

Roman held a mixed-metal ring with an oval center diamond flanked by two trapezoidal diamonds for her inspection.

"Oh, Roman. It's stunning." She was going to cry again. Still. Whatever. Hormones brought on so many fierce emotions. She should have been more patient with her pubescent daughters.

He slipped the circle onto her finger as Selah held her phone close.

That girl was videoing the proposal. Just like Wendy's abandoned camera was likely still doing, if no one had jostled it.

Selah winked at her then held the phone up. "Say hi to Adriel and Silas."

"You video-chatted them! Oh, my word!"

"Of course." Selah sounded matter of fact. "Now I'm gonna shut off your other camera, okay?"

"But we were supposed to do a New Year's segment with Julia. And with Roman..." Wendy's voice trailed off. "This was all a setup, right?"

"You're quick, Mom." Selah kissed her cheek and whisked herself away.

Everyone crowded around to see the ring and offer congratulations.

Wendy had never thought there'd be a diamond on that finger again. Never thought she could be happy again. Never really believed in hope for the future. But here she was.

Chris smiled at Wendy through what looked like tears of her own. "I'm happy for you." She gave Wendy a fierce hug.

"Me, too. I'm happy for me. Maybe your turn is still coming."

Chris shook her head. "I doubt it. God missed me in the first round, and there's no reason to think He'll remember me this time, either."

"Bruce?" Wendy whispered. If Chris couldn't have hope for herself, maybe Wendy could have enough for both of them.

"I doubt it. But I'm used to being alone, so it's no biggie." She stepped back as Laura and Audrey crowded in.

"So, you're going to be my sister for real." Audrey offered an awkward chuckle. "Who would have guessed it that day way back in Rossmoor?"

"Not me, for sure." Wendy hugged Audrey. "You've always been the closest thing to a sister I ever had. Remember the day we decided to be blood sisters?"

"Yeah, it was a dumb idea. It hurt like nuts."

"It did. Watching my daughters... I'd say pain is part of having sisters. It's worth it."

"You think?" Audrey eyed her.

"Yeah. I do."

Words she'd say to Roman one day soon as she pledged the remainder of her days to him. They'd have to figure out when and where that would take place, but for right now? At the close of this calendar year? They could look back on where they'd been and marvel at the way God had led them together after all that time.

Hope was a beautiful thing.

Epilogue

THE FOLLOWING MAY

Bliss.

There was no other way to describe the past ten days. With Roman's arms around her, Wendy stood at the rail of the cruise ship as it slid into its mooring in Seattle.

They'd married at Creekside Fellowship with both sets of parents and all of Wendy's children and grandchildren present. She'd wanted a small wedding, but that hadn't happened. They had too many friends. She'd also given birth too many times.

It had been a simple wedding. She'd donned an understated dress, especially compared to the massive lace explosion she'd worn when marrying Dave. One thing she'd learned over the past quarter of a century... the wedding wasn't the part that mattered. The marriage was everything. The man she married was everything.

Not quite everything. That was Jesus, the glue that held them together as they focused on Him.

Roman was different from Dave right there. Dave had gone

287

along with her faith, but Roman curried it. He asked her about her quiet time while demonstrating his own. He took the lead in praying for them. He was the spiritual leader she'd always longed for.

Roman nuzzled her neck. "It's been a good week." He sounded content.

She felt the same. Deeply satisfied. "It has been the very best. Thank you."

"Thank *you*." He turned her in his arms and kissed her properly. "Wendy Scala. It's growing on me."

She smiled, and he kissed her cheek. "I kind of like it myself."

"I can't wait to get home to Jewel Lake."

"I know." She sighed. "But first, a quick visit with my mom and dad and then the drive to Woodburn."

"Where I get my wife to myself in a nice hotel."

"In between family stuff."

"Right, right. Faith's grad. Do I have to make nice with Dave and Shyanne?" His lips grazed her jaw.

"We can ignore them as much as possible."

"Excellent. I can handle a few days for your kids' sake."

"Me, too."

"But then home. Sort of home."

They'd accepted Julia's offer to keep Wendy's staff quarters until they decided if they were staying in Jewel Lake or not. The days on the Alaskan cruise had reminded them both how much they enjoyed ocean breezes and vistas, so maybe they'd eventually settle somewhere along the coast… but not too close to Woodburn. As much as Wendy longed for her children and grandchildren, she didn't want to live near Dave. Thankfully, it wasn't a decision they needed to make today.

"It will be good to see Theo before he goes overseas," Roman said. "We could go visit him in Thailand sometime this summer."

"Good thing your channel is *Roaming with Roman*. We can take it anywhere."

He chuckled. "Now you're talking."

The ship steward's voice came over the sound system, asking everyone to prepare to disembark.

"Let's take the first step into the rest of our lives, Mrs. Scala."

"I'm ready when you are."

$\mathscr{A}$ Note...

Dear Wendy,

Your journey has been hard, and women (and men) every-where have been cheering for you. Continue to walk in hope, my friend!

Your loving author,

Valerie

Dear Chris,

I know you have felt unloved your entire life, but things are about to change, even though you've lost hope. You and I and Bruce are going to hang out quite a lot for the next while. Prepare your loving heart...

Your loving author,

Valerie

Dear Reader,

I hope you loved Wendy and Roman's story! It was a hard one to write, as I'm sure you can imagine. But next will be Chris's story — Chris, who's never been married. Never come close. Never been loved. I hope you'll be ready to cheer Chris on as she opens her loving heart!

Blessings, Valerie

https://valeriecomer.com/loving

Acknowledgments

Thank you, readers, for your words of praise for the free novella, *Her Waiting Heart,* and your enthusiasm to read the entire Christmas at Maranatha Inn series! I can't wait to keep writing the remainingstories.

Thank you to my reader group on Facebook who prayed me through an intensive round of revisions. I'm especially thankful to Amy and Ellen, who lovingly and painstakingly read an early draft and helped me shape Wendy's journey into one that honors the struggles so many women face. You are so very much appreciated!

Thanks to my writing buddies who check in with me often to encourage me and kick me in the rear as needed. Jan Thompson, Lynnette Bonner, and Elizabeth Maddrey — this writing gig would be so lonely without you! And I'm happy to return the favor. ;)

Thanks, Nicole, for editing over 60 novels and novellas for me! I appreciate your wit, your guidance, your honesty, and your faithfulness. This time around, you sent me back to the drawing board and then cheerfully re-edited the revised manuscript. Your advice was spot-on, and I hope I never need to find a new editor!

Thanks to my family for believing in me and giving me the time and space to work. To my husband, Jim, for his steadfast care and encouragement. To my kids and grandkids, thanks for your understanding, too!

But most of all, thanks to Jesus, the Author and Finisher of my faith. I write for Your glory, Jesus. Thank you for everything. Literally… everything.

Dear Reader...

Thanks for reading *Her Hopeful Heart*! I'm so honored that you chose to spend the last few hours with Wendy, Roman, and me. You are appreciated.

I'm an independent author who relies on my readers to help spread the word about stories you enjoy. Would you take a few minutes to let your friends know? Facebook, Instagram, Goodreads... wherever you hang out online.

Also, each honest review at online retailers means a lot to me and helps other readers know if this is a book they might enjoy. I'd sure appreciate your help getting word out!

I welcome contact from readers. At my website, you can contact me via email, read my blog, and find me on social media. You can also sign up for my newsletter to be notified of new releases, contests, special deals, and more! You'll receive *Her Waiting Heart*, the novella that introduces the Christmas at Maranatha Inn series, absolutely free as my thank you gift!

~ Valerie Comer

www.valeriecomer.com

https://valeriecomer.com/waiting

Books by Valerie Comer

You'll find the complete list of titles by Valerie Comer on her website: sixty books (and counting) in ten series (and counting)! Come on over to find farm-fresh romance, cowboy romance, and small-town romance, all with distinctly Christian themes.

https://valeriecomer.com/books

About Valerie Comer

Valerie Comer is constantly amazed that living, talking, dreaming characters appear in her mind and flow from her fingertips and, from there, to her delighted readers. She only hopes her creations enjoy their happily-ever-afters as much as she does hers, sharing rural life in western Canada with her husband, adult children, and adorable grandkids.

Valerie is a two-time *USA Today* bestselling author and a two-time Word Award winner. She is known for writing engaging characters, strong communities, and deep faith into her green clean romances.

To find out more, visit her website at www.valeriecomer.com, where you can read her blog and sign up for her email newsletter, where you will find news, giveaways, deals, book recommendations and more.